MIDNIGHT ENEMY

by

SERENITY WOODS

Copyright © 2025 Serenity Woods

All Rights Reserved

This book is a work of fiction. The names, characters, places, and incidents are products of the writer's imagination or have been used fictitiously. Any resemblance to persons, living or dead, actual events, locales or organizations is coincidental.

ISBN: 9798285191438

CONTENTS

Chapter One 1
Chapter Two 9
Chapter Three 20
Chapter Four 30
Chapter Five 42
Chapter Six 52
Chapter Seven 63
Chapter Eight 72
Chapter Nine 81
Chapter Ten.. 90
Chapter Eleven... 101
Chapter Twelve 112
Chapter Thirteen 121
Chapter Fourteen 131
Chapter Fifteen 141
Chapter Sixteen.. 149
Chapter Seventeen 161
Chapter Eighteen.. 170
Chapter Nineteen 179
Chapter Twenty.. 188
Chapter Twenty-One.. 196
Chapter Twenty-Two 206
Chapter Twenty-Three 215
Chapter Twenty-Four... 226
Chapter Twenty-Five 233
Chapter Twenty-Six 241
Newsletter 250
About the Author 251

Chapter One

Scarlett

"You'd better get going," Anahera says. "You don't want to be late."

It's a beautiful, warm March morning. Summer is hanging on by its fingertips, and the trees haven't yet donned their autumn coats. Bathed in buttery yellow sunshine, Waiheke Island off the coast of Auckland, New Zealand, is a paradise like no other. Seriously, there can't be anywhere in the world more amazing than this place, with its emerald hills and dark-green forests surrounded by the sparkling blue Pacific Ocean. I'd rather be here than anywhere else on Earth.

Which is why the absolute last thing I want to do is take the ferry to Auckland and spend the morning in the city.

"I honestly don't mind driving in with you," my sister says, passing me the last plate after washing it in the sink.

I take it from her, dry it with a tea towel, and place it in the cupboard. "No, it's okay. I'm looking forward to a bike ride."

"Go on," she says, "I'll finish up here. I don't want you to be late."

I hang the tea towel on the hook, lean a hip against the worktop, and look out of the window. A single mum and her thirteen-year-old daughter have recently arrived at the commune to stay in the retreat, and one of our members is giving them the tour, showing them the vegetable gardens and the chickens.

The Women's Refuge in Auckland referred them here, as they've just escaped an abusive husband and father. It's clear they've both suffered physically and emotionally, and they need serious healing. The woman has one arm in a sling, and I watch her put the other around the girl as they walk across the central lawn we call The Green, pausing to watch the ducks on the pond. The girl looks haunted, although she smiles as she gives the ducks some of the grapes we grow in the vineyard. I hope we can help her smile more often.

Well, that's why I'm going to the law firm, right?

"Okay." I hug Ana and kiss her cheek. "Wish me luck."

"You sure you don't want me to come with you?"

"No, I'll be fine. You go and have fun." Ana is a classroom assistant in the commune's tiny school, and she's taking the little ones on a nature walk this morning.

"Take care in the city," she says.

"I will. See you soon."

I go out of the refectory, walk the short distance to our cottage, and let myself in. Ana's right; I don't want to be late. It's warm and I'm going to be cycling, so I change into my jumpsuit—it's navy from the ribs down, and the top is white with red stripes. I'm not going to be able to shower and change when I get there, but I roll up a summer dress and put it in a bag—I can slip that on over the top of my cycling gear, and with a pair of sandals instead of trainers I should look presentable enough.

After braiding my hair into a long plait, I spot the red roses that Ana picked this morning in a pot on my dresser. Smiling, I choose one of the buds, break off the thorns, and slide it into my hair just above my ear. Mum planted the bushes, and we always try to have a few indoors to remind us of her. It makes me feel as if she'll be with me today, which gives me confidence.

I grab my money purse and a notebook and pen and put them in the bag, don my sunglasses, then go outside and over to the bike stand. I choose my favorite bicycle, which has a scarlet frame and a basket on the front, put my bag into the basket, then set off for the passenger ferry.

It takes me fifteen minutes to get to the marina. It's a beautiful journey through the luscious countryside, with the Pacific Ocean sparkling in front of me like a huge sapphire. Tui birds call from the trees, and I see several rabbits on the grassy borders before they bolt into the bush.

MIDNIGHT ENEMY

Luckily I've timed it just right, so I only have five minutes to wait before I board the ferry. I push my bike on, find a seat at the front of the boat, and lean the bike against the railings beside me. Before long, we're moving through the water heading west for Auckland.

I haven't been to the city in months. I don't enjoy going. The journey is pleasant enough, weaving past Rangitoto Island with its volcanic peak, past all the boats in the City of Sails, to the Downtown Ferry Terminal near Mechanics Bay. But soon I'll be confronted with the noise and smells and energies of the 1.7 million people who live here. I find it overwhelming, to be honest. So as the ferry docks and everyone starts disembarking, I pop my earphones in and start playing some music on my MP3 player.

Singing to Joni Mitchell's *Big Yellow Taxi*, I set off for Carter Wright Lawyers, which is at the edge of the Central Business District, not far from Auckland Domain—the oldest park in the city. I have a map, and I stop a couple of times to take it out and make sure I'm going in the right direction. It takes me about fifteen minutes to get there. It's hot here in the city, and humid, and by the time I pull up outside, I'm sweating and starting to wish I'd come by car.

I also realize I've forgotten to bring a bicycle lock. We don't need them in the commune, but I should have picked one up from the office. I don't really want to leave the bike outside because I've heard stories of people stealing them, crazy as it sounds. After resting it on the front window of the law firm, I go through the door.

The reception area is large and open plan, with light wooden floors and a curving front desk. The name Carter Wright Lawyers is carved into the front of the desk and surrounded by swirling Māori patterns. Elegant green plants stand in pots, and near the receptionist is a vase of white roses, soft pink Lisianthus, and green hydrangeas. It's cool in here, and I can't see a fan, so they must have air conditioning.

To the right is a visitor section with a water cooler, a coffee machine, and a row of cream chairs. A guy in a suit sits at one end of the row. He looks up as I cross the room, but I don't make eye contact and instead smile at the young woman behind the desk.

"Good morning," she says. "Can I help you?"

"I'm here for a meeting at ten o'clock with Mr. Carter," I reply. "Um… I've forgotten a bicycle lock, and I don't really want to leave my bike outside. Would it be okay if I brought it in and left it here?"

"Of course," she says. "I'll let Mr. Carter know you're here."

"Thank you." I go back outside, collect my bike, and return to the door. It opens outward, and it's either ridiculously heavy or the spring on it is super strong, because I struggle for a moment to hold it open and get the bike in, afraid of scratching the glass.

"Here." The guy in the suit gets up and strides across the floor to help me. He presses a hand against the door, somehow managing with super-human strength to both keep it open at an angle and move back to let me pass.

I lift the bike over the small step, positioning myself between him and the bike, because I don't want it to touch his suit. There's not a lot of room, and my back brushes against his chest as I squeeze past. He's a lot taller than me—I almost fit under his arm. His suit is beautiful, navy blue and fitting snugly to his body, very elegant. He's wearing a white shirt and a red and blue striped tie. His tie pin bears a silver eagle. I can smell his cologne, something vastly different from the natural scents the men tend to wear on the commune. It's sensual and spicy. It makes my mouth water.

I glance up at him. He's clean shaven and extremely handsome, with dark hair that has unusual white flashes at his temples, even though he's only young. He has a large graze on his right temple, amongst his hair, that looks maybe a few weeks old and has nearly healed. He looks down at me, and his eyes are a breathtaking, startling blue, the color of the Pacific in the morning sun.

Dropping my gaze, I make it past him unscathed, say, "Thank you," over my shoulder, wheel the bike over to the wall, and lean it there. Keeping my back to him, I unzip my bag, take out my dress, quickly pull it over my head, and let it slide down my body. Then I slip off my trainers and socks and replace them with the sandals.

Finally, I stuff everything back in the bag, zip it up, then go over to the waiting area. As I sit on a seat in the middle of the row, the guy in the suit, who's been at the water cooler, comes over with a cup and passes it to me. "Thought you might be thirsty after your bike ride," he says.

"Oh, thank you. That was very thoughtful." I take it from him and drink it as he takes his chair, two seats away. When I'm done, he holds out a hand. I put the cup in it, and he tosses it in the bin next to him. I smile. "Thank you."

"You're welcome." He doesn't smile back. But he does stare at me with those intense blue eyes, and for a second I can't look away. Wow,

MIDNIGHT ENEMY

he's so handsome. His eyes bore into me, and I'm conscious of my heartbeat speeding up, and my pulse racing in my throat. I get a funny feeling in my stomach too, a flutter, the kind I get at home when I'm about to jump off the waterfall into the Waiora—our healing pool.

With difficulty, I tear my gaze away and study my hands where they sit in my lap. He doesn't say anything, but he shifts on his seat, lifting an ankle to rest on the opposite knee.

We sit there in silence for about twenty seconds. I can feel him watching me. He inhales and opens his mouth as if he's about to say something, but at that moment he turns his head as footsteps echo along the corridor. I look up and see an older, gray-haired man approaching. He looks at the guy, then at me, and says, "I'm so sorry to keep you waiting. I'm Jack Carter." He holds a hand out to me. "You must be Mahuika."

I get to my feet and shake his hand. "Everyone calls me Scarlett," I say, conscious of the guy next to me getting to his feet too. Why's he standing?

"Then I'm pleased to meet you, Scarlett," Jack says. To my surprise, he then turns to the guy in the navy suit and says, "And you must be Orson."

"Good to meet you," the guy says, shaking his hand. His deep voice brings goosebumps out on my skin.

"And have the two of you been introduced?" Jack asks.

The guy, who appears to be called Orson, turns to me and says, "No, not yet."

"Oh, sorry," Jack says. "Scarlett, this is Orson Cavendish. Orson, this is Scarlett Stone."

Orson holds out his hand and looks me in the eyes. He still doesn't smile, but something tells me he's amused. He knew who I was. "Ms. Stone," he says, "I'm pleased to meet you."

I don't lift my hand. I stand frozen to the spot and just stare at him. "Orson Cavendish? You're Spencer Cavendish's son?"

He nods, lowering his hand slowly.

Fury spreads through my veins like lava. I turn to Jack and snap, "What's he doing here?"

Jack looks from Orson to me, clearly confused. "I'm sorry, I thought you knew. Orson was the one who arranged the meeting today. He wants to discuss the sale of the Waiora." The large pool sits between our lands. The Cavendishes have been after it for years, but my father always refused to sell.

I glare at Orson. He doesn't look amused anymore, but he meets my gaze evenly.

I'm so angry, I can barely form words. "My father died two weeks ago," I say, the words falling from my lips like sharp stones. "We've only just buried him. And my mother died just two weeks before him. I've lost both parents within a month, and now you swoop in thinking you can take advantage of my grief to get what you want? How dare you ask me here for this reason!"

The Elders told me that the lawyer's email requested a representative of the commune to talk about land ownership. Did they know that the Cavendishes wanted to discuss the sale of the Waiora?

"I'm very sorry for not being clearer," Jack says quickly.

My eyes blur. "Really? Because it seems to me that you were purposefully vague because you knew I wouldn't come here if he was here." I jab a finger at Orson, who just lifts an eyebrow. Then I say, "Well, it looks as if we've all wasted our time."

I spin on my heel and march over to my bike, intent on leaving. As I turn the bike, though, Orson moves to stand in my way. "Please," he says, "come and hear what I have to say."

"Get out of my way." My chest heaves with emotion.

"Scarlett, please. I just want to talk."

"I don't. I want to leave." I try to steer the bike around him, but he moves to block me. I change direction, but he blocks me again. Now I'm starting to feel panicky. One rule we have in the commune is that if someone wants to walk away from any situation or conversation, nobody is allowed to stop them, and this feels like a huge invasion of my privacy.

"Please move out of my way," I demand.

"No," he says.

Before I can think better of it, I push the bike forward, hard, and it bangs into his knee.

"Ow," he says. He moves then, but it's not to let me pass. Instead, he walks around the bike and rests a hand on my arm. "Please," he says.

"Don't touch me!" I shake his hand off, starting to tremble.

He holds both hands up. But then he says, "Scarlett, I'm so sorry that your parents died, especially so close together. I lost my mother six years ago. I do understand some of what you must be feeling. And I'm sorry I arranged this meeting so soon. I actually asked to meet with the Elders. I didn't expect one of Blake's daughters to show or of course I would have waited."

He's not touching me now, but he is standing close to me. He's so tall—he towers over me, with his broad shoulders and wide chest. I'm so tempted to push him aside and get out as quickly as I can. But his words, delivered in a gentle tone, mollify me, just a tiny bit. It makes sense. Most of those who live in the commune assume that the land belongs to it, but at the reading of the will it was revealed that my father never transferred ownership. As the eldest child, I've technically inherited the land, which is why the Elders asked me to come today. Orson probably wouldn't have known that.

My chest heaves with resentment, but I make myself stand still. My father and Orson's father have been bitter enemies for nearly thirty years. Dad made it very clear that the Cavendish family were our polar opposites, and they stood against everything that he and the other Elders have tried to build at the commune. The Cavendishes are rich, privileged, arrogant, and elitist. They believe everyone should earn their own wealth and use it as they see fit. You're from a rich, smart family and have every opportunity open to you? Lucky you. Screw all the others who come from broken homes and have no money for an excellent education, and no connections they can call on to give them a leg up with employment. It ain't what you know, it's who you know, right?

They have all this wealth, and what have they done with it? They could have helped those who are less fortunate than themselves the way my father did all his life, and organized medical facilities and disability programs and educational support and computers for schools. But no. Instead, they opened the exclusive Midnight Resort and Night Club on the land next to our commune. The kind that only extremely rich people can afford to go to, with helicopter pads and heated pools and swanky restaurants.

I hate them and everything they stand for. But the Elders have sent me here and want me to report back, and as much as I detest every second I'll have to spend in Orson's company, I don't have a choice.

"I'll stay," I tell him, my voice almost inaudible. "But I'm not promising anything."

"Thank you." He gently takes the bike from me and returns it to the wall. Then he gestures for me to precede him.

I walk past him, stiff and resentful, to where Jack is waiting. Jack gives me a smile and says, "This way," and walks down the corridor into an office on the left.

I follow with a rising sense of dread, not looking back to see if Orson is behind me, but feeling as if I'm being followed by a big cat—a tiger, or a black panther. I can almost hear him padding behind me, swishing his tail menacingly, his teeth bared in a menacing smile.

His family is known for being ruthless in business. If I make it out of here in one piece, I'll be incredibly surprised.

Chapter Two

Orson

I feel a little lightheaded.

I follow Scarlett along the corridor, my gaze sliding down the curves outlined beneath the short sundress. She's tiny—to me anyway. I'm six two and big all over, and most women look small to me. She's wearing flat sandals, so she's maybe five foot two or three at most, but everything is in proportion, and she's super cute.

The moment where she took the dress out of her bag and tugged it down over her tight cycling jumpsuit in the lobby was one of the most erotic things I've seen in a long time, and it made me hard immediately. The scene was totally incongruous with the professional business atmosphere of the firm, and it made me feel as if I was on the beach, watching her get dressed after a swim.

I couldn't stop staring at her. The dress is above the knee, made of a flowing material, and cream with tiny red flowers all over it. Her sandals are made from leather straps with a white and red leather flower on top of her toes. Her hair is in a simple braid, and it doesn't look as if she's put on any makeup—no eyeliner, mascara, foundation, or even lip gloss. And I'm pretty sure she's wearing a real fucking rosebud in her hair.

I honestly can't remember the last time I saw a woman like this. Every day I'm surrounded by businesswomen. In the office they all wear suits, smart blouses, and skirts or wide-leg trousers; their hair has highlights and lowlights and is styled to perfection; their makeup is faultless, with not a freckle or a blemish in sight. The women staying at the Midnight Club walk around in designer swimming costumes or expensive day dresses, and in the evening, they wear sparkling, tight gowns that have clearly cost a fortune. But Scarlett takes the words fresh and relaxed to a whole new level.

SERENITY WOODS

"After you." Jack gestures for Scarlett to precede him into his office. She walks in, and I follow her. Jack set up this law firm with a friend, and so his office is one of the largest in the building, with large windows that overlook a walled garden, an expensive-looking wooden desk in front of us with a black leather chair, and a dark-gray sofa and chairs on the far side.

"Please take a seat over there," he says, gesturing to the sofa and chairs as he collects a few papers from his desk.

Scarlett and I walk across the room, and she lowers herself onto one of the corner seats of the three-seater sofa. I sit at the other end, and she glares at me, presumably for not taking one of the chairs. I know that although her father was Pakeha or white, her mother was Māori, and this is reflected in her light-brown skin, dark-brown hair, and brown eyes. Her icy glare should have turned the blood in my veins to ice, but those eyes are far too dark and passionate for that.

"Did you know that the word scarlet comes from the Arabic word *siklat*?" I ask.

She blinks. "No."

"*Siklat* refers to silks dyed red with insects called kermes. Red symbolizes wealth and power. And passion and love in cultures all around the world."

Her cheeks gradually take on a reddish hue. Jesus, is she actually blushing? I didn't think women did that in this day and age.

Half of me expects her to tell me to fuck off. Instead, though, she says, "Mahuika is a Māori goddess of fire. When I was young, I used to wear red all the time because I wanted to be like her. So everyone started calling me Scarlett, and it stuck." She narrows her eyes at me. "Don't you dare make a joke about me being a scarlet woman."

"I wouldn't dream of it."

She keeps her eyes on mine. Oh… her lips have curved up, just a fraction. Or did I imagine it? Too late—she tears her gaze away as Jack comes over and sits in one of the armchairs, and the moment's gone.

He puts a folder on the table. On the front is a label that reads 'Blake Stone / Kahukura.'

"I'm going to take some notes, if that's okay," she says to him. When he nods, she opens the bag she was carrying on her bike and extracts a notebook. Not a laptop, but a proper old-fashioned spiral-bound notepad.

"Want a quill pen with that?" I ask, amused. "Why don't you just take notes on your phone?"

"I don't have one." She flips the pad open and clicks the button on the end of her ballpoint pen.

"You don't have a phone?" I'm completely baffled. My friends and everyone I work with are glued to their phones twenty-four-seven. "My whole life is on my iPhone. I'd be lost without it. How do you cope?!"

"We weren't allowed individual phones when we were kids," she says, "and you don't miss what you've never had."

"What if you want to look anything up on the internet?"

"I can use the computers in the commune library."

I'm stunned. I'm constantly checking financial data, reading the news on Reddit, writing business emails, looking at my calendar, or talking to friends on Snapchat. "Aren't you on Instagram or TikTok or anything?"

"I'm not interested in social media," she says. "I don't share my generation's interest in taking photos of every aspect of their mundane lives and sharing them with the world."

My lips curve up. "What if you need to text or call your friends?"

"They all live in the commune."

"And how is life in Brigadoon?"

She blinks, confused. I guess she hasn't seen the movie about the mysterious Scottish village that appears for only one day every hundred years. Do they even have TV over there?

Jack clears his throat. "Let's move on. Okay, Scarlett, first of all, I'd like to say I'm very sorry to hear about your father's passing. Our sympathies here at the law firm go to you and your family, and everyone else Blake was close to at the commune."

"I second that," I say.

She looks at me. "Oh, really?" Her voice is flinty. "You're so sympathetic toward us that you want to exploit us in our moment of grief?"

Ouch. "I apologize if that's how it comes across. But we'd heard that local *iwi* had expressed an interest in the land, and we wanted to put in an offer before you made a decision."

It's a complicated story. The land on which the commune sits originally belonged to Blake's Māori wife, Amiria. A river serves as the border between their land and the land my father inherited, which he offered as the site for the Midnight Club. The river culminates in a waterfall that tumbles into a large pool known as the Waiora, which is Māori for 'healing waters'. On a sunny day, rainbows can occasionally form in the falling water, which is why Blake called the nearby commune Kahukura, which means rainbow in Māori.

Māori consider the site *wahi tapu*, which means they think of it as a sacred, almost supernatural place where their *tūpuna* or ancestors would bathe, believing that the waters cleansed and healed their bodies and sustained their spirits at the same time. The retreat that the commune runs uses the pool's supposed healing properties in their treatments.

Technically, Blake's land extends in a loop around the pool. But because our land runs right up to the edge of the rest of the river, we've always maintained our side of the pool, and he never contested that—why would he, when we spent decent money to make his land look good? We created a neat gravel path to lead from the resort down to the pool, and because our guests often go on walks and like to explore the grounds, we've erected some seating there so people can sit and admire the waterfall.

"That's right," Scarlett says. "Local *iwi* have raised the issue of who owns the Waiora now my father has passed. We discovered that because my father never transferred ownership to the commune, the land is technically mine. But we all make decisions together at the commune, and I'll be reporting back to the Elders later."

"I understand the cultural significance of the site," I say. "We'd like to offer to buy the Waiora so we can develop the land in a respectful way."

"Respectful?" Her eyes blaze. "You want to exploit and commercialize something natural and pure."

I frown. "It's an underdeveloped site that's going to waste. I want to make it beautiful and functional. I promise I'll honor the space and make sure it's safe and secure."

If her spine gets any more rigid, it's going to snap. "I don't want it to be safe and secure," she says, her voice hard. "It should remain untouched and wild. It's a tranquil place where vulnerable people can find clarity and peace. It's not underdeveloped, and it's not going to waste. It's a sacred place of healing. You can't disturb the god of the waters."

That pushes me over the edge, and my patience—which hasn't been great lately anyway—snaps. "Oh, come on. I accept it's a peaceful place and that people enjoy meditating and other crazy stuff there, but let's keep your batshit religion out of it." Out of the blue, a stab of pain runs from my shoulder down to my elbow like lightning, and I twitch irritably. "I don't want my chakras located, and I don't need to know if the moon's in Uranus. I just want to talk business."

Silence falls in the room.

Jack rests his head on a hand and massages his brow.

Scarlett looks astonished, as if she doesn't believe that someone would ever say anything like that to her.

A seed of guilt blooms in my chest and spreads through me. I shift in my chair and roll my right shoulder with a wince. "I'm sorry," I say grumpily. "I came off my motorbike a few weeks ago, and I'm in pain this morning. It's no excuse for being rude, though. I apologize."

She blinks, and then her gaze skims down my body, as soft as a brush of her hand would be. I wait for her to say, 'Good, I'm glad it hurts,' or something similar.

Instead, she says, "I saw the graze on your temple and wondered how you got it."

"He had a concussion," Jack says, because he knows I wouldn't have admitted it.

She frowns. "Are you getting headaches?"

I give a terse nod.

Sympathy flickers on her face. "I'm sorry I banged my bike into your knee."

Surprised, I say, "That's okay. My knees are fine. Well, they were."

Her lips twitch. Then she says, "I'm very sorry to hear you had an accident. What happened?"

"Another driver took his eye off the road to check his phone, swerved across the road, and rammed my motorbike."

"Orson's dog was in the carrier on the back of the bike," Jack says. "Unfortunately he was killed."

Her eyebrows lift, and her mouth opens. "Oh no."

As always, when I think about Doyle, my throat tightens, and I have to swallow hard.

"I'm so terribly sorry," she says, and she rests a hand on my arm. "I know dogs are a man's best friend."

I look down at it, shocked that she'd offer me comfort after I've been so rude to her. This girl has just lost her parents, and she's being kind enough to console me on the death of my dog.

13

She has light-brown skin, and her hands are smooth and unlined, with short, neat nails, absent of fake painted talons or French polish. She squeezes my arm lightly, then removes her hand, although her gaze lingers on mine. I'm so taken aback, I don't know what to say.

"Why don't we start again?" Jack asks. "So, about the sale…"

"I'm here to gather information," Scarlett interjects, "and take it back to the Elders for discussion. But I can tell you now that I am vehemently opposed to the sale of the Waiora, and I will fight that every step of the way."

"Let me explain our plans," I say, "and maybe you'll change your mind. We'd like to offer fifteen million dollars for the Waiora and the strip of land surrounding it."

Her eyebrows rise. I know that the Elders would have had the land valued, just like us, and she would know it's worth around ten million. So fifteen is a very generous offer.

I continue, "Along with that, I'd give the commune permanent access to the Waiora in the form of a right-of-way easement. We would also invest a significant amount of money into developing the area to make it safer and more accessible. We'd create well-signposted walking paths from both the resort and the commune that lead to a paved area around the pool with seating and sheltered areas, bathroom facilities, a changing room, maybe even a small cafe…" I stop as Scarlett inhales, her eyes widening. "Don't pop a blood vessel," I say sarcastically. "Everything would be negotiable. Let me show you the plans."

"I don't want to see the plans."

I ignore her, take the roll of paper from Jack, and spread it out on the table, holding it down both ends with books. "Look," I say, directing her gaze down. "These would be the paths, and there would be a safe paved area on either side of the pool here and here. I'd also suggest a bridge across the top of the waterfall where the stepping stones are now. You must have noticed that some of the stones are uneven. It won't be long before a kid falls in and goes head first over the waterfall."

Her gaze skims across the plan, and she studies it silently for a while. I let her look, glancing at Jack, who lifts his eyebrows, suggesting he's glad she's considering it, at least.

"What are those?" she asks stiffly, pointing to a series of circles on her side of the pool on the right.

"I thought it would be cool to create a series of nooks for you. Maybe like small gazebos, covered over to provide some shelter for when you take groups down there. They'd be private, and fitted with whatever you'd like to make it pleasant there, like outdoor cushions, fairy lights, as much kale as you can eat..." I'm half-teasing.

But her eyes flare. "Fairy lights? Kale? We're not running a mind, body, and spirit fair. The retreat is a serious place for women and children to escape from abusive relationships and to recover and heal."

Jack massages his brow again.

I knew the commune ran a retreat, but I hadn't looked into it, and I'd assumed it was some hippie bullshit thing where they all sit around chanting and striking bells or dancing naked under the moonlight.

Not that I'm against watching someone like Scarlett Stone dancing naked under the moonlight...

She's still glaring at me. I clear my throat. "I'm sorry, I'm sure the work you do is useful..."

"You throw apologies around like they're tennis balls, but you don't mean them," she says heatedly. "We had a mother turn up yesterday with her thirteen-year-old daughter. The woman's husband beat her so badly he injured her arm, and he sexually abused his daughter. The two of them are physically and emotionally scarred, and absolutely terrified."

I blink, thrown by her passionate retort, as well as what she's saying.

"The Women's Refuge sends women like this to us," she continues, "so they can spend some time recovering in a place that's an escape from the harsh world they're used to. I'm in charge of the healing program at the retreat. Yes, we hold yoga and meditation classes, but that's so we can teach them techniques to control their fear and anxiety, which help to lower blood pressure, and I also teach self-defense. We are all vegetarian, but that's because a vegetarian diet has lower levels of saturated fat and cholesterol, and more fiber, potassium, and vitamin C than other eating patterns, and we're trying to help them heal. We want them to feel better about themselves, and to be able to return to the real world feeling more confident and in control. So I'd appreciate it if you aren't facetious and stop mocking what I do."

When she finishes, her cheeks are flushed again, and her eyes are blazing. Fuck me, she's beautiful.

SERENITY WOODS

Shame spreads through me. I've insulted her twice now, and that would be unforgivable even if she wasn't obviously doing worthwhile work. Why has my father never told me what they do at Kahukura? Does he know? I can't believe he doesn't, but he's always spoken about Blake Stone with derision, and calls the commune a 'crystals-and-kumbaya retreat.' I've felt vaguely exasperated at the thought of having a cult-like settlement next to the Midnight Club, and I have to admit that part of the reason I wanted to develop the Waiora was so we could keep our half separate from the 'tree-hugging, granola-munching patchouli brigade', as Dad has called them in the past.

Now, I'm disgusted with myself for insulting the valuable work she does. She would have no idea that the Midnight Circle—the consortium of rich men and women who run the group of Midnight Clubs, of which I am a part—meets regularly to decide which charities we should spend the profits from the clubs on. Although we're ruthless in business, I'm proud that we're all driven by altruism, compassion, and a desire to change lives.

And now look at me—insulting this beautiful young woman and the honorable work she does.

I fucking hate myself sometimes.

I look down at the plan on the table, and see us through her eyes for the first time—as a faceless corporation taking over a smaller but well-meaning establishment, like a huge new supermarket putting the local Farmers' Market with its organic fruit and vegetables out of business.

I'm not prepared to give up on my idea. But I'm not going to achieve anything by acting like this. What's the fable about the wind and the sun trying to remove the traveler's cloak? Proving that gentleness is more powerful than force?

Thoughtfully, I reach out, pick up the plan, and roll it back up. Then I throw it like a dart so it lands in Jack's rubbish bin.

I turn toward Scarlett, lean forward with my elbows on my knees and my hands clasped, and look into her startled eyes. "I'm truly sorry," I say, injecting as much feeling as I can into my words. "I've been extremely rude and thoughtless."

She narrows her eyes. "So walking in and throwing money at me didn't work, and now you're going to try to win me around with charm? I wasn't born yesterday, Mr. Cavendish."

"Call me Orson, please. And no, I'm not trying to charm you, I'm attempting to be sincere."

"You're trying to tell me you've changed your mind about developing the site?" She gives a short, humorless laugh. "I don't believe you. Why do you have to change anything? Why can't things just stay the way they are?"

"Because progress is good, when it's done the right way."

"You just want to commercialize something that's sacred to me."

"No, I want to preserve it and make it safe. And I have an idea."

Jack's eyebrows rise, but he doesn't say anything, trusting that I know what I'm doing.

I continue, "My suggestion is that the Midnight Club still purchases the Waiora for fifteen million dollars, but afterward we place the land into a stewardship trust co-managed by the Midnight Club, Kahukura, and local iwi. The Club would retain certain rights to protect our investment, but we would ensure that the trust allows for regulated access for everyone, including the general public, as well as safe walking paths, a secure bridge, and some level of maintenance. We would be free to make respectful developments to our side of the site, but because we would own the land, we'd also agree to pay for any improvements you felt appropriate for your side, like the nooks we mentioned. Those developments would be up to you. If you wanted to keep it as it is, that would be your decision."

Silence falls again in the room. Scarlett is breathing fast, but she's not immediately refusing.

"How do I know that 'respectful development' won't alter the spiritual nature of the Waiora?" she asks.

"You'd have to trust me."

She snorts.

My lips curve up. "Look, let's be honest. We would gain legal access, control development, and strengthen the resort's appeal without steamrolling local interests. We might even score some good PR for preserving a sacred site. But the trust would make sure the Waiora was protected from over-commercialization, and that it remains sacred and stays under shared guardianship."

She looks at Jack and says, "Did you know about this?"

"No," he says. "But Orson has a head for business and finance, and you can trust him. With the fifteen million he's offering? I have to say, it's a win-win for the commune, and it's a very generous offer."

She studies her notepad, but she doesn't write anything down.

I know she won't be able to give me an answer today because she'll need to talk to the Elders. I'm sure she wants to reject my offer, but I'm also convinced the commune would benefit greatly from a cash injection, as Jack said there have been rumors of it having financial difficulties.

"Can I make a suggestion?" I ask. "Would you meet me at the Waiora and let me show you the kind of developments we're suggesting? We'll take a walk around the site, and you can explain to me what you do there. We can discuss what we'd like to do with our side, and how that might impact on your business."

It was the right thing to say. She looks slightly mollified and says, "Maybe."

"How about midday tomorrow? Would that suit you?"

She gives a stiff nod.

"All right, I'll meet you there," I say.

She puts her notepad and pen back in her bag, then gets to her feet.

I hand her a business card. "In case you need to contact me." Then I extend my hand. "Thank you for coming. I really am sorry about your parents."

She slides her hand into mine. "And I'm sorry about your dog."

As her warm fingers close around mine and our eyes meet, I experience the same feeling that I had when I did a charity parachute jump last year—the sharp intake of breath you take before you freefall, and the uncomfortable flip in my stomach, thrilling and terrifying at the same time.

Then she withdraws her hand, says goodbye to Jack, and walks to the door.

"Midday tomorrow at the Waiora," I call out.

She nods, then disappears down the corridor.

I watch her go, then look at Jack. He's smirking. "Orson Cavendish falling for a sweet summer child," he says, "who would have thought it?"

"Shut up."

"Don't worry. It happens to the best of us."

I scowl and rub my shoulder. "Don't mock a man in pain."

"Have you still got a headache, too? Sit down and I'll get you a couple of painkillers. And then we'd better discuss that plan you just came up with. Your father won't be happy with it—you know that, right?"

"He left the details up to me," I say stiffly.

He holds up a hand. "I know. I'm just saying, he won't like the idea of Blake's family having any control over the developments. I'll get the pills and a cup of water." He leaves the room.

I sit back down with a scowl. Yeah, she was hot, but I've hardly fallen for her. No way would I ever be interested in a girl from Brigadoon who wore real flowers in her hair and didn't even own a phone.

I think of the way she pulled the dress over her cycling jumpsuit and blow out a long breath. Women were put on this earth to torture us.

I'm not going to give her another thought.

Chapter Three

Scarlett

"Fifteen million?" The eyebrows of Richard—the leader and spokesperson of the Elders—shoot up toward his rapidly retreating hairline. "That's crazy money."

"And we'd be part of a stewardship trust?" Dani, who's in charge of the commune's small school, sits back with a laugh. "We'd be crazy not to accept."

It's seven p.m., and I'm sitting in the meeting house with the Elders after dinner, relating the details of what happened at the law firm earlier today. I'm not an Elder. That position is reserved for a small group of eight older members, voted on by the rest of the commune, but they invited me to the meeting today to report back on my visit to the law firm.

I sit with my hands in my lap, perched on the edge of the chair, my spine straight. I've been brought up to respect the Elders, and I know they all want the best for the commune. I also know that Kahukura is struggling financially, and fifteen million dollars would rejuvenate the commune and allow it to thrive and even expand rather than just muddle along.

"I appreciate that it's a very attractive offer," I say carefully. "And that being part of a trust would at least allow us to have some control over what happens on our side of the river. But we have to remember that we would no longer own the pool. The Cavendishes would have free rein to do anything they wanted to their side. Orson specifically mentioned the possibility of opening a cafe. I mean, can you imagine what that would do to the atmosphere of the Waiora?"

They exchange glances. "A cafe sounds kinda nice," Dani admits. "It would be cool to be able to get a coffee while you're down there."

I stare at them, shocked. "You're not serious?"

They all look a tad embarrassed.

"We understand your feelings, of course," George says. He's an accountant, the same as my father was. They worked together to run the commune's finances and were also best friends, and I think of George like a favorite uncle. I know he's under pressure to get things sorted right now. "But we think it's possible to retain the spiritual nature of the site, even with a few developments."

"It would be great to have a proper path down to the Waiora," Lee, the Head Caretaker, says.

"And several of us have slipped and nearly fallen off the stepping stones," Dani adds. "A bridge would be terrific, especially if we didn't have to foot the bill."

"A bridge would mean that resort guests would be able to cross easily to our side," I point out. "They'd disrupt my classes."

"We could add a signpost saying private property," Lee suggests. "Or even a locked gate."

He's right, and I can see that they want me to agree. But I can't get rid of the anxiety that's lying heavy in my stomach like a stone.

"I don't trust him," I snap. "He gave this spiel about being respectful and honoring the nature of the site, but once he owned the land he could do anything he wanted to it. He could turn it into a flashy tiled pool with spotlights and disco music and a restaurant and bring bus loads of guests there with their fake tans and designer bikinis and coiffured hairdos."

They all look uncomfortable at that suggestion, because they know I'm right.

"Look," George says, "we all know that Blake and Spencer hated one another's guts. But from what I've heard, although they can be ruthless in business, the Cavendishes are always true to their word."

"Are they really billionaires?" Dani asks.

"Yep," George says.

My eyes nearly fall out of my head. "Orson is a billionaire?"

"Nine zeroes in his bank account," George confirms.

I'm astonished. "But he's so young. Is his family rich?"

"I'm not sure," George replies. "Spencer, his father, obviously is. He runs Cavendish Finance and is supposed to be brilliant. Orson and his friend Kingi Davis co-run Te Aranui Developments. It means 'the great path', and it's a property business. Apparently the two of them are completely ruthless and make an absolute fortune. But they are honorable. I think we can trust them."

The thought of him being mega wealthy makes me uncomfortable. In my experience, rich people don't stop until they get what they want. They assume everyone has a price, and they're usually right, which I hate.

George leans forward. "The thing is… I think we can push Orson for more than fifteen million."

My eyes widen. It's already a small fortune for us, and his greed shocks me. "More?"

"I think he'll be prepared to go to higher. This site would be hugely attractive to his guests, plus preserving the Waiora for local iwi would mean great PR for him."

I know he's right because Orson said the same thing. But the thought of pushing him to pay more than his already generous offer leaves a horrible taste in my mouth.

But the others are excited by this. "Higher than fifteen million?" Richard says. "Seriously?"

"We could finally get the new schoolroom built," Dani states.

"And rebuild the fence around the outside," Lee confirms. "I've repaired it so much it consists of more wire and tape than wood."

"We could double the size of the retreat," George says. "Get twice as many women and children to stay. Think of the good we could do, Scarlett." His eyes are earnest. He's done more than most others here bar my father to better the commune, and I trust him implicitly. And he's not wrong.

I sit there, breathing fast, knowing he's right and I need to consider Orson's offer. But it goes against everything I've been brought up to believe.

"My father would be furious if he thought I was considering selling the Waiora to the Cavendishes," I say desperately. "Shouldn't his views count?"

"The problem is that his issue with Spencer Cavendish was personal," Dani points out. "None of us knows what was at the root of it because he wouldn't talk about it. Look, we all miss him terribly, but he's gone, Scarlett. It's incredibly sad, but it's the truth, and we can't change that. All we can do is move forward and do our best to keep the commune going."

"And we need a real injection of money," George says gently. "Or we might not be here this time next year."

That stuns me. I hadn't realized it was quite that bad.

"Orson wants me to meet him at the Waiora tomorrow," I say reluctantly. "He wants to show me what developments he has in mind. I'll go, and I'll report back tomorrow night."

"Good, thank you." Richard nods. "We have a bit more business to talk about, so you can go, Scarlett. Our thanks for going to the lawyer today; I know it wasn't easy for you."

I say goodbye, leave the meeting room in the town hall, and go out into the late-summer evening. The kids are playing football on the green, and there's a lot of shouting and running around, although I can't make out which team's which.

Smiling, I sit on the bench that overlooks the green, close my eyes, and turn my face up to the sun.

My stomach is churning, and I try to take deep breaths to calm myself. But it doesn't work. I don't want to see Orson tomorrow and try to talk him into giving us more money. The thought sickens me. I don't like him or what he stands for, and I thought he was arrogant, rude, and condescending, but that doesn't mean we should fleece him for everything he owns.

If I'm honest, I'm anxious about seeing him for another reason, too. It's impossible not to think about the moment we said goodbye and shook hands… the way he looked into my eyes… and the heat that was in his gaze. It seared right through me, and it made me extremely uncomfortable. I bet he's had a hundred girlfriends, and he knows exactly how to turn on the charm. Dad always said that Spencer was smooth but ruthless, and he practically spat whenever his name was mentioned.

I think about what Dad would say if he knew we were considering selling the Waiora to the family he hated so much, and my eyes well with tears. The pool is precious to me, a place of peace and solitude, and a spiritual focus. I scattered Mum's ashes downstream from the pool just a week before Dad died, and his followed literally a few days ago. It's more than a piece of land. It's a part of me and my family.

But what am I supposed to do? The Elders make the decisions regarding the commune, and even though I inherited the land, I have to do what they say. So I'll have to swallow my pride, ignore my misgivings, and meet with Orson tomorrow. I'll do my best to take on board his suggestions, and I'll keep my thoughts to myself.

*

Tuesday, 11:15am

I meant it. I really was going to try.

But when I turn up early at the Waiora to have some quiet time alone before I meet Orson, I discover three men wearing suits and carrying clipboards in the process of measuring up the Club's side of the pool. Two guys in shorts and tees are moving stones from the shallows at the top of the waterfall, and another appears to be working out dimensions for the bridge that Orson talked about.

I climb the path to my side of the stepping stones and stare at them in fury. "What are you doing?" I yell.

They all look over, then exchange confused glances. The guy who's measuring for the bridge comes across the stones toward me. "Morning ma'am," he says.

"Don't you 'morning ma'am' me," I snap. "What on earth are you doing here?"

He looks startled. "Um… we're mapping out the improvements to the Waiora…"

"Did Orson Cavendish send you?" I know it must have been him; who else would it have been? So I'm not surprised when he nods. "Right," I say. I slide off my sandals, then, lifting my long dress with both hands, I start walking across the stepping stones toward the Club's side of the river.

Halfway across, I tread on a wobbly stone and stumble. One foot slips and plunges in, spraying water over me.

"For fuck's sake," I mutter under my breath, glaring at the Māori guy who rushes over to extend a hand. I take it because I don't want to go completely under, but by the time I get to the other side I'm half drenched and cross as a cat when you stand on its tail.

"You okay, ma'am?" he asks as he releases me.

I scowl. "I'm going to see Mr. Cavendish. At this moment, the land belongs to the commune, and we haven't yet given our permission for any developments. So I suggest you stop working right now until we've cleared this up."

They exchange looks again. "I dunno," the Māori guy says. "Mr. Cavendish likes his work to be completed on time…"

Furious now, I put on my sandals, stride down the bank, and start heading toward the Midnight Club. Behind me, one of them calls out something, but I ignore them and keep walking.

I follow the gravel path west. I admit it's been nicely done, flanked by flower beds, and with the occasional bench facing out across the ocean view. Soon it leads through a small copse of trees, and then it opens out, and before me stretches the Midnight resort in all its glory.

I stop, astonished.

Because the main road to the commune comes straight from the ferry, I've never come this way. I'm sure some of the kids at Kahukura have snuck over at some point, but this is private property, and we all know it's out of bounds. We're taught from an early age that our little community is all we need, and Dad was always so dismissive of the Cavendishes' lascivious lifestyle that I've never given the resort a second thought, and never been interested in wanting to take a peek, afraid that somehow even a glimpse of it will taint me.

Now that I've met Orson, though, I'm a little curious. Because I'm on high ground, I have a good view of the entire complex. The resort sprawls from the top of the hill all the way down to the ocean. There's a central large building with two wings, all built in what looks like white plaster with natural stone accents in a Greek style, with columns and porticoes. The left wing looks like it could be a hotel, as every window has a private balcony. The right wing has a huge Neon sign above it, currently switched off, with the word Midnight and a clock. I think that might be the nightclub.

On the left side going up the hill is a series of individual villas, carefully situated to give them maximum privacy. Behind the buildings, small gardens are dotted between a couple of large swimming pools, smaller plunge pools, and hot tubs. A sheltered bar is serving drinks to those swimming; a couple of people are floating on inflatable loungers, sipping cocktails. Talk about decadent. Alcohol during the day! In the pool!

I continue down the path toward the resort, growing increasingly furious the closer I get. The place is incredibly opulent. I admit it's tasteful, which for some reason annoys me even more. Everything is clean and well-tended, from the neat flower beds to the manicured bushes to the paving slabs that are free of weeds and sparkling white in the sun. As I near the main building, I can see that the windows are freshly cleaned and the front steps have been swept. The porter who is carrying the luggage for a couple of guests who have just arrived is wearing a smart suit.

I climb the steps and go into the main building. The lobby is huge with high ceilings and large windows that overlook the view of the well-maintained gardens and pools to the back. The reception desk to the left and the tables and chairs in the waiting area by the windows are made from a light wood, probably kauri I think, and everything smells of polish and coffee from the bar to the right. The staff is dressed in black with white shirts and they all look professional and give pleasant smiles.

"Good morning," the man behind the reception desk says as I walk up to him. His gaze skims down me super quickly, and suddenly I'm conscious of dripping water onto the floorboards. "Can I help you, ma'am?"

"I'd like to see Mr. Cavendish," I say stiffly, trying to act as if I come to places like this all the time.

"Do you have an appointment?"

I shake my head.

"He's very busy," the guy says. "But I will see if he's available." He picks up his phone and is in the process of calling when he looks up and says, "Oh, there he is. Mr. Cavendish? There's a lady here to see you."

Heart racing, I turn—then stop and stare at the man walking toward me. It's not Orson. This guy is about the same height as him but older, maybe in his late forties. He's clean shaven, and his hair has the same white flashes at his temples, although the rest of it is also sprinkled with gray. Oh my God. I think this is Spencer Cavendish—Orson's father, and my dad's bitter enemy.

He stops before me and gives me a pleasant smile. His gaze appraises me briefly, the way the man's behind reception did, but he's polite enough not to comment on my state of disarray.

"Good morning," he says. His voice is deep and resonant. "Can I help you?"

I blink at him, my heart hammering and my chest rising and falling quickly. I can't form a single thought. I've been programmed to hate this guy and everything he stands for. I'm not sure if I can even be civil to him.

When I don't reply, he exchanges glances with the guy behind the desk, then frowns at me and says, "Is there a problem?"

"Scarlett?"

We both turn at the sound of Orson's voice as he strides across the lobby. "Jesus," he says, staring at me. "What the fuck happened to you?"

"Orson," Spencer scolds.

Orson throws him an icy glance, which surprises me. Clearly there's no love lost between father and son.

"Are you okay?" Orson stops before me.

I look down at myself and realize it's worse than I thought. Much of my dress is soaked and clinging to my legs and breasts. Oh no. I wrap my arms around myself, trying not to shiver.

"Here." Orson flips the button of his jacket open, slides it off, and places it around my shoulders.

"I'll get it wet," I protest.

"I don't care about that." He tugs it closed around me. "What happened?"

"I slipped off the stepping stones." I tremble under the gaze of the two men in front of me.

"Scarlett?" Spencer repeats, his eyebrows rising. "Scarlett Stone?"

"Yeah," Orson says.

"Amiria's daughter," Spencer says softly.

I frown, surprised that he didn't say 'Blake's daughter,' and I give a short nod. I've never felt so intimidated in my life. Wealth rolls off these guys like smoke. Spencer's suit is navy and Orson's is dark gray, but they're both obviously tailor-made and fit them like a dream. They're both wearing cufflinks and tie pins and polished black leather shoes. Their haircuts are razor sharp as if they were done yesterday, although Spencer's hair is a little longer all over and is combed back neatly, while Orson's is fashionably spiky on top and fades almost to bare skin at the nape.

"What are you doing here?" Spencer asks.

I direct my glare at his son. "We haven't come to any agreement yet."

Orson lifts his eyebrows. "I know. I thought that's what we were going to discuss today."

"So why are your men on our land?"

He blinks. "What?"

"There are men measuring up at the Waiora," I say hotly, my fingers tightening on the two sides of his jacket. "The land belongs to the commune, and they have no right to be there." I stop as my voice turns husky with emotion. I am *not* going to cry in front of these guys.

Orson's face goes carefully blank. "Hold on," he says. Then he pulls a phone out of his trouser pocket. He dials a number, holds the phone to his ear, and turns away a little.

"Ed?" he says when the person on the other end obviously answers. "It's me. Where are you? What? Why? I distinctly remember asking you to wait until I'd spoken to Ms. Stone. No. I said midday. Today, Ed. Jesus. Get the guys off there—the Waiora belongs to the commune, and we haven't signed anything yet. Yes, I'll call you." He ends the call, slides his phone back into his pocket, and turns back to me.

"I'm so sorry," he says. "They weren't supposed to go until they'd heard from me."

"So you assumed I'd agree to the sale," I say heatedly. "It didn't enter your head that I might turn you down."

He tips his head to the side. "Not really."

"You're so sure of yourselves," I snap. "So arrogant. You think money can buy anything."

"That's because it usually can," Spencer says, amused.

"Not me," I say, close to tears. "It can't buy me. You can't just throw zeroes at me and expect me to drop to my knees in front of you."

Orson's eyebrows rise again. Spencer opens his mouth to say something, then closes it again.

"I meant in thanks," I say, feeling my face flush. "Goodness."

Spencer stifles a laugh. Orson's lips curve up slightly.

I rub my nose, not knowing whether to laugh or cry.

"Hey," Orson says, "come on. I really am sorry. It was totally out of order for those guys to be there. And I didn't mean to imply that I assumed you'd sell. Of course I didn't. I know what the place means to you. I just hoped we'd be able to come to an agreement, that's all." He lifts a hand and rests it lightly between my shoulder blades. "Why don't you come to my office, and we'll see if my PA can find you some fresh clothes?"

"These will dry," I mumble, feeling the warmth from his hand even through the jacket, as if he's branding me.

"Come on." He gently steers me past his father.

"Nice to meet you, Scarlett," Spencer says.

"Mmm," I mumble.

"I don't think the feeling's mutual," Orson calls out wryly as he leads me across the lobby and along a corridor. "I'm sorry you slipped," he says as he steers me through a doorway. "Can you see why I thought a bridge might be a good idea?"

"Maybe," I admit grudgingly.

I find myself in a large office overlooking one of the gardens. It's cool, so clearly air conditioned, although the sun streams through the windows across a light-gray sofa and chairs. A desk sits to one side with a laptop, a tablet, and a pile of papers, spreadsheets, and books.

"You're very messy," I inform him.

He smiles at that—the first time he's given me a proper smile. It's a bit wolfish and makes me think of the big cat again. "Come and sit in the sun," he says. "That'll help warm you up."

"I'm not cold."

"You're trembling."

It's not because I'm cold, but I don't correct him. I let him lead me to the sofa, and I sit, feeling the sun on my legs.

"Can I get you a drink?" he asks. "A glass of champagne or something?"

"It's eleven thirty," I say, astonished.

That makes him laugh out loud. Oh my God he has amazing teeth, all white and straight, with slightly longer canines that only enhance his wolfish smile.

A shiver runs down my spine. I feel as if the big cat has dragged me back to his lair, and now he's about to have me for dinner.

I'm really in trouble.

Chapter Four

Orson

Scarlett looks at me as if she's completely baffled as to why anyone would ever want to drink a glass of champagne while it's still daylight. She's obviously never drunk alcohol when she 'shouldn't'—never snuck a bottle of vodka out with her friends for a camping trip, never stolen a third of her dad's whisky and watered the rest down; in fact maybe she doesn't drink alcohol at all. I can't imagine growing up in a community that's so restrictive.

The commune isn't closed doors exactly, but it is very private. In its early days, while they were in the process of setting up, they came under a lot of local media scrutiny, and after a reporter wrote a scathing article mocking their hippie ideology, they tightened their ranks and created a set of rules to keep their structure and systems private. There are lots of rumors. Some people say that newcomers have to take a vow of silence about anything that happens within its walls. Others are convinced that some rules are only revealed once a member reaches a specific level of trust.

Because of my father's dismissive attitude toward Blake and Kahukura, I assumed it was just a group of long-haired unwashed vegans who sat around chanting 'om' and making flyers about global warming, and as a consequence I've never paid the commune much attention. However, after Scarlett revealed the true nature of its purpose yesterday, I did a little research. The retreat is highly praised for the work it does with victims of domestic and family violence. It works closely with the Women's Refuge to provide sufferers with a place to heal and recover, while also helping with accessing healthcare and counselling, giving legal assistance and obtaining protection orders if necessary, finding a place for the victims to live, and even meeting basic needs like food and clothing.

I confronted my father about it last night and asked him if he knew what the commune actually did at Kahukura. It turns out that he did.

"Why didn't you tell me?" I demanded, furious that I made a fool of myself in front of Scarlett. The Midnight Circle gives millions to charity, and the commune is right next door to our club. I'm stunned that he's never put it forward as a potential recipient for donations when I assume it relies on them to survive.

"Because I knew you'd want to go riding in on your white horse and I didn't want you to have anything to do with Blake Stone and his family," he snapped.

"What the fuck?" I yelled. "You made me think he was a delusional religious freak! But the guy set up a place that's helped thousands of innocent people."

"Just because he helped people doesn't mean he wasn't a lunatic," Dad stated flatly. "Blake always claimed he could heal, but just like Jim Jones, he was never able to offer any real proof. Don't forget that even the Peoples Temple helped the poor."

"Do you have any evidence?" I asked, shocked that he was comparing a harmless living facility to a destructive cult. "Have you actually seen them drinking the Kool-Aid? It's a harsh accusation to make if it's unfounded."

"I don't need proof that Blake was a fucking nutcase. I know it to be a fact."

"We should consider giving them some money," I told him heatedly.

"I'm not giving that man's family a single cent," he replied, and turned away.

I walked out then. I knew there was no point in asking him why he was so bitter toward Blake because I've asked him before, and he always refuses to answer. Their feud goes back to their teenage years. It continues now, even though Blake has died, and I have no doubt my father will hate him until he also eventually leaves this mortal coil.

But I'm secretly fascinated. Although once again she has a red rosebud in her hair, Scarlett doesn't sound like a lunatic country bumpkin who's part of a crackpot community where men can have numerous wives and cousins can marry and have six toes on each foot. She might not possess a mobile phone, but she sounds smart, educated, and hardworking. Has my father got it completely wrong? And if so, why?

"How about I get us a takeaway coffee to have while we walk back to the Waiora?" I ask Scarlett.

"That would be very nice, thank you," she says stiffly.

"What kind? Is a latte okay?"

"Yes, thanks."

I buzz for Anne, my PA, and say, "Can you ask the barista to make us two lattes in takeaway cups, please?"

"Of course."

"I'll collect them from the bar in a few minutes."

"No worries."

I end the call. I turn back to Scarlett and stop. She's opened the front of my jacket and tipped back her head, eyes closed, to feel the rays of the sun that are slanting across her. Her long brown hair, free from yesterday's braid, tumbles over her shoulders like chocolate-colored silk. Splashes of water across her white dress have turned much of it transparent, and… holy fuck… I can see the lace of her bra on her left breast, and through it a glimpse of light-brown nipple. She's also slipped off her flat sandals, presumably because they're wet, and she's resting the balls of her feet on the coffee table, curling her toes over the edge. Her feet are small and clean, and the toenails are neat but unpainted.

Despite not having a foot fetish, I immediately get an erection and, as she opens her eyes, I grab a folder from the desk and hold it in front of me.

I clear my throat. "Are you okay? You didn't hurt anything when you fell?"

"Just my pride." Her lips twist. "It's been a while since I used the stepping stones. I suppose I can see that a bridge might be a useful addition. Although I wouldn't want your guests to think it means we'd be allowing access to our land."

"I understand. My idea was a kind of viewing platform, actually, so anyone who wanted could stroll across and get the beautiful view over the waterfall and downstream toward the ocean. It would have to be carefully planned though to avoid blocking the river in the event of high rain. But you could have a gate on your side with a 'No Entry' sign if you wanted."

She nods. Then she glances at the folder in my hand. "Does that have more plans in it?"

I look down at it. "Ah… nah… It's just serving a purpose."

She frowns. "What do you mean?"

"Just for God's sake, put your sandals back on if you want me to be able to walk out of here."

She looks at her feet. Blinks a few times. Lifts her gaze to the area I'm covering. And then her eyes widen.

She goes completely scarlet. "Oh my God." She immediately bends to pull her sandals back on. "I don't believe you."

I try not to laugh. "Why? Because I'm a normal, healthy, twenty-seven-year-old guy whose body is reacting to a gorgeous young woman with pretty feet?"

"Stop saying such kinky things."

That does make me laugh. "I don't think admiring someone's feet is necessarily kinky."

"Jesus, stop it."

I chuckle and put the folder down. She sits back and looks with alarm at my crotch.

"It's gone away," I tell her. "You're safe. Look, I am sorry for making an inappropriate comment. Blame the fact that I've been single for a long time." I gesture to the door with my head. "Come on. Let's get our coffees and we can start walking over to the Waiora. I'm sure your dress will dry on the way."

She gets up. "Do you want your jacket back?"

"You can keep it for now if you like." I take out my cufflinks and leave them on my desk, then start rolling my shirt sleeves back.

She watches, her gaze sliding up me. "Do you only possess one tie?"

"No…"

"I've seen that one before."

I finger the tie with its red and blue stripes. "I like it. It belonged to my great-grandfather. He was English, and he supported Crystal Palace Football Club. The Eagles." He gestures to the eagle on the tie pin.

"Oh. Well, that's kinda nice."

"They won the FA Cup recently so I'm wearing it for him."

She looks surprised, as if she hadn't expected me to be into family. Giving me a small smile, she pulls the two sides of the jacket close, and we head for the door.

"I'm just walking over to the Waiora," I call out to Anne as I pass her office, and she nods and waves. I lead the way back to the lobby and over to the bar, where the two takeaway lattes are sitting there waiting.

"Thanks," I say to the bartender. "Sugar?" I ask her. She shakes her head, so I pass her one of the cups.

"Have you been to the club before?" I ask.

"No. It looks very…" She frowns.

"Go on," I say, amused. "Spit it out."

"Nice."

"I don't think that's what you were going to say."

"Maybe not, but I was brought up to be polite."

"I don't think politeness has ever featured before in our families."

She sends me a wry look. "No, you're right there."

"I'm guessing your father was as bitter as mine?"

"Ohhhh yes. As a lemon that's been passed over for a promotion."

That makes me laugh out loud, and she smiles. Wow. It's the first time I've seen her smile, and it lights up her whole face.

"You should do that more often," I advise.

"You too," she scolds.

We exchange amused glances. Without meaning to, our gazes lock, the way they did in Jack's office, and for a moment I can't look away. Something flares inside me, like striking a match in the dark—bright, sudden, and impossible to ignore.

She wrenches her gaze away, shading her eyes as she looks around the lobby. "What's that room there?"

"A restaurant. And that's the club." I gesture at the double doors. "Lots of people come here just for that."

"Is it a sex club?"

I stare at her, startled. "What? No! It's a nightclub. What… how… why would you think it was a sex club?"

"There are rumors."

"Jesus. Really?"

"You can tell me the truth."

"I *am* telling you the truth! It's not a sex club. Although that would be fun, I'm sure. Come on, I'll show you around."

"Oh, er…"

I grin. "You won't be corrupted just walking through the doors, I assure you." I lead her over, the automatic doors slide open, and we go inside.

It's quiet now because it doesn't open until six. I'm very proud of it. It's decorated with silver and midnight-blue furnishings, and at the back, beyond the stage, is a huge, magnificent clock.

"When it strikes midnight," I tell her, pointing up at the nets on the ceiling, "they release those, and balloons and silver foil come fluttering down."

"I feel sorry for the person who has to clean that up."

I laugh. We walk slowly around, and I can see her taking in the gleaming tables, the spotless carpets, the way the nooks are placed to allow for privacy.

She glances at the smaller stages with the dance poles and says, "So you have dancers here?"

"We do."

"Do they wear clothing?"

I chuckle. "Yes. No nudity."

"Do they offer lap dances?"

My lips curve up. "Sometimes."

"But it's not a sex club."

"Nope."

"You're sure?"

"I'm positive. I think I'd know."

She frowns. "Have you been to one?"

"No," I say, amused. "Not really my thing."

"I would have thought it was exactly your thing."

"Why?"

She shrugs, trailing a finger along one of the polished bannisters. I guess maybe her father must have painted the Cavendishes as hedonists, focused only on money and pleasure. That stings a bit. I like food, whiskey, and sex as much as the next guy, but I'd never call myself a hedonist, and for some reason it makes me uncomfortable that people think of me as one.

"Why is it called Midnight?" she asks.

"Because it sounds cool."

She gives a short laugh. "It's part of a chain of clubs, isn't it?"

"Yeah, there are seven others across New Zealand, and one in London. They all have a similar theme to this one, with the clock on the wall."

"All run by rich guys like you."

"We're a consortium. The Midnight Circle. If you want the truth, if we meet to do any business it's not normally until after midnight. That's how we came up with the name."

"I'm always in bed by ten," she says.

"So would I be if I had a girl like you." I say the words before I can vet them fully. They earn me a glance that's half-bashful, half-exasperated. I'm not sure whether she likes me flirting with her or not.

"What do you really think of the resort?" I ask as we go through the doors and cross the lobby, heading outside.

"Honestly?"

I squint in the bright sunlight and slide on my sunglasses. "Always."

"I'm shocked at the sumptuousness and decadence. The wealth on display." She gestures at the cars parked out the front. "I mean nobody needs cars as extravagant as those."

"Wealth isn't about having what you need," I tell her. "It's about having what you want."

"And you always get what you want, I imagine?"

"See, want, take. It's a family motto."

"Really?"

I laugh. "No. You're incredibly gullible."

She pokes her tongue out at me, then returns to looking at the cars.

"Do you drive?" I ask.

"Yes."

"Do you own a car?"

"No. We have a pool of cars, and I use one of those. My favorite is a small Suzuki. It does everything I need." She stops by a silver Aston Martin DB12 Volante. "I mean, who really needs a car like that? Look at it! Talk about over the top. All that leather. And a convertible! How ridiculous. Clearly that belongs to an arrogant poser who's compensating for a tiny penis."

We stand and look at it.

After about ten seconds of silence, she says, "It's yours, isn't it?"

"Yep."

She looks at me. Then we both burst out laughing.

"Fucking cheek," I say as we continue walking.

"You asked for it," she scoffs, "driving about in something like that."

"She's beautiful. I love her with all my heart."

"I wasn't sure you had one."

"It's small, sure, but it's loyal to my one true love."

She laughs, then gives me an appraising look. "I thought motorbikes were your thing."

"Not anymore," I say gloomily.

"The accident wrote yours off?"

"Yeah. It was a magnificent Kawasaki Ninja H2R. Black and stunning. I loved that thing." I sigh.

"I am sorry," she says softly. "Especially about your dog."

I roll my right shoulder, which always aches whenever I think about him. "Thank you."

"What breed was he?"

"A Dachshund. A rescue dog. I went to the shelter to get a dog to run with me, but I saw him and fell in love, even though he had little legs and didn't like running. He was dignified, placid, and very funny. He was my best friend." I swallow as my throat tightens.

"We've always had dogs at the commune," she says, seemingly unbothered by my emotion. "They belong to everyone, but there was a sheepdog called Shadow who stayed with me most of the time. I missed him a lot when he died."

I clear my throat and nod. "They're good company."

"What was the Dachshund's name?"

"Doyle. After Arthur Conan Doyle."

"Oh, you're a Sherlock Holmes fan?"

"I am."

"You sound surprised that I recognized his name."

"I am," I say, still smarting a bit at her insult about my car. "I thought you only read books about unlocking your inner goddess."

"No need," she says, "my inner goddess is unlocked and raring to go twenty-four-seven."

We both laugh again. Jeez. When I first saw her in the lobby, glaring at my father, I didn't envisage that I'd be exchanging smiles with her later.

We leave the grounds and enter the copse of trees leading down to the river. They close over our heads, leaving us in a quiet, sheltered world far removed from the busy opulence of the resort.

"Are you okay being alone with me?" I ask, suddenly aware it's just the two of us.

She frowns. "What do you mean?"

"I mean would you rather I ask my PA or one of the other women at the resort to come with us?"

"Why?"

"Because… you might not feel safe being alone with a man?" Most of the women I know would have balked at the idea, especially if nobody knew where they were.

Scarlett just snorts. "Try anything with me, sunshine, and I'll have you flat on your back in seconds."

"Is that a promise?"

"Don't flirt with me."

"You started it."

She throws me a glare. "I hate you and everything you stand for."

"I love you too."

"Mr. Cavendish…"

"Jesus, I'm not in my sixties. Call me Orson."

"Mr. Cavendish, I think it's probably best that we maintain some kind of professional decorum, don't you?"

"Absolutely not." I hold a branch back for her. "I need you to explain exactly how you would have me flat on my back in seconds."

"I'm a black belt in Jiu Jitsu."

My eyebrows shoot up. "Seriously?"

"Yes. You have been warned."

"I'm tempted to tackle you now to see if you're fibbing."

"Just try it."

Without warning, I grab her arm and pull her toward me with the intention of snatching a kiss to prove my male superiority.

About two seconds later I discover myself on my back amongst the dead leaves. Scarlett had dropped to a crouch and charged her shoulder into my midriff with a double-leg takedown, completely taking me by surprise.

"Holy fuck." I look up at her, astonished. "That was impressive."

She gives me a smug look. "Told you."

Her eyes are the same color as the earth beneath me, and the dappled sunlight reveals autumn highlights in her hair—light browns, reds, and golds.

I slide an arm around her waist and, before she can react, I lift up and twist, reversing our positions so she's underneath me, and then grabbing her wrists and pinning them either side of her head. She fights me, but I'm a foot taller and much heavier, and without the element of surprise she doesn't stand a chance.

She stops moving, and for a long moment we look into each other's eyes. Christ, she's gorgeous.

"Submit?" I ask softly.

Her eyes flare. "Never."

I give a short laugh. "Stubborn to the end."

"I always win," she says. "I'm just being kind." She glances down, and I follow her gaze to discover her knee resting about an inch from my family jewels.

That should have alarmed me, but all I can focus on is the way the skirt of her dress has risen to her hip to reveal her thigh with its expanse of smooth, light-brown skin.

"This'll hurt more if you have an erection," she points out.

"Bit late for that."

"Jesus." She struggles to free her wrists. "Does that thing ever go down?"

"Apparently not, when you're around."

She can't get her wrists free, and glares up at me. "Is this your way of making a single woman feel safe?"

I study her mouth, which is free of lipstick. Her lips are a light pinky-brown with an attractive Cupid's bow.

"Don't you dare," she says.

I lift my gaze back to hers, amused. "Is it true that you practice free love at the commune?"

Her eyes widen. "What?"

"I can see the appeal."

"I bet you can. I bet you practice it all the time. Spreading your seed around Auckland like it's oats and barley."

"Oats and barley? Where are you from, medieval England?"

"Deny it."

"I do deny it. I'm a serial monogamist. I don't sleep around."

"Yeah, right," she scoffs.

"I don't." I look at her mouth again. "I don't kiss just anyone."

Her lips part, but no words come out.

I look back at her eyes again, and we study each other for a long, long time.

The loud call of a tui bird directly above us jolts me out of my reverie. What the hell am I doing? What if someone were to come along the path and see us?

I blink, then release her wrists and push up to my feet. I extend her a hand, and she takes it and lets me pull her up.

39

We brush ourselves down, clear our throats, then continue along the path heading east.

"Lovely day," she says.

"Yes, although I think they've promised rain later."

"It's been dry for a long time. I think the ground needs it."

"Absolutely."

As if I wasn't kneeling between her legs thirty seconds ago, pinning her down and wondering whether to kiss her.

What on earth am I doing? Scarlett Stone is the absolute last girl I should get involved with. She is the polar opposite to me. She hates my way of life, and disagrees with every single principle by which I stand.

"Do you really believe everyone is born equal?" I ask, puzzled.

She gives me an amused look. "Of course."

"You can't really believe that, surely?"

"We're all blank canvases at birth. It's our opportunities and experiences that influence the person we become."

"So you think that Einstein and the guy who cleans the toilets were born equal?"

"I do, as it happens."

I laugh.

She glares at me. "Why are you laughing? And why are you so rude about the way I live? I don't criticize you and your beliefs."

"That's because mine are sensible and normal."

Her eyes blaze. "You're so incredibly arrogant."

"And you're the naivest person I've ever met. You think everyone's born equal, money is the root of all evil, and society should be one big group hug."

"And you think you're better than everyone else, that money can buy anything, and society should be a kind of caste system where us poor minions should be permanently excluded from your privileged world."

"Sounds about right."

She puts her hands on her hips. "You're an elitist arsehole."

"And you're a communalist."

"That's not even a word."

"Sure it is."

She throws her hands up in the air. "I can't believe you think some people are just naturally better than others."

"Not better. Smarter. More capable. More ambitious. I believe we make our own luck."

She opens her mouth to say something. Closes it again. Then says, somewhat curiously, "Are you really a billionaire?"

I feel the first tingle of warning deep inside, but I ignore it. "Yes, and I didn't get there by being born the same as the guy down the road."

"Yeah, I get that. You were born into a rich family."

Resentment flares inside me. It's not the first time someone's assumed my success is purely down to my connections.

"I was," I say stiffly, "but that's not what I meant. I've worked extremely hard to get where I am. I'm not a genius; I'm not even close. I had to work harder than most of my friends to get my first-class degree and a Master's in Finance. I barely left my room at uni. I spent all my time studying. Since I graduated, I've worked fourteen-hour days. Sometimes longer while Kingi and I were setting up our business. Was I born privileged? Sure. Is that the reason I'm successful? I acknowledge it's played a part. But I haven't sat back and let the money do all the work. I've earned everything I've achieved."

We walk in silence for a minute or so.

Eventually, the trees part, and ahead of us we can see the path winding toward the Waiora.

Scarlett stops walking, and I turn to face her.

"I'm sorry," she says.

My eyebrows rise. "What for?"

"I made assumptions, and they were unfair. I assumed you were a rich playboy whose father had given you everything you have. I apologize."

I'm so astonished I just stare at her. "I don't think anyone has ever said anything like that to me before."

"Don't get all mushy on me. I still think you're a knob."

I give a short laugh. "Come on. Let me show you what I have planned."

She precedes me along the path, and I watch the swing of her hips as I follow.

I still think she's batshit crazy. But her words warmed me through, and she fascinates me more than any woman I've met in a long time. Maybe ever.

SERENITY WOODS

Chapter Five

Scarlett

We walk up the steep path to the top of the waterfall and turn to look at the Waiora. It's a beautiful view from up here. The river tumbles over the rocks in a sheet of sparkling silver. The rainbow after which the commune is named arcs across the pool, its seven shades shimmering in the sunlight. The pool itself is wide and deep, and luckily has no rocks beneath the surface near the waterfall, which means it's a relatively safe test for young people's courage as they leap into its depths.

The far side—my side—of the pool is covered in thick bush. There are Ponga or Silver Ferns; Nikau palms, which is New Zealand's only native palm; Mānuka trees with small white flowers, which is what the bees draw from to make their special honey; Kawakawa with its heart-shaped leaves that have many medicinal uses; Rengarenga or rock lilies; Makomako or Wineberry, which are small trees with reddish leaves and edible berries; and New Zealand Jasmine, which fills the air with a delicate fragrance. The small, cleared area near the middle is where I bring people to meditate and bathe in the healing waters.

Orson's side of the pool is more cultivated, with a gravel path, neatly trimmed plants, a small gazebo, several benches, a rubbish bin, and a display board that tells the visitor a little about the history of the Waiora and its spiritual properties.

"Terrific view," Orson says.

"Mmm." I'm distracted by his closeness. He's next to me, not touching me, but his arm is only millimeters from mine, and I can feel the heat from his skin. I turn my head a little, looking down at where he's rolled up his shirt sleeves. His skin is tanned, which surprises me considering he must spend all day in the office. His hands are big, with clean, neat nails. He's wearing a large watch, one of those expensive ones that does everything but tell the time. He could probably run NASA from it. He has a scattering of brown hairs on his arms. Does he have the same amount of hair elsewhere?

I lift my gaze and discover him looking at me.

We keep doing this. He does something to my brain. His eyes are like superglue. I look into them, and I get stuck in them—I can't look away.

I think about when I took him down, and how easily he flipped me over onto my back. I'd never have admitted it, but that impressed me. The feeling of him on top of me, pinning me down as he gazed into my eyes, will remain with me for a long time.

He looks away and runs his tongue over his top teeth. Then he says, "Right. So this is what I was thinking."

He proceeds to run through the plans he has for the Waiora. I listen silently, half resentful, half intrigued. He wants to secure the stepping stones above the waterfall, and maybe also install a footbridge further up to give everyone a safe crossing. The river here is mostly shallow where it flows over the stones, but after heavy rain it can become precarious, and a bridge would definitely be a useful addition.

On his side of the river, he wants to create a more formal swimming area, with changing rooms, easy access in and out of the pool including a shallow ramp for disabled people, and seating for those who just want to enjoy the view. He insists it would be done respectfully, and that I would be able to okay the plans before he begins building.

He then turns to the commune's side of the Waiora. "I understand that you want to keep it natural," he says. "So I'm having my architect design some new ideas that incorporate more rustic designs. Natural is good but it doesn't provide for longevity. The bank is already eroding on the left side, and again it's not safe, especially for kids who are going to be climbing out after jumping in. The architect is working with an engineer to explore reinforcing the bank from there to there, with steps and a slope so people with disabilities can use the pool."

"I guess that would be an advantage."

"And I know you hold classes down here. I thought it would be nice for you to have private spaces for people to sit and meditate or talk or whatever you do. I think it would be best if they were made from wood, and then my architect could have a Māori artist carve patterns or stories in them."

"I'm not great at visualizing," I admit.

"That's okay. The architect will provide sketches. She's pretty good."

"She?"

His lips curve up. "Yeah."

"She an ex-girlfriend?"

He gives me a baffled look. "No, of course not. Why would you say that?"

"Dunno. You seem like the kind of guy who would have slept with half the population of Auckland."

"I told you, I'm a serial monogamist."

"Serial as in one a day, every day?"

His glance this time is sarcastic. "No. As it happens, I don't believe in sleeping around, which is another area where I suspect we differ."

I glare at him. "We don't all sleep in one huge bed at the commune."

"I'm not saying I don't see the attraction."

I give up. "I accept that the developments you're proposing are interesting. But it still concerns me that you would own the land. If you changed your mind and decided to turn it into a nightclub, there wouldn't be much we could do about it."

"True. I guess you'd just have to trust me."

I give a short laugh. "Yeah, right."

He turns to face me, sliding his hands into the pockets of his trousers, tips his head to the side, and raises an eyebrow.

"What?" I say, my heart beginning to pound.

"Would you like me to supply you with professional references?"

"George said that although the Cavendishes are ruthless in business, they're always true to their word."

He looks startled. "You really say what you think, don't you?"

"Do I? I suppose. I don't know any other way."

"I wouldn't call myself ruthless. Determined, maybe, when I see something I want."

His blue eyes fix on mine again, and for some reason it makes me think he's talking about me.

"No," I say without thinking.

His eyebrows lift. "No, what?"

God, he's so handsome, and the look in his eyes is… well, I don't know how to describe it. Hungry, maybe. Like the big cat he reminds me of, it's like he wants to ravish me. My mouth has gone dry, and I'm trembling a little.

"Stop it," I say.

His lips curve up, a frown appearing on his brow at the same time. "Stop what?"

"Looking at me like that."

His gaze turns sultry. "Like what?"

"Like you're planning to act out your family motto." See, want, take. That's exactly what he's thinking.

He doesn't protest, so I know I'm right. But he does say, "Not where girls are concerned. I'm only interested if they're willing."

I take a step back. "I don't believe you. I know men enjoy the chase. You've seen something that's not fallen immediately into your hands and so now you're interested."

His eyebrows lift and he extends a hand toward me. "Scarlett…"

"Well money can't buy everything, Mr. Cavendish, so if you think you can—"

"Scarlett!"

"No!" I move back, scared because I know that if he touches me, I'm not going to be able to resist him… and then the world gives way beneath me.

I hadn't realized I was so close to the edge. I fall backward into the river, completely submerging. Before I can scramble to my feet, I immediately feel the tug of the current, which rolls me over and disorients me. My arms and legs flail, and alarm spears through me at the thought that I'm perilously close to the edge of the waterfall. I've jumped off several times and survived, but that was a controlled fall after I'd taken a deep breath, and this time I'm already confused and spluttering.

I bump against a rock and squeal, then cough as water pours into my mouth. Oh shit. I'm really in trouble here…

But even as the thought enters my head, I feel something grasp my wrist, and I'm hauled up out of the water. The momentum sends me shooting forward, and I land on him, forcing him to stumble and lose his footing. A strong arm wraps around my waist, though, and then he gets to his feet, bringing me with him.

"Scarlett?" Orson is standing waist-high in the water. "Are you okay?"

I tremble, partly from the cold, partly from the realization that I had been extremely close to tumbling over the edge. Without meaning to, I burst into tears.

He sighs, bends and slides an arm beneath my knees, then lifts me into his arms and carries me to the side. Still holding me, he sinks onto the ground, legs crossed, and lets me sit in his lap while he tightens his arms around me.

"It's all right," he murmurs. "You're safe now."

I bite my lip to try and stop crying, still shivering from the cold. Then I sit up in alarm as realization hits me. "Your jacket!" I spin around to look for it, but of course there's no sign of it. "Oh no, it must have gone over the edge."

"It did, I saw it."

"I can look for it."

"Don't worry about it."

"It'll stay in the pool until the current picks it up."

"Don't worry about it," he says again. "It doesn't matter."

"Was it from Italy?"

"Milan, yes."

I wipe my eyes, which is useless because my hands are wet. "I'll replace it, if I can take out a small mortgage to cover the cost."

He laughs and kisses my forehead, then tightens his arms around me. I rest my cheek on his shoulder, because I don't have the strength to break free.

"I thought I was a goner there for a minute," I mumble.

"Nah. I wouldn't have let you go over."

I think about that, as he rubs my back and arms to warm me up.

"You smell nice," I whisper.

"Thank you."

"Is it a very expensive cologne?"

"Six hundred bucks a bottle."

"Jesus. What is it?" I sniff his neck. I can smell vanilla and tobacco, spices, and something sweet—brandy, or rum.

"It's a Penhaligon's Picture scent."

"A what?"

"It's called The Tragedy Of Lord George. Very British. They say 'it's the perfect scent for a gentleman with something dark hidden away.'"

I close my eyes and inhale. "What secret are you hiding?"

"I'm not hiding anything. I'm an open book."

"I sincerely doubt that," I mumble.

We sit there for a minute or so, while my heartbeat gradually slows.

"You smell nice, too," he says eventually.

"River water?"

"No. Something soft and flowery."

"It's rose water."

"Really?"

"Yes. Water infused with rose petals."

He gives a short laugh, but doesn't say anything.

The sun is hot, and I'm warming up a little. I should move… but I discover that I'm reluctant to. Orson's shirt is mostly transparent, the cotton stretching tight across his biceps where his arms are around me. He has huge biceps. He's quite a big guy close up, bigger than he looks in his suits, which fit so well they hide his athletic build.

I shift on his lap… and then freeze. Slowly, I look up, into his blue eyes.

"Jesus." I scramble to get away from him.

He laughs. "Steady or you'll end up falling back in."

Flustered at the memory of what I felt in his trousers, I try to unstick my dress from my legs. "I don't believe you. I just nearly died and you're all aroused!"

"I wasn't aroused by the near-death experience. I was aroused by the proximity of a gorgeous young girl."

"Just because my dress is transparent, God you men are so predictable…"

"Look, I defy any man not to get an erection when they have a water nymph sitting in their lap smelling of rose water."

The word erection makes my face heat. "Goodness."

He just laughs. "We should get you home so you can change out of that wet dress."

I think about what Ana's going to say when I walk in and groan.

"Come on." He holds out a hand as he walks toward the stepping stones.

"I know the way home," I tell him, ignoring it.

"I'm not letting you fall in again while you're all wet and slippery. Hold my hand."

I try not to think about being wet and slippery with Orson Cavendish and fail miserably. "I'm not holding your hand."

"Hold my arm then. Scarlett!" He grabs for me as I slip on the first stone. Before I can argue, he lifts me into his arms again and starts walking across the stepping stones.

"Put me down!" I squeal, conscious of his bare arm touching my thighs.

"Not until we're on the other side. And stop wriggling—do you want us both to end up in the water again?"

I stop, fuming, and loop my arms around his neck as he navigates the stones. "Your shoulder," I say, remembering his injury. "You're going to hurt it carrying me."

"You're like carrying a pillow," he scoffs. "Anyway, my shoulder's almost healed. It's my head that hurts."

"You had a concussion?"

"Yeah. It's taking its time to heal."

I try not to look at the way his biceps bulge against the tight cotton. Or the sight of light-brown hair through the transparent shirt. Or the bulge of his Adam's apple. Or how smooth his chin is.

Instead, I look at his hair, and the white flashes at his temples. Spencer had the same, so it obviously runs in the family.

"How old are you?" I ask as he steps carefully from stone to stone.

"Twenty-seven. You?"

"Twenty-four." He looks younger up close. He has no lines on his face and no scars. His mouth is attractive, his lips narrowish and firm. I bet he's an expert kisser.

He glances at me. "Stop it."

"I'm not wriggling."

"Stop staring at me like that or I'll end up kissing you and then we'll go over the waterfall, and it will all be your fault, but I'll have to pretend it was mine because I'm a gentleman."

I drop my gaze to his tie, which is also mostly soaking wet, and touch a finger to his silver tie pin with the tiny eagle on it. I'm glad he didn't lose it in the water. "Did you ever meet your great-grandfather?"

"Once. He died when I was thirteen." He steps over the last stone onto terra firma, then stands there for a moment, looking at me.

"Are you going to put me down?"

He purses his lips, looking at my mouth.

Oh my God. I despise him and everything he stands for. But I really, really want him to kiss me.

Instead, he slides his arm out from under my legs and lowers them, real slow, until my feet touch the floor, keeping one arm around my shoulders so I end up pressed up against him.

MIDNIGHT ENEMY

I place both hands on his chest. But as I feel his muscles through his wet shirt, my fingers curl rather than push him away.

He's so tall, and muscular, and handsome, and he smells so good… There's nobody at the commune like this. In fact I don't think I've ever met a man in real life who's as attractive as Orson.

He's wealthy and experienced and accomplished and confident, borderline arrogant. It's infuriating, but also extremely sexy. Some of the men at the commune wear suits to work, but they're nothing like Orson's. They're not sophisticated or elegant or refined. They're just normal working guys. They don't have the nonchalant, cavalier, 'I can do anything I like and you can't touch me' attitude that money brings.

I have to remind myself it's the fact that he's so different from other men which makes him seem so attractive to me. That doesn't mean that if I delved under the surface, there'd be anything interesting at all. It's like seeing a fantastic Pavlova on a table, a foot high with cream and fresh fruit, and you can't wait to eat it, but when you do, you discover it's ninety-nine percent air.

"What are you thinking?" he asks, amused, as he lifts a hand to unstick a strand of hair from my cheek.

"I'm comparing you to a Pavlova in my head."

"Elegant as a ballet dancer?"

"*A* Pavlova not *The* Pavlova."

"Sweet and creamy?" His eyes dance.

"Full of air," I say sarcastically, then gasp as he bends his head and touches his lips against my ear.

"You smell divine," he murmurs, his hot breath fanning across my skin.

I tremble. "Get off me."

"Just one kiss." He brushes his lips along my jaw to my mouth.

I shiver. "Mr. Cavendish!"

"You know that turns me on, right?"

"Orson!" I squeal and push him, terrified I'll give in.

He straightens, rolls his eyes, and releases me. I'm bitterly disappointed and incredibly relieved at the same time.

"Come on," he says, leading the way down the bank. "I'll walk you back to the commune."

"I know the way."

"I know you know the way. I just want to make sure you make it back without falling over again."

"I don't make a habit of falling over," I say as I follow him down.

"Even so. I wouldn't be a gentleman if I didn't keep you safe."

"You're not a gentleman," I scoff, taking his hand as he offers it to help me climb over a fallen log. "You're like a big cat. You're just identifying my weak spots so you can pounce."

"I've had worse insults."

"I bet you have."

He laughs and sets off along the track. "Jeez, this is overgrown," he complains, brushing aside the branches leaning down from the trees. "It's going to need some work."

I realize the truth then. "You just want to check out the land and see what needs doing. This has nothing to do with my safety."

"I can't do both?"

I send him a wry look, but he's studying the ground, obviously thinking about how the path could be improved, and maybe what it would cost.

The sun slants through the trees across him, showing that his hair is dark brown, not black, and putting gold flecks in his blue eyes. His shirt is drying out a little, but still clings to his big biceps. He's so handsome.

I hurriedly tear my gaze away from him and concentrate on where I'm walking so I don't fall over.

I feel a little panicky at the thought of him coming back to Kahukura. Some of the Elders will be there and will want to talk to him if they see him. And Ana will also be around. I surprise myself by feeling a flare of jealousy. Ana is prettier than me, more outgoing, and better with men. I don't want Orson to meet her.

Then I get cross with myself. I'm being ridiculous. I don't know why he's coming with me anyway. I hardly need protecting.

At that point I walk straight into a tree branch and nearly decapitate myself.

"Jesus," he says, catching my arm as I stumble. "Girl, you gotta be more careful."

"It's your fault," I complain before I can think better of it.

"Why is it my fault?" he asks, amused.

Because I'm having trouble concentrating on anything else but you.

"You keep distracting me," I complain. "Go home."

"I'd like to look around the commune."

"No," I say with alarm. "Absolutely not."

"You take visitors around, don't you?"

"Yes, but—"

"Then I'd like to visit. I'd like to know what you do there."

"There won't be any group sex sessions going on, if that's what you're hoping to see."

He laughs, and our eyes meet. "I want to see your world," he says mildly.

I hesitate. Then I say, "I don't want you to make fun of it."

He snorts. "Because you would never make fun of mine."

He's right, and I feel ashamed of that, especially now he's told me about how hard he works, and how much he studied to get where he is.

He's looking at me, and now he says, "I won't make fun of the commune, I promise. I am sorry I teased you." He frowns. "There's something about you that…"

"That what?"

"Riles me up." He looks amused and perplexed at the same time.

I don't know what to say to that, so I just look away as we exit the trees and start walking across the field. It slopes down to the commune, which lies spread out before us. It's busy today—a car heads up the drive, probably with some kind of food delivery; Dani's taking the younger kids for a walk through the vineyards; Lee is out digging post holes for a new fence. A car is parked out the front, and Isobel, one of the Elders, is greeting the two women who are currently exiting it.

We stop and look down at the view. Orson surveys it thoughtfully, scanning the vineyards, the vegetable gardens, the quiet but busy life taking place in the peaceful surroundings, a world removed from his opulent resort with its rich patrons, flash cars, and swanky buildings.

Is he secretly laughing inside? Having to hold himself back from mocking my way of life? I lift my chin. I don't have to prove anything to him or anyone else.

"If you're coming, let's get on with it," I say, and begin to walk down the hill. "Just please refrain from calling anyone a communalist. They won't appreciate your sense of humor the way I do."

Chapter Six

Orson

She appreciates my sense of humor, then? That makes me smile as I follow her down the hill toward the commune.

I admit that I'd half-expected to see a kind of medieval settlement, with dirt tracks for roads, ramshackle houses, filthy kids playing with sticks and hoops, and dogs and chickens running wild.

Instead, the small town, while definitely having a medieval feel, looks well planned and maintained. Neat roads form a simple grid system around a central village green with a duck pond in the center. A few shops line one side of the green, while on the other is what looks like a village hall, possibly a chapel although there's no cross on the top, and a couple of other larger buildings. Behind them are several rows of small cottages that are hardly bigger than the villas our guests stay in at Midnight. But they're all surrounded by a decent patch of land, with mown lawns, painted fences, flower borders, and veggie patches. On one side, there's a large vegetable plot, so they obviously grow their own, and I can also see a couple of cows in the nearby field, and several goats. There are chickens, but they're in a large coop.

They're obviously modernized here—there are Sky dishes and my phone has a signal and Scarlett mentioned they have computers with the Internet in their communal library. The cars are newish, just not ostentatious. But there's a sense of peace about the place that speaks of another time, before the craziness of the modern world became the norm.

I follow her down the slope and through the gate at the bottom. "There," she says, stopping, "you delivered me safely. You can go now."

"I told you, I'd like a tour."

Her brows draw together. "Please go."

"Why? I'm serious. I want to look around." The truth is that I'm intrigued. It's clear my father hasn't told me the whole truth about Kahukura. He's always painted Blake Stone, his family, and the commune with crazy paint, but Scarlett's recent comments have suggested he's offered a highly fictionalized account, which puzzles and angers me at the same time. I'm not sure what's the truth and what's made up, and I want to discover the reality for myself.

She glares at me. "I—" Immediately she stops as someone calls her name from behind her. We both turn, and I see a slightly younger version of Scarlett jogging up to us. She has the same build and the same color hair, although she sports a quirky pixie cut.

"Hello," she says, slowing as she nears us. She gives Scarlett an amused look. "Who's this, and why are you both soaking wet? Has it been raining?"

"I fell in the pool," Scarlett says.

"That explains why *you're* wet…"

"I rescued her," I tell her.

Ana grins. "That was kind of you. She does have a habit of getting herself into strange situations."

"I'm beginning to realize that."

"I'm standing right here," Scarlett says crossly. "Orson, this is my sister, Ana. Ana, this is Orson Cavendish."

Ana stares at me, and her smile slowly fades. "Cavendish?"

"Spencer Cavendish's son," Scarlett adds.

Ana's mouth forms an O. Her gaze slides down me slowly, from my tie, down my shirt, all the way down my trousers to my shoes, and then slowly back up.

"No forked tail," I announce. "And no horns either."

"I beg to differ," Scarlett says sarcastically. "Come on, then, if you want to look around."

"You're giving him a tour?" Ana asks, astonished.

"He wants to check out the enemy so he can make fun of us more accurately," Scarlett says.

"That about sums it up," I reply.

Ana's lips twitch, but I can see she's puzzled. "Dad wouldn't be happy knowing you've let him on the premises," she says.

Scarlett looks down at her sandals for a moment. Then she lifts her chin and says, "Well, Dad's not here anymore, and we've got to get on without him." She marches past her sister toward the central buildings.

I give Ana a quick smile and say, "It was nice meet you," and stride out after Scarlett.

She's walking quickly, and I fall into step beside her.

"You okay?" I ask.

"I'm fine." She slows down, then stops. "Would you rather my sister shows you around?"

I stop too and frown. "No, why?"

"I just wondered. I don't mind."

"I don't want your sister. I want you."

She meets my eyes again. We study each other for ten seconds. Then she drops her gaze and starts walking, and I join her.

She clears her throat. "So this is the main communal area around the green. This is the Haven." She stops outside the building that looks like a chapel.

"It's a place of worship? For what religion?" Dad has inferred they follow some kind of New Age wacky paganism here.

But Scarlett says, "Anything and everything. We're not a religious-based commune. Any faiths are welcome. We have Christians of all denominations, a few Muslims, one Jewish family, pagans, a Hindu couple, several Buddhists… Many aren't religious at all."

"What about you?"

"If I tell you, will you mock me?"

"Almost certainly."

She gives me a wry look. "I'm guessing you're not religious?"

"Nope."

"Why not?"

"My dad is far too practical to have faith in anything or anyone except himself."

"What about your mother? Was she?"

I look away, across the green. "She was Anglican. She told us some of the Bible stories when we were young. But Dad didn't want us to go to church—he said we should make our own minds up when we were adults."

"I can understand that," she says, surprising me. "When you're not religious it makes sense to feel that you shouldn't force children to think the way you do. But religion brings a lot of people comfort. And it's good sometimes to give children structure and a strong moral code."

"You don't need religion to do that."

"No… that's true. But most people are comforted about the thought of there being more than what we can see around us."

"I dunno. What's around us is pretty amazing. Snowflakes and sex and all that. I don't know why there has to be more."

Her lips curve up. "Snowflakes and sex?"

"First amazing things that came to mind."

"Well at least you put snowflakes first."

We both laugh. "Come and have a look," she says softly, and she goes up the steps and pushes open the door.

I follow her inside. The Haven turns out to be a hall with white walls, light-wood furniture, and high windows, including one rather beautiful stained-glass window that's decorated with religious symbols from all religions, with a table at the front. There are chairs and bean bags, and a low table with paper and coloring pencils for the kids, with their drawings pinned to a large board. Two huge displays of fresh flowers on either side of the front table bring a splash of color. There's also a stand for votive candles, incense holders, and several bookcases.

"Our library of wisdom," Scarlett says as I wander over to it. It contains a carefully curated selection of religious texts, philosophical treatises, and explorations of spirituality from across lots of different cultures.

I pick up one and show it to her with a raised eyebrow. It's called *Reveal Your Inner Goddess.*

"I'll show you mine if you show me yours," she says.

I laugh and put it back. "I like the fact that it caters for all religions."

"We believe everyone's faith is important and valid here."

I think about that as I follow her out of the Haven, into the bright sunshine.

"This is our town hall." She opens the door of the big building next to the Haven, and I follow her inside. It's a basic community hall, with white walls, polished wooden floors, exposed beams, long benches and tables, and stackable chairs, and a noticeboard near the door. Handmade tapestries hang on the walls, presumably crafted by members of the community. Pots holding more fresh flowers are placed at regular intervals along the walls.

Open doors reveal smaller meeting rooms off to the sides. "The Elders meet here every evening," she says. "I saw them last night to put forward your proposal."

"Oh?" It's the first time she's mentioned this. "What did they say?"

"They're interested in your offer. They want me to report back on our meeting today, and then they'll discuss it." She looks down.

I tip my head to try to see her face. "Do you get a say in it?"

"We trust the Elders to make the decisions for the commune."

"I get that. But you own the land now, right?"

She frowns. "Technically."

"So you should have the final say on what happens to it."

"It's complicated." She turns and starts walking, and I fall into step beside her. "This is the retreat," she says, and she stops before the largest building. "Come on."

I hesitate, though. "Are you sure? If this is a sanctuary for abused women and children, the last thing they would want is a strange guy wandering through the corridors."

Her gaze scans me, and then her expression softens. "You wanted to see all of it, right? It's important that they don't think they're coming here to get away from men. Men make up half the population of the world, and the vast majority of them are good people. They need to reestablish trust by connecting with the good ones, that's all."

I blink. "And you're including me in that group?"

Her eyebrows lift as if she's surprised herself. Then she gives me a quirky smile. "Looks like it. I don't think you're a bad person, Orson. Just misguided." The smile turns mischievous. "Anyway, you're with me. You'll be fine." She gestures with her head for me to follow her.

Stunned at that little revelation, I go inside with her.

We walk slowly through the building. There's a big meeting room, classrooms for group workshops, and smaller offices for one-on-one counseling. A gym with a space for yoga, ballet, and Jiu Jitsu classes. I discover that Scarlett herself runs many of those. A kitchen backs onto the vegetable patches, and she tells me that everyone is encouraged to spend time helping out there, because they believe a connection with nature is integral to healing.

"We run a mind, body, and spirit holistic healing program," she says as we slowly climb a central staircase to the next floor. "Physical healing is obviously important in cases of abuse, but healing the mind and the soul is also essential. Relationships are all about the balance of power, and in the cases of most of these women, they feel as if they've lost all their power. We try to help them regain some of that control over their lives by showing them how to eat better, exercise, and

MIDNIGHT ENEMY

meditate, as well as to help them deal with some of the more practical aspects of their situation."

"You offer legal and financial advice, right?"

"Well not me personally, I'm clueless about that side of things. But yes, some of the members of the commune are experts in those fields, and they offer their help if needed."

We get to the top of the stairs, and she shows me around. It's like a hotel, with individual rooms for the women and children, playrooms for the kids, and spotless bathrooms. As we're walking along the corridor, a woman comes out of a room with a teenage girl. She sees us, stops, and takes an involuntary step back. I stop walking, horrified to think my presence had that impact on her.

But Scarlett just smiles and says, "Morning, Tina, morning Bella! Are you heading down to lunch?"

Tina, the mother, gathers herself and nods. "We're going to make a sandwich."

"We had some Brie delivered with the groceries earlier, and some fresh cranberries, so Julie's made some cranberry sauce. That would make a nice sandwich."

"Ooh," Bella says, "yum."

"This is Orson," Scarlett says, resting a hand on my arm. "He's a friend of mine. He lives nearby, and he's visiting the commune. I'm betting he'd add chips to his sandwich. Am I right?"

"A sandwich isn't a sandwich without at least six ingredients," I reply.

Scarlett rolls her eyes. "I knew it." The other two chuckle.

The girl looks down at Scarlett's wet dress and my wet pants and whispers something to her mum.

"Scarlett fell in the Waiora," I tell them. "And I tried to be the white knight and jumped in to save her, then fell over myself."

"Don't listen to him," Scarlett says. "He was very heroic." She smiles. "Come on, I'll take you around the rest of the commune now."

"Nice to meet you," I say to Tina and her daughter, and they both wave goodbye as Scarlett and I head downstairs.

"You think I was heroic?" I say as we go outside.

"I was playing to the crowd."

I snort, and her lips twist. She steers me to the next building, which turns out to be a large communal kitchen and dining hall.

I look briefly inside. "You all eat together?"

She nods. "It's a major part of being in the commune. We take turns preparing the food and clearing up afterward."

"Not sure how I'd feel about that," I say, letting the door close. "I like cooking my own food."

"You cook?" she asks as we continue on.

"Sometimes. Why are you smiling?"

"I thought you'd have had your own personal French chef bringing you your every whim."

"I do sometimes," I admit. "If I'm entertaining. But mostly I cook for myself."

"Where do you live?"

"In an apartment in the city. And I have a suite at the Midnight Club too. I divide my time between the two."

"I thought you'd have had a mansion somewhere with tennis courts and swimming pools and a staff of thirty to wait on you hand and foot."

"I don't live in Downton Abbey," I point out.

"I'm going to call you Sir from now on," she teases.

"Ah, I wouldn't go down that road," I advise. "I'm having enough trouble keeping myself restrained as it is."

She blinks and stares at me, obviously bemused.

"Never mind," I say, stifling a laugh. "But yeah, I don't think I'd like to eat communally. What if you fancy something different from the day's meal?"

"Well, you can prepare your own food, of course. But most people find it easy to just have what everyone else is having—pasta, casserole, whatever."

"How often do you go to a restaurant?"

"I've never been to one."

I stare at her. "Sorry, what?"

"Scarlett!" A guy in his early sixties with grey hair approaches us and smiles.

"Hey George," she says. "Orson, this is George Bush—no relation to the US President—he's the commune's financial expert. George, this is Orson Cavendish."

"Pleased to meet you," I say, and we shake hands.

"Scarlett giving you the tour, is she?" he asks.

"Yes, I asked if I could have a look around."

"You've been to the Waiora?" He glances at our wet clothes.

MIDNIGHT ENEMY

"And surveyed the water," I say cheerfully.

He chuckles. "So Scarlett has mentioned our request?"

She glares at him. "No, I haven't had the chance yet."

"Request?" I ask.

"He's talking about your offer," Scarlett says stiffly.

"We're interested," George says. "But we don't think it's enough."

I lift an eyebrow. "You don't think that offering five million more than what the land is worth is enough?"

George clears his throat. "Developing the Waiora would be financially beneficial to you and your resort, and it would also smooth over any issues with the local iwi."

I hold his gaze for a moment. We both know that fifteen million was more than generous.

I look at Scarlett, irritated at being blindsided. Why didn't she tell me about this earlier?

"Do you support this?" I ask her.

Gradually, her face matches her name, and she lowers her lashes to shield her eyes. Oh... George's outspokenness has embarrassed her. She didn't want to sell to the Cavendishes anyway, and it looks as if the thought of haggling is causing her to curl up and die inside.

But she says, "Yes." No doubt duty is forcing her to back them, even if she disagrees. "We need the money," she adds. "For the commune."

George frowns, clearly annoyed that she would share that.

"It must be tough having to organize all the finances of the commune," I say. "Do you have any help?"

George meets my gaze and holds it for a moment. Then he looks away and says, "I don't need help. I know what I'm doing."

"Well," I say softly, "I'll think about it and talk to Scarlett."

"The decision will be made by the Elders of the commune," he says, looking back at me.

"The land is Scarlett's," I point out.

His cheeks flush. "That's just semantics."

"Not really. It's the legal position."

"Please," Scarlett says, "don't argue. George is right. The Elders have the final say over what happens here."

George nods. "I'm going to the city. Scarlett, do you want anything?"

"No, thank you."

"Come and see us tonight, okay?" he says to her.

She nods. "Of course."

We both watch him walk away.

Scarlett glances at me, and then we continue walking.

"Why did you ask if he has any help?" she asks.

I slide my hands into my trouser pockets as I think about how to answer. "Do you know if the commune has any kind of audit system?"

"What do you mean?"

"Does anyone else check the books? Or does George do it all on his own?"

"He does it on his own. He's very competent."

"I'm sure he is. But it's always important to have financial systems checked by an independent party."

"Why?"

I frown at her. Is she really that naive? "To make sure the books aren't being cooked."

"Cooked?"

"Altered."

She stares at me. "George would never do that."

"Sweetheart, I understand that the success of the commune depends on everyone trusting everyone else, but if you are going to make a decision about your land, you need to take off your rose-tinted glasses."

She looks astonished. "What are you implying?"

"I'm not implying anything. I'm just saying it's not a great idea to have one person in charge of a company's finances."

"Because you think everyone can be tempted if the price is high enough."

"Absolutely."

"That's bullshit." Her face flushes. "I trust every single one of the Elders."

"That's commendable and sweet."

"Don't talk to me like I'm five years old."

"Then don't act like it. I'm an expert in finance. I run my business with my best friend. I've known him since high school and I'd trust him with my life, and vice versa. But we still have an independent company come in to audit us. It helps us trust one another—it doesn't destroy the trust."

She blinks. That's hit home.

"It's none of my business," I say more gently. "I have no skin in the game where Kahukura is concerned. If you want to trust George with your money and the future of the commune, it's nothing to do with me."

She gives me a wry look. "That statement wasn't loaded by much."

"Maybe a little. Look, do you know any other accountants?"

"No."

"I'd offer to do it myself, but I don't think anyone would appreciate that. If I was to send my friend your way, would you put it to the other Elders that you'd like an audit done?"

Her jaw drops. "I… don't know… it's not my place…"

"Of course it's your place. You're a democracy here, right?"

"I don't know the technical term," she says stiffly. "The Elders are elected by the rest of us."

"Are other members allowed an input?"

"We can attend Elder meetings, but the Elders make the final decisions."

"So it's Elder Council Governance rather than a Guided Democracy."

"I guess…"

That makes it trickier. Some 'intentional communities' involve individual ownership and autonomy, where members rent their own houses but share meals, chores, maintenance of the communal areas, and possibly values and ideology, with the intention of fostering a sense of community and belonging. Kahukura obviously takes it one step further, though. I'm guessing its members form a fully income-sharing community that practices egalitarian decision making, with no one person in charge. And I'm getting a prickling feeling that tells me the lawyer was right—they're struggling financially, and that's why George and the others are pressuring for a higher price.

"You own the land, Scarlett," I say. "And as a member of the commune, and as a human being, you have the right to ask that the people who are in a position of trust are doing their jobs."

She looks puzzled. "I suppose."

I realize that if she's grown up here, and she's not been to university, she's probably never been taught to question.

"I'll get Kingi to call you," I say. "Have a chat to him and see what you think. I want to help, if I can."

She stops walking and lifts her gaze to mine. "Why?"

"I… don't know," I say honestly.

"We're enemies," she says. "Aren't we?"

I frown. It's true that our fathers were. And before I met her, I would have agreed with her.

But she's standing before me with her huge eyes and wet dress and a fucking rosebud in her silky brown hair, and I realize I can't think of her as an enemy at all.

But she turns and walks away before I can answer, and I bite back my retort and follow with a frown.

Chapter Seven

Scarlett

"What time are you meeting him?" Ana asks.

It's Sunday, and the two of us are working in the vegetable garden. I straighten, arch my back, and look at my watch. "Three o'clock. I suppose I should get going soon."

Five days have passed since I showed Orson around the commune on Tuesday. It's not been an easy week. And this morning he called the commune and left a message asking if I'd meet him at the Waiora this afternoon to talk.

I don't want to see him again. He gets under my skin. He hasn't yet agreed to the higher offer, and the Elders have called me in several times to try and convince me to push him to sell. But when I've called him twice to talk to him about it over the phone, his secretary has told me each time that he's in a meeting. I suspect it's been a ploy to make sure I meet him, but I can't be certain.

"Have fun," Ana says as I take off my apron.

I glare at her. "Fun is the last thing on my mind."

"Your mouth says one thing but the blush in your cheeks says another." Her words are mischievous, but her smile is kind.

I was so sure he'd prefer her, but I still think about his answer when I asked if he'd rather she show him around: *I don't want your sister. I want you.*

Shaking my head to try to dislodge it, I say, "Whatever, I'll see you later," and head off to the house to get ready.

I take a quick shower because I'm hot and sweaty, and put on a red summer dress and sandals. Then I take it off and pull on jeans and a tee. Take them off. Put the dress on again. I brush my hair. Braid it severely. Then unravel it, brush it again, and scowl at myself in the mirror. I don't know why I'm bothering. It's not like either of us is interested in the other in that way.

That doesn't mean I shouldn't look nice though. I slot a red freesia above my ear, then slick on some red lip gloss. Trying to block out the memory of the look in his eyes when he stared into mine, I realize it's 2:55, curse under my breath, and head out of the door.

It's a blustery March day. The sun was hot earlier, but the clouds are moving quickly now, and the sky is turning a deep gray. As I walk up the hill, I begin to wonder whether I should have brought an umbrella, but I can't be bothered to go back.

By the time I get to the Waiora, it's nearly ten past three. As soon as I exit the bush, I see a guy on the other side of the pool, sitting in the gazebo there, reading on his phone. For a moment I don't recognize him. He's wearing dark jeans, a faded gray T-shirt, and Converses, his hair is a little ruffled, and he looks completely different from the suave, sophisticated man in his suit. But then he looks up and sees me, and he stands, pockets his phone, and waves before walking up the bank to the top of the waterfall.

I do the same, heart racing, and we pause at the top, facing each other across the stones. A drop of rain falls on my cheek, then another.

"Hey," he calls, and he lifts a hand and beckons to me. "Come over this side and we'll talk in the gazebo—I think it's going to rain."

For some reason, the way he beckons to me irritates me, as if I'm a dog. I bet everyone in his life does his bidding without question. Well, I don't work for him, and I'm not going to do what he says.

"No," I snap, "you come over this side."

He lowers his hand and looks up at the sky. More droplets land on my face. Unfortunately, I think he's right, but now if I go over I'm letting him win, and I'll be damned if I'm going to let that happen.

He looks back at me. "Please, come on. It's the only shelter out here."

"I don't mind getting wet." I brush a hand over my cheek to remove the drops.

He puts his hands on his hips. "Scarlett…"

I shake my head.

He runs his tongue across his top teeth, then starts traversing the stepping stones. I glare at him, hoping he slips and falls, but I know that despite us not agreeing on a sale yet, he's had someone up here securing some of the stones, and sure enough he strides out surefooted and swift.

It's starting to rain properly, and I'm beginning to regret my decision, but it's too late now. I watch him approach, impressed with how elegantly he moves, like the big cat I've compared him to before. The sleeves of his tee stretch tightly across his biceps, making me wonder if he works out. Surely they're not natural. Would they give under pressure, like a firm cushion, or would they feel solid, like carved wood?

He covers the last few stones and jumps onto the bank next to me. His light-gray tee is now covered in dark blotches from the rain, and his hair is turning spiky.

"I should have brought an umbrella," I begin to say as he walks up to me, but my words fade away as I realize he's not stopping. He closes the distance between us, bends quickly, and hoists me up and over his shoulder.

I squeal loudly and kick my legs, but he wraps one arm tightly across the back of my thighs, turns, and heads back over the stepping stones. Upside down, I whack him on the backside, but he just says, "Are you trying to turn me on?"

"Orson!"

"Serves you right for not behaving."

I reel off a string of curses.

"Language," he says. "I didn't know you Peaceful Percys knew words like that."

"Fuck off."

He's halfway back by now, and he stops and shifts my weight on his shoulder. "Stop wriggling or I'll drop you."

I do, because I don't want to be submerged again and end up falling off the waterfall, but that doesn't stop me giving him another earful as he continues.

He covers the last few stones onto the bank, then lowers me down. As he straightens, he rolls his shoulder.

"I hope it's really painful," I snap, tugging my dress down where it's risen up. It's really raining now, and we're quickly getting soaked.

"Don't worry," he replies. "Your wish is granted. Now, will you come down to the gazebo?"

"Will you stop bossing me about?"

He closes his eyes and massages his temples with a hand for a moment, and I remember that he also had a concussion. Guilt twinges inside me, at the same time that the heavens really open, and rain begins to fall in torrents. "All right," I concede.

"Thank you."

We turn and make our way hastily down the bank, but sub-tropical rain like this can easily soak you in seconds, and by the time we reach the gazebo, we're completely drenched.

"Fuck me," he says as we climb the steps. It's covered over, but of course it doesn't stop rain being blown over us as the stiff breeze whips it around. "Jesus that came down quickly." He scowls at me. "This was a mistake. I just wanted to ask if the Elders were still pushing for the higher price."

"You could have asked me that on the phone."

"You weren't around," he pointed out.

"I rang you, but you decided you were 'unavailable.'" I put air quotes around it.

"I *was* 'unavailable,'" he says, repeating the air quotes. "I was in a meeting."

"Twice?"

"Yes, both times."

"Yeah, right. You just wanted to make sure I came here today."

He meets my eyes. Then his lips curve up. "Maybe."

"I knew it!"

He chuckles and runs a hand through his wet hair. "So have you had a chance to speak to the Elders yet?"

His T-shirt tightens across his chest and arms as he moves. God, he's gorgeous. "They're deliberating," I tell him. "They still want the higher price."

"Kingi said he'd spoken to you."

I nod. He rang on Wednesday and introduced himself as the friend who runs Te Aranui Developments with Orson.

"I haven't approached the Elders about an audit yet," I told Kingi nervously on the phone.

"That's okay," he said easily. He had a deep, gruff voice with a slight hint of a Māori accent, which is a little different from the standard Kiwi accent. "I just wanted to introduce myself and have a chat. Orson told me that at the moment you don't have anyone to audit the commune's finances. I wanted to echo his suggestion that you get someone to do that, even if you'd rather use someone else. It's so easy to make mistakes, and a second pair of eyes can catch all kinds of errors."

"That's his bad attempt at diplomacy. He doesn't trust our finance manager."

"I'm sure that's not true," Kingi said.

"It's totally true, and he's way off the mark."

"I'm sure he didn't mean to imply anything…"

"Yes he did." My throat tightened, and my eyes pricked with tears. "The success of the commune relies on us trusting one another," I told him, my voice a little husky. "He doesn't understand that."

"I think he does," he replied gently. "Much of business relies on trust. Auditing provides reassurance, that's all."

It was similar to what Orson said, so it made it difficult to argue with him. I told him I'd speak to the Elders and let him know, and he reiterated his willingness to help before ending the call.

"Yes, he offered his services," I tell Orson.

"And?"

"I put the suggestion of an audit forward."

He waits. Then, when I don't answer, says, "And?"

I hesitate. Then I drop my gaze to the floor. "A couple of the others said it would be a good idea. But George went ballistic. Said it went against the ethics of the commune. He said if we didn't trust him, we should find someone else to do the finances. They spent half an hour talking him down."

"Huh," Orson says.

"It's why I don't have an answer for you. They asked me to leave, and they're still trying to sort it all out, as far as I know."

He massages his head again.

I frown. "Do you have a headache?"

"I always have a headache."

I sigh. "Come here," I say softly, lowering myself onto the wooden floor. It's rain spattered but not too wet in the middle. "I want you to lie down."

His eyebrows rise. "Why?"

"So I can do some voodoo on you."

His expression turns wry, but he sits on the floor. "Seriously?"

"Yeah. Turn around and lie down, and put your head in my lap."

His eyes meet mine.

"Don't get any ideas," I scold. "I want to help the organ in your skull, not the one in your pants."

He gives a short laugh. Then he turns around, lowers onto his elbows, and lies back, resting his head on my crossed legs.

I look at him upside down. "Close your eyes," I tell him, unable to bear the intensity of his blue eyes as he looks up at me.

He does so obediently, and I let out a long breath. My hands are cool, and I rub them together for a moment to try to warm them a bit. Then I place them above his face, not quite touching, covering his eyes.

He exhales, his breath whispering across my palms.

"Try to relax," I tell him softly. "We're not going anywhere anytime soon. Listen to the rain and the waterfall. Listen to Kahukura singing to you. Let her waters heal you. Now, concentrate on your breathing. Put your hand on your belly, and breathe from there—not from your chest. You're going to visualize a flower blooming. As its petals unfurl, you inhale to the count of six. When it's fully bloomed, you imagine the flower closing at nighttime and exhale for a count of six. Ready?" I count to show him the pace. "Inhale, two, three, four, five, six, exhale, two, three, four, five, six."

I stop counting out loud and close my eyes. The water tumbles over the rocks into the pool, the sound like the crescendo of an orchestra. The wind has eased a little, and the rain now falls straight down, pattering on the roof of the gazebo, and on the ferns and stones around us. The light breeze ruffles the leaves of the palms and the trees.

After about a minute, I open my eyes and move my hands, resting them over his temples.

Now I can see his face. I usually do this with women, and I'm fascinated by his different bone structure. Women tend to have softer, more rounded contours, their brow ridges less pronounced, their jawlines narrower, and their chins more pointed. Orson has a prominent, angular facial bone structure, with a stronger brow ridge, a broader chin, and a more pronounced jawline. He has a long, straight nose, and a well-shaped mouth. His lashes are dark, quite beautiful actually, long and as curved as a woman's. I'd tease him about them, but I do want him to feel better, and don't want to disturb him.

The few times we've met, he's been clean shaven, but today his skin bears a light touch of bristle. Before I can stop myself, I brush my thumbs across his cheeks. They rasp slightly, which fascinates me.

Orson inhales deeply, then lets out the breath in a long sigh. This happens often when people who are touch starved receive healing—they're so unused to the touch of another person that even a light brush of someone else's fingers can make them feel emotional. Is he touch starved? It wouldn't surprise me. I can't imagine that Spencer Cavendish is the touchy-feely type of father. Orson's mother died. He said he hasn't had a girlfriend in a while. And even if he's the sort of guy who greets friends with a bearhug, men are unlikely to touch each other often.

His headache might have been started by his accident and his concussion, but I believe a person's power to heal themselves is affected by their mental, emotional, and physical health. He has a high-powered job, so he will suffer from stress and anxiety, even if he thinks he handles it well. All men struggle with the weight of duty and responsibility, and the need to appear in control. These things are like anchors weighing him down and will affect his body's natural repair tools: his immune system, his heart rate, and his blood pressure.

I'm a big believer in the power of touch, and so I decide to give him a face massage. I start by brushing my thumbs across his forehead, starting in the center and sweeping them to the temples. I do the same with his eyebrows, and very lightly stroke over his eyes and the eye sockets. Resting my first two fingers on each temple, I massage them gently, admiring the unusual white flashes of hair there, and being careful not to press too hard on the graze that is still visible there. Then I move my fingers down each side of his face and cup his jaw.

Sliding my hands down, I stroke his neck and throat above the top of the tee. My fingers brush over his Adam's apple—possibly the thing that's most different from a woman's face. He swallows and I feel it rise and then lower again. I smile and see his lips curve up too.

I dip my thumbs into the hollow at the base of his throat and brush away the drop of rain that has moistened the skin there. I can smell his cologne rising from his damp clothes, the same as before—vanilla, tobacco, and brandy. What did he call it? The Tragedy Of Lord George. 'The perfect scent for a gentleman with something dark hidden away.' I wonder what dark things he's hiding, what his secrets are. What he shares with women in bed after the sun goes down.

Even though he protested he's a serial monogamist, I have no doubt he's had many partners. He will be skilled in bed, and know his way around a woman's body. Know how to touch her and please her, how to tease her to a climax.

I brush my thumbs up over his mouth, tracing the shape of his Cupid's bow, imagining what it would feel like to press my lips to his. I realize with surprise that I like him, even though we're supposed to be enemies, and even though my father would be angry to know I'm even talking to him, let alone touching him like this.

To my surprise, he puckers his lips and kisses my thumb. My heart bangs on my ribs. And before I can think better of it, I lean forward and press my lips to his.

His eyes are still closed so he obviously didn't expect that, and he inhales sharply. I move back a fraction, shocked at myself, wondering if he's going to scold me. His bright blue eyes open and stare up into mine. Then he lifts a hand, rests it on the back of my neck, and pulls me down to him again.

I give him a Spiderman kiss, upside down. He doesn't move, just accepts the kiss, but he also doesn't remove his hand from my neck, and I feel him brush his thumb across my throat.

I shiver, my nipples tightening, my lips parting as I inhale, and then I jump as I feel his tongue touch my bottom lip. He stops and waits, and I take a few seconds to debate whether I should push him away and get up. I ought to. I should.

But I don't. It's too wicked, too delicious. His cologne winds around me, and I know that his secret is his passion, kept locked away inside him like a feral big cat. When I lower my lips back to his, he gives an approving growl deep in his throat, like a purr, and it makes firecrackers go off inside me, tiny little fizzes and bangs and sprays of color in my head and my heart and my stomach.

He slides his hand into my hair, opening his mouth, and I gasp as he probes with his tongue, stroking it against mine. Mmm that's so erotic, and my body stirs like an animal coming out of hibernation.

I continue to brush my hands over his face, stroking his cheeks, his jaw, his throat, and across his shoulders. He sighs as he kisses me, and I feel his shoulders release some of the tension they were holding. I rub his right shoulder, where I know he's sore, massaging it lightly and willing the healing power of the Kahukura to penetrate his muscles and tendons and ligaments and bones.

At the same time, he runs his fingers over the nape of my neck and through my hair, and I give a little moan, tingling all over. In response, he tightens his fingers, clenching my hair, opens his mouth wider, and deepens the kiss, plunging his tongue into my mouth until I'm gasping for breath. I'm shocked at the intensity of it, how I feel invaded and ravaged, and he's hardly touching me really.

When I moan again, he shifts suddenly, turning and lifting an arm around my shoulders. Before I can understand what he's doing, he pulls me across him, lifting me as easily as if I'm a pillow, and adjusting our position until I'm lying fully on top of him, stretched out.

"Oh!" I'm stunned at how easily he manhandled me. But there's no time to react, because he cups my head and brings it down so he can crush his lips to mine.

Oh my God, I thought the previous kiss was deep, but this is intense, lighting fires inside me, and I'm powerless to fight against it. I know that if I yelled stop, or pushed up, or wrenched my head away, he'd stop immediately. I don't know how; I just know. I trust him. But I don't want him to stop. I'm burning, and he's driving me crazy, and if he stops I honestly think that, like a rose deprived of sunshine and water, I'll just curl up and wither and die.

So I kiss him back, and he's hard through his jeans against my stomach, and my heart bangs against my ribs so fast I feel dizzy, and I don't know where this is going, but I want it to go on forever, until the stars come out to watch us, and the moon rises in the night sky.

Chapter Eight

Orson

My head is spinning.

I couldn't believe it when Scarlett kissed me. And I can't believe that now she's lying on top of me, still kissing me, and not fighting me off with a stick.

Jesus… she's so incredibly soft all over. She doesn't possess a single angle. Her breasts are two small pillows squashed to my chest, my erection is pressed into her soft stomach, and when I run my hand down her back to her bottom, my fingers automatically clench the plump muscles there.

Something hits me then, and I run my fingers up her sides, feeling for any elastic at her hips or in the middle of her back. I don't find any.

She lifts her head and gives me a mischievous look.

"You're not wearing any underwear," I say flatly.

She shrugs. "It was a warm day."

"Holy fucking shit."

"Orson!"

"I'm so fucking turned on right now."

She laughs, her expression lighting up at the thought that I desire her. I lift both hands to her face and hold her as I kiss her. She responds with such enthusiasm that it only serves to fire me up even more.

My senses feel heightened, turned up to eleven by the wind and rain, the sensation of the wet clothes against my skin, and the way her hands moved across my face, neck, and shoulders, stroking and massaging. I know I'm probably imagining it, but the ache in my right shoulder and even in my head has vanished. But then that's probably because all the blood in my body has flown south for the winter. Her hands on my face warmed as she held them there, and it's impossible not to believe she was somehow drawing on healing power, even if it was only internal.

Fuuuuck... I have no idea why, but this girl drives me crazy... Her sundress—scarlet with white swirls—is short, loose, and flowing and looks like something that might have been worn at Woodstock. Her bare legs are smooth and brown. She was wearing red lip gloss when she first walked up, and when she kissed me, her lips stuck to mine, then peeled away in such an erotic manner that I nearly came on the spot.

She's shifted up my body a bit, and I don't know if she realizes she's doing it or if it's unconscious, but she's moving her hips slowly, arousing herself on my erection. The head of it nestles in her softness and slides up to the top as she moves, and she gives a little groan and circles her hips, presumably feeling it pressing against her clit. Ahhh... that's incredibly erotic. I slide my hands down her back to her bottom and pull her toward me, moving with her to encourage her.

"Ohhh," she says softly, just an exhalation really, her breath whispering across my lips, and her teeth tug on her bottom lip as her eyes close, so I know she's feeling the ripples of pleasure like shockwaves through her body.

"Mmm," I murmur, kissing her jaw, her neck, her throat. "Slowly..."

I stroke up her body to her breasts and fill my palms with them. They're probably a C cup, generous but still high, and they fit my hands perfectly. It's not cold exactly, but the rain is cool, and her nipples have tightened where her wet dress is clinging to them. They're like buttons on her dress, and when I tease them with my thumbs, she moans softly against my lips.

This is like heaven, the rain falling around us like a curtain on a four-poster bed, shutting out the world. I'd worry that someone might be watching, but there isn't going to be anyone else out here in this weather, and anyway we're surrounded by ferns and palms that shelter us from prying eyes.

Her breathing has changed, her breaths coming faster; I don't think she's far from coming. I hold her in place with one hand at the base of her spine and tease a nipple with the other, and she lifts her head, her eyes wide and unfocused.

"Orson," she whispers, "oh my God..."

"Come for me," I murmur, lifting my hand to the back of her head to pull her mouth back down to mine.

She mumbles something against my lips and puts both hands on my chest as if she's about to push herself up, but I deepen the kiss, and instead she moans and circles her hips. Her fingers clutch at my T-shirt, and I return my hand to her nipple.

I take a chance and slide the other hand beneath her dress, up her silky thigh, and onto her bare bottom. Her skin is velvety soft and damp, like rose petals. In response, she parts her legs so she's astride me, then positions herself so the tip of my erection is pressing against her entrance through my jeans, and moans. Ah, fuck… I lower my other hand to clutch at her bare ass and hold her as I rock, and that does it—she shivers, goes still for a second, then gasps against my mouth as she comes.

Aaahhh… the beauty of a woman's orgasm, sweet as a whole bowl of strawberries and cream. I bet she tastes like it, too. I wrap an arm around her waist, wishing I was inside her and could feel her clenching around me. But this is pretty good too, her mouth hot on mine, her soft body draped over me. Fuck me, she's hot.

She collapses on top of me and pries her eyes open, and stares straight into mine.

"Oh," she whispers.

"Mmm." My lips curve up, and I kiss her gently. "You're right. This place does make you feel better."

She gives a shy smile, moving her hips against mine. Her big brown eyes study my face, and she lifts a hand to stroke my forehead. "How's your headache?"

"What headache?"

Her smile widens. She brushes a thumb over my mouth, her gaze turning sultry. "You're incredibly handsome."

"Thank you," I say, genuinely flattered. "I feel like I'm making love with a water nymph. With Kahukura herself."

"Making love?" she teases.

I shrug and slide a strand of her silky hair through my fingers. "Did you know that another name for the New Zealand red admiral butterfly is Kahukura? It makes me think of you." It symbolizes Scarlett's fragility and lightness of spirit perfectly.

She kisses me. Then she kisses me again. I sigh, opening my mouth so she can slide her tongue against mine. I'm still hard, and as she moves against me, it's hard to stifle a groan.

She lifts her head again and studies me for a moment.

"What?" I ask, amused at her hesitancy.

"Do you have a condom?"

I blink. "Yeah… in my wallet."

She just meets my eyes, breathing fast.

My lips part, but no words come out. Heat rushes through me. "Here?"

She nods and glances around. "There's nobody around."

"Scarlett…"

"Please," she whispers, rocking her hips again.

Christ, what's a man to do? How can I turn down such a beautiful girl when she's actually asking me to fuck her?

I wrap both arms around her, lift up, and flip her onto her back, and she laughs, looping her arms around my neck as she says, "That was smooth."

Then she can't say anything else because I crush my lips to hers.

On top, I can direct the action more, and I make sure I leave her in no doubt as to how much I want her. I kiss her until we're both breathless, until her breasts are heaving and she's moaning against my lips. She tugs up my wet T-shirt and slides her hands onto my skin, and both of us sigh as she strokes all the way up to my shoulders, then drags her nails lightly back down to my hips.

I raise my head and look into her eyes. "Are you sure about this?"

She nods, then gives another shy smile.

I lift up, extract my wallet from my back pocket, and take out a condom. She's looking at my jeans, her eyes wide as she stares at my erection.

Opening my arms, palms up, I say, "You want to do it?"

Her eyebrows rise. Then she quickly starts unbuttoning my jeans. Carefully, she slides the zipper over my erection, her lips parting in wonder as it protrudes through the opening, coated in the black cotton of my boxer-briefs, eager for action.

I hold the condom out to her, but she shakes her head, so I take off the wrapper, push my underwear down, and roll the condom on.

Next I slide her dress up her thighs, exposing her to the summer air, and exhale at the sight of her smooth light-brown and pink skin glistening with her moisture. Lowering a hand between her legs, I slip my thumb down to make sure she's lubricated, and pause to circle it over her clit, making her moan. I guide the tip of my erection down to her entrance. Then I lean back over her, a hand on either side of her shoulders.

"You're sure?" I say again. I feel kinda dizzy, high on lust, my heart racing, blood speeding around my body at a million miles an hour, pooling in my groin and making my erection rock hard. The breeze sweeps a layer of rain across us, but neither of us reacts.

She moistens her lips, then nods. Fuck me, she's so beautiful. Consumed by lust, I lower onto my elbows and kiss her deeply, and at the same I push my hips forward and bury myself inside her.

"Ow!" She jerks and squeals, an involuntary action that startles me and makes me stop in alarm. We stare into each other's eyes for five seconds, and I register her horrified face before I lift up, sit back on my heels, and ease myself out of her.

There's blood on the condom.

For a moment I can't think straight. My brain spins like a centrifuge, flinging thoughts to all corners of my mind. In the end, all I can come up with is: "You're a virgin?"

She covers her mouth with a hand and bursts into tears.

"What the hell?" Anger flares inside me as I strip off the condom and shove it in my pocket, stuff myself back into my underwear, and zip up my jeans. I yank down her dress. "What's going on? Did the commune send you here to seduce me?" Scenarios flit through my head like bats—of George and his cronies sacrificing her virginity in a scene reminiscent of *The Wicker Man* because they want me to pay more for the Waiora.

But Scarlett shakes her head, tears pouring down her face. "I liked you," she says through her sobs. "I'm sorry. I'm twenty-four. I didn't think it would hurt." She moves back against the bench that looks out over the pool, wraps her arms around her knees, rests her forehead on them, and cries.

Slowly, my anger dissipates like mist. Ah… *shit.*

"Hey…" I move to sit beside her, then put an arm around her shoulders and try to pull her toward me. She resists, her body stiff and unyielding. "I'm so sorry I got angry," I murmur. "Come here, honey. It's okay."

Eventually she lets me lift her onto my lap, and she curls up there and cries into her hands while I hold her.

"Shhh." I rub her back. "It's all right."

"I'm sorry."

"It's all right, sweetheart. But why didn't you tell me?"

She tries to wipe her face, which is pointless because we're both wet from the rain and she's crying too much. "I thought you wouldn't want to if you knew."

I frown, cradling her as if she's a wounded animal. "Well, you're right, I wouldn't have, but only because your first time should be in a comfortable bed with someone you like and trust."

"I like you," she says. "I trust you. That's why I wanted to do it."

I'm so taken aback, I don't know what to say.

I rest my lips on the top of her head and hold her as her sobs turn to snuffles.

"I can't believe you're still a virgin," I murmur.

"Well, I'm not now."

"You know what I mean. You're beautiful and warm and funny. How have you got to twenty-four and not had sex? Are you not allowed in the commune? Do they make you wait until you're married?"

She shakes her head, wiping her face again. "No. There's just nobody there I like, and I don't get out much."

I think about how it must have been for her, isolated in the small community, and not attracted to any of the limited number of young guys in there. It's a world away from my teenage years at university. My lifestyle was a lot more conservative than some, but there were still nightclubs and parties and a scattering of girlfriends.

"You didn't want to save your virginity for your husband?" I ask.

"It's not nineteen-fifty."

I chuckle. "No, I know."

"I hate it," she says fiercely. "It's like an anchor weighing me down. Any man I meet would want a girl who knows what she's doing. I wanted to get rid of it."

The elated feeling I got when she said she liked and trusted me sinks a little. That might be true, but for her those feelings were just a means to an end. She was attracted to me, and maybe because of my position and status and the fact that I'm respected in the community, she felt she could trust me, and therefore I was a suitable contender to rid her of her innocence. I'm not sure how I feel about that. I feel as if I've somehow despoiled a fresh mountain stream by washing my dirty clothes in it.

But I don't say that. I hold her, lending her my warmth as she shivers and cuddles up close to me.

"You smell nice," she whispers.

My lips curve up. She lifts her face to look up at me, and I study her mouth, with the beautiful Cupid's bow, then lower my head to press my lips to hers.

It turns into a smooch, and then she raises an arm around my neck and opens her mouth to slide her tongue against mine.

I lift my head and say, "Whoa."

She blinks and looks confused. "What?"

"Honey…"

"Don't stop. Please."

I summon every ounce of willpower I own and kiss her forehead. "No, love. Not here."

She moves back a bit and frowns at me. "I don't understand. You were happy to do it five minutes ago."

"Yeah… but my ardor has cooled somewhat since I made you bleed."

"I'm okay." She sends me a pleading glance, but I harden my heart.

"Scarlett, it's not going to happen, not now."

She looks upset again. "Why not? I want you to."

"I know, but it's not right."

She stares at me. "You're serious?"

"I am."

She shifts off me and gets to her feet.

I rise quickly, and we face each other across the gazebo. She stands there defensively, her arms wrapped around her body. The wind blows a sheet of rain across us, and we both shiver.

"I don't believe this," she says. Her face has reddened. "We've gone this far, why not go all the way?"

"Because a) you're going to be sore, and b) I don't want your first time to be in a public place like this."

"So it would be okay if it was my second time? Or fifth? Tenth? What's the appropriate number of fucks I need to have had before I advance to public sex?"

I put my hands on my hips. "I understand why you're angry, but you've just admitted I'm your first, and you need to think about how that makes me feel."

She blinks; she hadn't considered that at all.

"I'm not a robot," I tell her. "I hurt you, and it shocked me. We shouldn't have been having sex anyway, but I got carried away because you're gorgeous and I was turned on."

"You think I'm gorgeous?"

"Of course I think you're gorgeous. You're stunning, Scarlett."

Her eyes are huge, and I feel a brief flicker of regret. Am I doing the right thing? She wants me. And she's right—we've gone this far, why not go all the way?

Then I feel a sweep of shame. "Look, I know that many girls' first experience of sex is at a party or in the back of a car, but yours shouldn't be. You should be wined and dined and taken to a top-class hotel, undressed slowly, and laid in a soft bed so you can be kissed all over, before the guy tenderly and gently makes love to you."

"What if I don't want that? What if I just want to get it over with?"

That makes me glare at her. "Oh, how romantic."

She looks around the gazebo, then sends me a sarcastic look. "I didn't think this was about romance."

I look at my shoes, a tad embarrassed as I think of how I just unzipped my jeans and slid inside her. "Yeah, well, it was a mistake. I shouldn't have done it."

"So now I'm a mistake." Her eyes fill with tears.

I close mine for a moment. Then I open them again and move toward her. "No, of course not. I'm just saying—"

"It's all right, I know what you're saying." She turns and jumps down from the gazebo.

"Scarlett..."

But she's already running up the bank in the rain.

"Scarlett!" I yell, furious at her. I jump down as well and follow her, but she's quick, and by the time I reach the top, she's already halfway across the stepping stones.

I stop, watching her leaping from stone to stone. She reaches the other side and jumps onto the bank, and then she heads down the hill. In less than a minute, she disappears into the undergrowth, heading for the commune.

Shit.

It's still pouring down, and I stand there, completely soaked, feeling upset and angry. I run a hand over my face, then through my wet hair. Now I've hurt her and made her feel worthless and unwanted. Could I have fucked this up any worse?

I think about what my father would say if he knew what I'd done, and wince. If she felt vindictive, Scarlett could report me to the police and accuse me of assault, and I wouldn't be able to offer a defense, because they always believe the woman in situations like this. At the least, she might tell the commune, who could then make life very difficult for me, and they would probably refuse to sell the Waiora, too.

But although I feel anxious about what my father's reaction would be if he knew what I'd done to his enemy's daughter, more than anything I feel terrible for what I've done to her. I hurt her and embarrassed her, and that was unforgivable. There's no way I could have known she was a virgin, but that doesn't excuse what I've done. I shouldn't be screwing any girl in a public place where anyone could have seen us. I'm not eighteen. I'm a pillar of the community.

What the fuck did I think I was doing?

Chapter Nine

Scarlett

"Scarlett? There's something for you at the office."

I've just finished a Jiu Jitsu class, and I pause on the way to the showers, sweating profusely and red-faced. Maria, who's in charge of our stores and who orders in our food and other supplies, hovers in the doorway, eyes dancing.

"I'll just have a shower," I tell her, "and then I'll pop over."

"You might want to go now," she says, "before the whole commune sees them."

"Them?"

She just winks at me and walks away.

Frowning, I grab a towel and loop it around my neck, then head outside. It's a cooler day today, as if Tāwhirimātea—the god of the weather—and Rūaumoko—the god of the seasons—decided that my foolishness yesterday marked the end of summer, and today is the first day of autumn.

I wince as I step down from the retreat building. I should have worn looser yoga pants. I'm still tender underneath, and these ones keep irritating my sore skin.

I scowl as I head across the green toward the main office, dying a little inside at the memory of what transpired in the gazebo. I was such an idiot. I assumed that because I ride a bike and use tampons I wasn't going to bleed, and I'd hoped he wouldn't notice that I hadn't had sex before. I couldn't have been more wrong. I groan silently at the thought of how I squealed, how quickly he shot back, and the shocked look on his face as he saw the blood. The poor guy. It wasn't his fault. No young guy is going to turn down a girl when she offers herself on a plate to him like that.

SERENITY WOODS

No, it's my fault that I feel embarrassed and humiliated, not his. It was actually rather sweet that he refused to continue. I think. Maybe he was just so turned off by the whole virgin thing that it killed any desire he had. My spirits sink even lower, and tears prick my eyes. But I cried enough last night; I'm not going to give in to self-pity again. I lift my chin, push open the door to the office, and go inside.

Various people take turns manning the desk here. I fill in from time to time. You have to answer the phone, take messages, watch over the library and computers, accept deliveries, and generally help out with the day-to-day running of the business of the commune and the retreat.

Today Lou is on the desk, but she's not alone; Ana's here too with a couple of her young friends, as well as Richard, the leader of the Elders, and George.

They're all looking at something sitting on the table in the corner. As I walk in, they part and stop talking.

"Hello," Ana says with a mischievous grin.

I don't reply, because the object on the table has rendered me speechless. It's a bouquet of red roses. Oh my God, how many are there? There must be three dozen at least, and they're absolutely beautiful, half open and half in bud, glistening with water droplets. They're wrapped in cellophane, and I think they've come in the vase because I don't think it belongs to the commune—it's round and glass and painted with more red roses.

"They came with a card," Lou says, passing it to me.

I take it. The front bears one word—my name, Scarlett, and above it someone has hand-drawn a fancy red heart. My face heating, I open the envelope and take out the card. Like the envelope, the card also bears one word: Orson. Inside the O, someone has drawn another red heart.

Richard takes the card out of my hand, and the others look at it. At the commune there's little privacy, and we're used to sharing everything. I don't have any secrets from Ana or any of the others. But for maybe the first time in my life, I hate the fact that they've all seen what suddenly feels like a very private message.

"Ooh," Ana says. "Orson!"

"Orson Cavendish?" Richard asks. "What's he doing sending you flowers?"

"Hmm," George says, eyes gleaming.

"Is it a business gesture or a personal thing?" Lou asks.

"No kisses," says one of the other girls. "Business?"

"You don't send roses for business," the other girl says. "Or put a heart on the card."

"He wants to buy the Waiora," Richard tells them, frowning. "That's all. He's trying to flatter you."

"That's not it," Ana says impatiently. "He likes her. It was written all over his face when he came here."

I blush even more. "That's not true."

"You can't go out with him," one of the girls says. "He's a capitalist pig who's only interested in money."

"He's not," Ana protests, "you obviously didn't see him the other day. He's gorgeous, and he's really nice."

"Don't let his looks distract you from the fact that he's here for business," Richard warns. "He's well known in the city for being ruthless and cutthroat. He's not the sort of guy who'd send flowers without having a seven-point plan in place."

I swallow hard, thinking about how tenderly he kissed me, and how he held me when I cried. Was it all a ploy to get around me? Surely not? But then he himself said *you're the naivest person I've ever met*.

"Can I talk to you for a moment?" George asks me. He exchanges a look with Richard before gesturing with his head for me to follow him into the library.

After taking the card from Richard, I follow George, and he closes the door behind him. The library is empty this early in the day, with most of the women in the retreat busy with exercise classes or workshops. I stand in front of the shelf of gardening books and look at George awkwardly. He worked closely with my father, and I know Dad trusted him implicitly, but Orson's comment about it not being a great idea to have one person in charge of a company's finances has sown a seed of doubt deep inside me.

Who should I trust more, though? A guy I've grown up with, who's part of the commune, who my dad loved and trusted, and who's been nothing but supportive of me and my family? Or a ruthless businessman who's only interested in acquiring my land, and who'd no doubt resort to any sneaky tactic to get what he wanted?

Except I don't believe Orson is like that. I think he sent me the flowers because he likes me, and he was sorry that he hurt me, and he regrets what happened and how it ended.

Or am I being naive again?

"I think we can use this," George says.

I blink. "Use what?"

He flicks his fingers toward the office. "The flowers. His interest in you."

"So now you think he's interested? That it's not just about the Waiora?"

He tips his head from side to side. "Can't it be both? And can't we use that to our advantage?"

"What do you mean?"

"I mean that I think you should encourage his interest and use it to push for more money."

I stare at him, genuinely shocked. "Are you serious?"

His expression hardens. "Do I have to tell you again about our situation?"

"No…"

"Do you want the commune to close, Scarlett? Do you want us to go under?"

"Of course not," I say sharply.

"We all have to do what we can to make this work," he says. "It's what your father would have wanted."

"He wouldn't have wanted me to pretend to like Orson Cavendish to get his money."

"I think that would be exactly what he would have wanted."

That stuns me into silence, because I realize he might be right. He'd have been horrified to think I like Orson, and furious at what I'd let happen at the gazebo. But what better way to get revenge on Spencer Cavendish than for me to pretend to like his son in order to push him for more money? I know he'd have thought that was most amusing.

Maybe it would just be playing the game. Orson pretends to like me to get the Waiora; I pretend to like him to get more cash. We all know it's happening, so where's the harm?

But the thought makes acid rise from my stomach, and I press my hand over my heart. "I can't believe you're asking me to do this."

His expression turns impatient. "I'm not asking you to do anything you don't want to do. You're a young woman and he's a good-looking guy—it's hardly a chore. I'm just saying you should play along with him a bit. Let him take you out to dinner, wine and dine you. Turn the charm on. Come on, Scarlett, you're not fifteen anymore. You're a woman of the world now, and you know how men work."

My face is so hot you could cook eggs on it. "I don't know what you're implying, but I'm not going to prostitute myself, I don't care how many million dollars it's for."

He rolls his eyes. "Scarlett…"

I turn around and walk out of the office, pick up the vase and flowers, stride past the others who are still standing there, and go out into the sunlight.

"Scarlett." George comes out after me, Richard on his heels. "We agreed last night that we will sell the Waiora to Orson for seventeen and a half million, providing he puts the land in a trust like he said, and that we get to decide over what developments he makes to our side of the pond. So I suggest you deliver that news to him and do your best to convince him to raise his offer."

I stand there with the two men looking at me, the smell of the roses rising to my nostrils, my chest heaving with indignation. I could refuse. Say I'm not going to play a part in this ridiculous charade. Tell them how insulted I am that they think I would practically sell myself to save the commune.

But I don't want it to close. What would I do if it did? I'd have to join the real world, which I find incredibly scary. A world where the only things that people care about are money and designer labels and fast cars and fancy restaurants and who's posting what on Instagram. It's not my world at all, and I would end up like the butterfly Orson mentioned flying into the rotor blades of a lawnmower and being chopped up into little pieces.

"All right," I say stiffly. "I'll go and see him."

They both nod with satisfaction. "Thank you," Richard says. "Good luck."

The two of them turn and walk back into the office, passing Ana as she comes out. She glances at them, then walks up to me, studies my face, and asks, "Are you okay?"

I force myself to smile. Even though she's only twenty-one and therefore only three years younger than I, sometimes it feels as if the two of us are a completely different generation. She has bought herself a phone and is more au fait with social media and the things that are important to young people in this day and age. Both of my feet remain firmly in the commune, but she has one foot in the real world, and even talks about getting a job in the city. Despite this, she's struggled more than I have after our father's death. She was his baby, and although he did his best to protect both of us from the harsh realities of the world, he was more open and honest with me because I was the eldest, so I've always felt the need to protect her.

"I'm fine," I say. "They want me to go and see Orson, that's all. They've decided to sell the Waiora."

She studies my face. She knows how I feel about selling the pool, but she didn't want to go with me when I scattered Mum's ashes, and she isn't a part of the healing program, so it doesn't hold quite the same meaning for her.

"Are you okay with that?" she asks.

I look away, across the duck pond. What do I say to that? The whole issue is now knotted up inside me like a tangled ball of wool, and what happened yesterday has only complicated matters.

"They are beautiful," she says, bending to sniff one of the roses.

"I'll go and see him later," I say reluctantly. I haven't told her about the Elders wanting an extra two and a half million for the Waiora, and I'm not going to, because that means admitting what they want me to do, and I know she won't approve.

"All right," she says. "You can tell me all about it tonight." She kisses my cheek, then heads off.

I go home and place the vase with the roses in the middle of the coffee table in the living room. They are such a vibrant color, a true scarlet. Did he choose that shade on purpose? I take out the envelope, remove the card, and look at both my name and his name. Did he call a company and tell them what to put on there? Or did he write them personally? I brush my thumb across his name with the heart in the middle of the O. It's true that he didn't add any kisses. But if he just wanted to say sorry, why put the heart?

We have a landline, because my father used to work from home sometimes, so I go over, pick up the receiver, and dial the mobile number on the business card he gave me rather than his office number. It rings a few times, then goes to voicemail.

"It's me," I say, my heart racing. "Scarlett Stone, I mean. I… um… just wanted to say thank you for the flowers. And to tell you that I need to see you. For business reasons. Can I… um… make an appointment? I'm not sure whether you'd rather see me at your office in the CBD? Um… maybe you could let me know sometime. That would be great, thank you." Jesus, could I waffle any more? I end the call, cursing myself, and head off to the bathroom to take a shower.

I've just got out when I hear the phone ringing in the living room. Wrapping a towel around me, I run through the house to answer it. "Hello?"

"It's me," he says. "Orson Cavendish."

"Very funny," I reply sarcastically. "Don't mock me. I get nervous on the phone."

He chuckles. "You liked the roses?"

"I did."

"I went to three different florists to find one that sold the shade I wanted."

For some reason, that makes me soften inside. "Really?"

"Yeah."

"You wrote the card?"

"Yeah. Took me an hour to come up with the message."

That makes me laugh.

I walk across the room to look out of the window at the kids in the playground next to the duck pond. I feel suddenly and inexplicably shy.

"You okay?" he asks.

"Yeah."

"I'm sorry."

I fiddle with the catch on the window. "For what?"

"You know what for. I'm so sorry I hurt you. I feel really bad about that."

My lips curve up. "It wasn't your fault."

"Even so. If I'd have known… but even if I had… I mean…" He clears his throat. "I've never been someone's first before."

I straighten the curtain. "Really?"

"Really. So it took me by surprise for several reasons." Voices sound in the background. "I can't talk much now," he says, "I'm due in a meeting, but I'll be at the club around four this afternoon if you want to come over."

"Are you sure? I just want to talk business, and I thought you'd rather do that at your office."

"We do business at the club, too."

"Oh yes, but not until midnight, right?"

"Normally, but you said you go to bed at seven, so…"

"Ten," I say, laughing. "I'm not twelve years old."

He chuckles again. "So you'll come over?"

"Okay."

SERENITY WOODS

"I'll see you then."

"All right."

He hesitates. Then he adds, "I look forward to it," and ends the call.

I switch mine off and return it to its holder, then go over to the roses on the table and pick up the envelope and card. He wrote it himself. I brush my thumb over his name again, looking at the heart in the center.

Then I put it down and head off to get dressed.

*

In the afternoon, I help out in the retreat. It's a non-profit organization and a registered charity, affiliated with the National Collective of Independent Women's Refuges. It's partially funded by the Ministry of Social Development, but relies mostly on donations, both monetary and of clothing and other items. We work with another refuge in the city, also set up by my father, and they run an office where people can drop off their unwanted stuff and a shop that sells everything on. Some of the members of the commune work in the shop and help with sorting, washing, and ironing the clothes. Ana does this a few days a week. But I prefer to stay in the commune and work in the retreat.

Today I help prepare lunch in the main refectory—pita breads loaded with lettuce, cucumber, tomatoes, grated carrot, olives, crumbled feta cheese, spinach, parsley, and an Italian dressing I make myself, along with some homemade coleslaw and air fryer French fries for whoever wants them.

Afterward, when everything's washed and put away and the kids are back in the schoolroom, I take some of the women on a walk to the Waiora. We sit by the side of the pool, and I give them a guided meditation.

It's quiet there, with no sign of any of Orson's men, and I'm pleased about that, as a couple of the women are new to the retreat and very anxious and jumpy. For the first time, as we sit on the uneven ground around the water's edge, I think about how nice it would be to have a gazebo like the one on the other side where Orson and I… no, not going to think about that. But it would be cool to have a small platform with comfortable outdoor bean bags to perch on, and maybe some screens we can pull around in case there are other people present.

Well, if we accept his offer to purchase the pool, he's said he will pay for any developments, so maybe we should take him up on the offer. If I think about it from the angle that it will improve the experience for these women, it might help me justify accepting his help.

While we sit in silence, letting the autumn breeze drift across us, I try to clear my mind, but instead memories of the moment that I told him what we do at Kahukura creep into my mind. He teased me at first, suggesting we'd want fairy lights and 'as much kale as you can eat', but after I reacted angrily and explained we were actually a Women's Refuge and highlighted the work we do at the retreat, he looked genuinely shocked. He didn't know. That interests me. Had Spencer Cavendish not told his son about what we do there? I find that interesting.

Well, it's three fifteen now, so I guess I should start thinking about making our way back. I want to get changed before I head over to see Orson. Only because I want to smarten myself up for our business meeting.

I don't want to make myself look nice for him.

That doesn't enter my head at all.

Chapter Ten

Orson

"Orson? Ms. Stone is in the foyer."

"Thank you," I say to Anne, who's stuck her head around my office door.

"You want me to bring her through?"

"No, it's okay, I'll get her."

She winks at me.

"Stop it," I scold. "She's here on business."

"Of course she is." She chuckles and disappears. Rolling my eyes, I get to my feet and pull on my suit jacket. I do up the buttons, glancing at my reflection in the window to make sure my hair looks okay. Briefly, I wonder what she thinks about the white flashes at my temples. Sometimes I wish I hadn't inherited them from my father, but some women seem to like them.

Not that it matters—Scarlett is here on business today, and I have to focus on that. I take a deep breath and blow it out slowly, and it's impossible not to think about when I lay with my head in her lap, and she taught me how to meditate and breathe from my belly. Shaking my head, I go out of the door and along the corridor to the foyer.

I see her immediately, leaning on the front desk, talking to the receptionist. I stop in my tracks. She's wearing a scarlet blouse and a long black skirt, and she's pinned her long brown hair up in a bun, although untidy strands tumble around her face and neck. I think she's attempting to look businesslike, but there's still something bohemian and wayward about her.

God, this girl… She drives me crazy no matter what she's wearing.

Hana, the receptionist, glances over and sees me, and Scarlett follows her gaze and turns. I walk toward her, conscious of my heart banging on my ribs.

"Afternoon," I say, stopping before her.

"Hello." She tucks a strand of her hair behind her ear. Her cheeks flush slightly. Our eyes meet, and immediately I'm transported straight back to the moment when I pressed into her and felt her close around me, warm and wet.

I blink, suddenly aware that about ten seconds have passed, and glance at Hana to see her studying her computer screen with a small smile, so I know she's witnessed our silent exchange.

I clear my throat. "You want to come through to my office?"

"Um, sure."

I glare at Hana, who tries not to laugh, then lead Scarlett through to my office. I gesture at the sofa, and she sits while I try not to remember the way she curled her toes over the edge of the coffee table last time.

"Would you like a drink?" I ask as Anne appears in the doorway.

"A coffee would be great."

"Two lattes, please," I say to Anne, and she nods and goes off to get them.

I flick open the buttons on my jacket and take a seat. Scarlett watches me. I can't read her expression.

"Your father has the same white flashes at his temples, hasn't he?" she asks.

I nod. "All the men in my family have had it."

"Your sons will probably have it too, then."

"I suppose," I say with some surprise. I hadn't given it any thought.

"I'm sorry about your mother," Scarlett says. "You said she died six years ago?"

"Mm. Also of breast cancer." I know her mother died of the same.

She hesitates as if wondering whether to ask me something. "Did she have Enhertu?"

It's the more common name for Trastuzumab deruxtecan, a drug used to treat advanced breast cancer that has shown superior progression-free survival compared to other treatments. I nod. "It gave her four more years with us. What about your mum?"

She looks at her skirt and smoothes out a wrinkle. "The drug isn't funded in New Zealand."

Ah, fuck. There would have been other drugs available, but Dad did his research at the time, and Enhertu was by far the most successful, so that's what mum got. Without a second thought.

We sit in silence for a while, during which Anne comes in with our coffees and a plate of brownies, glances at us both, then leaves them on the table and goes, closing the door behind her.

"I'm sorry," I say.

Scarlett leans forward and picks up her takeaway cup. Then she smiles at me, surprising me. "It's not your fault."

"No… that's true."

She has a sip of the coffee, looking around the office. "You said you do business here sometimes with the other members of the Midnight Circle."

"Yes."

"After midnight?"

"Often. We all work long hours."

"So it's the equivalent of handshakes over golf?"

"Not quite." I've debated whether to tell her this, but although we tend to keep it quiet, it's not a secret as such. And the truth is that I want her to know that I'm not as shallow as she thinks I am. "The Midnight Clubs aren't quite what you think they are."

Her eyebrows rise. "They're not decadent nightclubs for the rich and famous?"

"Well, if you put it that way…"

She smiles and sips her coffee.

"They are," I say. "But once all the bills are paid, the profits go to charity."

She stares at me. When she lowers her cup, I can see her jaw has dropped.

"You're kidding me?" she says.

"Nope. I was approached by a guy called Oliver Huxley, who runs a business club in the city, also called Huxley's. He told me he was inviting a selection of wealthy business people to invest in a nightclub, with the intention of donating the proceeds to charity. I told my father, because he'd recently inherited this land when his father died, and I suggested we use this as the site for the club, and he came up with the idea for a resort which would make even more money than just a club. So Midnight in Waiheke was born. That was six years ago, and since then the Circle has created another seven clubs across the country, and one more in London."

"And all the proceeds go to charity?"

I nod and lean forward, elbows on my knees, studying the cup in my hands. "Scarlett… I want you to know that I wasn't aware that Kahukura was a Women's Refuge. I don't know why, but my father has always implied that the commune is some kind of wacky retreat for aging hippies, and I'm ashamed to say I never investigated it myself."

"It's okay."

"It's not." My tone hardens. "I don't understand it, but I will have it out with him at some point."

Scarlett's mouth opens, but she hesitates and then closes it again. She examines her coffee cup and fiddles with the lid.

"Go on," I say, amused. "Spit it out."

"I… was just thinking about you giving to charity. It's… not what I expected."

For some reason, I don't think that was what she was going to say, but I can't force her to speak her mind. "You thought I stored all my gold coins in a vault and sat there sifting through them like Scrooge McDuck?"

That makes her laugh. "I can see you with a top hat and walking stick," she says, and I smile. "You should do that more often," she says softly.

Our eyes meet, and lock, as they seem to do more often than they should. We study each other quietly for a moment.

"Do you like my hair?" I say eventually. "I was thinking of getting it dyed."

She gives a short laugh. "Don't do that. It's distinguished."

"I'm twenty-seven."

"Nothing wrong with being distinguished at twenty-seven."

I inhale and let it out as a sigh. "I dunno. Sometimes I feel old before my time." I rub the back of my head. "I'd feel better if I could get rid of this damn headache. It did go briefly at the Waiora, which surprised me, but unfortunately it soon came back."

"It won't go until you resolve the things that are bothering you," she says.

I lean back. "Don't go all New Age on me. I have a headache because some idiot crashed into my motorbike and gave me a concussion."

"That might have started it. But the reason it won't go away is because of the emotions you're carrying in here." She presses her hand over her heart.

I sip my coffee, not saying anything.

"How do you feel about losing Doyle?" she asks.

I frown. "How do you think?"

"I don't know. That's why I'm asking you. I wouldn't presume to try to understand someone else's grief."

I shift in my seat and glare at her.

"Are you going to tell me to mind my own business?" she asks mildly. "Because that's fine; you're within your rights to do that."

I swirl my coffee in the cup. I know she's thinking it would be a predictable retort. I don't particularly want to talk about my feelings. What guy does? But I also hate being predictable.

I think for a moment. "I'm angry that he was taken before his time. Furious at the guy who caused the accident, but I don't feel I can express it because he didn't mean to do it, and he's gutted that he injured someone and killed his dog. And I'm sad at losing my best friend." I stop as my throat tightens and have a mouthful of coffee.

"It's always good to get things out in the open," she says. "And I know that's not everything. I know you're angry and resentful at your father, and I suspect that's not a recent thing. He's obviously been a huge presence in your life. All sons feel a need to impress and prove themselves to their fathers, and some are harder to please than others."

I don't say anything.

"You're still grieving over your mother's death," she continues. "Of course you are, because the loss of a mother never goes away. Most of us who lose someone to cancer have lots of blame to throw around—we blame the disease and we blame ourselves for not working hard enough to find a way to fix them and we blame the hospital and the doctors and nurses for letting them die, even though of course we know it wasn't their fault."

I look away, out of the window.

"And on top of all that," she continues relentlessly, "maybe because of the way your father is, and also because it's a part of your nature, you're imbued with this incredible drive to succeed and to make something of yourself, so you work fourteen-hour days, and subject yourself to incredible stress. And it's like lying down with a stone monolith on your chest. If you don't have support, it will eventually crush you. It's too much for one person to bear. Are you seeing a therapist?"

Speechless, I shake my head.

"You should," she says. "You should talk to someone who can listen and give you ways to work on releasing that stress."

"I'm talking to you," I reply.

"I think after what happened between us, I'm not the right person to help you."

"I'm sure you can think of a way to help me release my stress." I let my lips curve up.

I thought it would make her blush, but instead she lifts an eyebrow. "You think turning this conversation to sex will distract attention from the fact that you're struggling and hurting and need help?"

I've never had anyone talk to me like this before. Even men who are good friends don't discuss thoughts and feelings. Women I know through work would also never talk about personal issues. And it's only now that I realize the few women I've had serious relationships with were never interested in me like this. They only wanted to know how I was feeling or what I was thinking when it impacted on them in some way. I'd come to assume that everyone is selfish and concerned only with themselves. So maybe that's why Scarlett's open discussion shocks me to the core.

"You're a qualified therapist?" I ask.

"I don't just weave flax and eat kale over there." Her lips twitch as she leans forward and picks up one of the brownies. She takes a bite and chews, then says, "Mmm. These are lovely."

I pick one up and take a bite. "Yeah."

"They've got cherries in."

"Have they?" I look at it in surprise. "I guess."

"You didn't know?"

"Well, I didn't make them myself."

She laughs. "No, I guess not. Although you said you liked cooking."

"I can fry a steak. I'm not a great baker."

"Pity. I can see you with the white hat and checked trousers."

We both chuckle.

"I suppose we should talk business," she says, "rather than continue embarrassing you."

"I'm not embarrassed," I say, realizing with some surprise that it's true. "But you're probably right."

"The Elders have authorized me to tell you that they are willing to sell the Waiora to you. For seventeen and a half million."

I lean forward, elbows on my knees, and study her as I suck a few crumbs from my thumb. "And they sent you to deliver the message. Interesting."

"It's my land," she says firmly, lifting her gaze to mine. But there are twin spots of red on her cheeks.

They've told her to come here because I sent her roses. They know I like her, and they want her to try to talk me into increasing my offer.

That fills me with such fury that it blazes through me like wildfire, turning everything in its wake to ash. I hate being manipulated like that, in both my business and personal life.

And I'm mainly angry because I know it's going to work. I'll pay whatever Scarlett wants for the Waiora because I want to make her happy. That shocks me. I've never let my feelings influence my business decisions before.

I don't want to say yes immediately because I don't want to give them the satisfaction. Equally, that's going to force Scarlett to play their game. And how do I know that if she spends time with me, it's not because she's been instructed to do so?

I finish off the brownie, then wash it down with a mouthful of coffee. "Can I ask you a personal question?"

"I am wearing underwear today, if that's what you're going to ask."

I laugh. I adore this girl. "No. I was going to ask you how your father died."

The humor fades from her face. "He had a heart attack."

"I'm sorry. Were you with him?"

She shakes her head. "George was."

"Oh?"

"They were in the office. It came out of the blue. George called an ambulance, but he was pronounced dead on arrival at the hospital."

"Was there an autopsy?"

"No. Why should there be? There was nothing suspicious about his death. He was overweight, had high blood pressure and cholesterol, and often forgot his pills."

I don't say anything. I can't raise my suspicions with Scarlett. She's been brought up to respect her literal Elders, and she would never suspect that her father's death could be anything but natural. And of course she might be right. If the authorities didn't find anything amiss, surely that means there's nothing wrong? I've become jaded and distrustful, that's all.

Still, I can't quieten the tiny bell of doubt ringing inside me. And because I can't silence it, I don't want to give in to George and the others just yet.

Also, it gives me a reason to persuade Scarlett to see me again.

"I need time to think about it," I say.

It prompts her to give me a sarcastic look. "You don't need time. You've already decided what your reply will be."

"Not at all. I need to get another surveyor's valuation and take a look at the market, and also examine my own books. Two and a half million is a lot of money to pull out of nowhere."

"Says the man with nine zeros in his bank account."

I smile. She pokes her tongue out at me, and my smile spreads.

"I have an idea," I say.

She rolls her eyes. "What?"

"Come to dinner with me tonight. It'll give you the opportunity to convince me."

Another sarcastic look. "That's not fair."

"Nor is attempting to fleece me for another two and a half million dollars. We all have crosses to bear."

We survey each other. I'm amused; she's bemused.

"Why?" she asks eventually.

"What do you mean?"

"Why do you want to go to dinner with me? I might be naive, but I'm not stupid. You're rich, handsome, successful, sophisticated… You could have any woman you want. Why are you pursuing me?"

"I don't want any woman. I want you."

"Again, I ask why?"

"Are you looking for compliments?"

"No. I'm genuinely baffled."

"You honestly can't understand what I see in you?"

She blinks. "No."

Jesus, she really does mean it.

"I want to see if you meant it when you said you weren't going commando."

That earns me a third sarcastic look. "There will be no exploration beneath my attire on this dinner date."

I try not to laugh at her use of the word attire, and fail. "So you do agree to come?" Her gaze goes unfocused. "To come to dinner," I correct, my smile widening. "You have a dirty mind."

"You started it."

"That's probably true." Our eyes meet, and my stomach flips the way it does every time I see her. "I want to say sorry," I say softly. "Please come to dinner with me."

Her warm brown eyes crinkle a little at the edges. "Okay."

My heart leaps, but she's already getting to her feet, so I rise with her, hiding my joy that she accepted. "I'll pick you up at six," I tell her, "and I'll take you somewhere nice in the city."

Suddenly, she looks uncertain, and I remember that she's never been to a restaurant. "What should I wear?"

"This is New Zealand," I remind her. "Half the clientele will be in shorts and tees. Whatever you want will be fine." When she continues to look worried, I add, "I'll make sure it's somewhere relaxed, honey. I want you to have a nice time."

"I'm vegetarian."

"I know that. Most restaurants offer veggie options now. I'm not going to take you to CowsRUs."

She tries not to laugh, and fails. "Okay." She chews her bottom lip. Then she walks forward and extends a hand. "Thank you for your time."

I smile and shake it, closing my fingers around hers and holding her hand for longer than necessary. "I'll see you later," I say softly, looking into her eyes. "I look forward to it."

She looks up at me with those big brown eyes that are full of trust. I love that she's so open and honest, but I also worry about the fact that she's worn rose-tinted glasses for so long that she's never learned to take them off.

"You're incredibly beautiful," I murmur, looking at her flushed complexion, her silky hair, and her soft mouth. "Inside and out."

Her gaze drops to my lips, and my pulse picks up speed—she's thinking about kissing me. Still holding her right hand, I slide my left onto her waist as I move closer. Her eyes widen, but she doesn't move back, and she lifts her face to mine as I lower my head.

Behind us, someone clears their throat. I straighten immediately and release her, and Scarlett steps back. It's my father, standing in the doorway, his expression heavy with disapproval.

"Excuse me," Scarlett says. She flicks Dad a brief smile, but he just glares at her. Dropping her gaze, she slips past him, and I hear her footsteps tapping rapidly as she runs down the corridor.

"That was fucking rude," I snap, furious that I missed out on a kiss.

"What's she doing here?" he demands.

"We were talking business."

"Yeah, it sure looked like it."

I glare at him. "This has nothing to do with you."

"She's the daughter of Blake Stone. This has everything to do with me."

"I'm tired of this," I say irritably. "Of your eternal feud with Blake and his family. He's gone now. The guy's dead. It's time you moved on."

He puts his hands on his hips. "Midnight might be your baby, but the land is mine. I said you could be in charge of the purchase of the Waiora, but I'm not going to let you screw up the sale. If you can't seal the deal, I'll do it myself."

"I'll do it. But they've added two and a half million dollars to the price."

He lets out an incredulous laugh. "Jesus."

"Yeah. So forgive me for wanting to take time to think about it."

He gives me an appraising look. "You know they've sent her to soften you up."

Privately, I think it's to give me the opposite effect, but I don't say that.

"I know," I say instead. "My eyes are open."

"She's never been around money like this," Dad says, gesturing around us. "I told you years ago that you have to be careful with women. Most of them are treasure hunters, and if you let yourself be blinded by a pretty face and a pair of tits, you'll never be sure that they're not after your fortune until it's too late."

I know he's right, but that doesn't mean I have to like what he says. I'm fully aware that Scarlett is after my money, but I don't believe the connection between us is entirely due to that, and I'm not going to let him come between us because of his bitterness.

I turn away. "I need to get back to work because I'm going out in a few hours."

"With Scarlett?"

I don't reply.

"You're a fool," he says. And then he turns and walks out.

I sit in my leather chair, then slide down in it a little and stare moodily out of the window.

SERENITY WOODS

The terrible thing is that I know he's right. And I don't give a fuck.

Chapter Eleven

Scarlett

"Oh my God, oh my God, oh my God." I go through the clothes in my wardrobe frantically. "What am I going to wear?"

"First, calm down or you're going to hyperventilate and black out," Ana says from where she's lying on my bed. "Second, you'll look beautiful in whatever you wear, so it doesn't really matter."

"You're not helping. He's taking me to a posh restaurant."

"I thought he said it would be somewhere relaxed?"

"He's a billionaire. It's not going to be a burger bar, whatever he says." I take out a black dress. "This is slimming, don't you think?"

"You're hardly fat. And it's dull." She gets up and joins me at the wardrobe. "He's used to women in designer clothes and gold jewelry with coiffured hair and long painted nails."

"And I'm none of those things. How am I going to match that?"

She starts looking through my clothes. "That's my point. He's interested in you because you're different. You're like a sunbeam in a gallery of neon lights. You're natural and fresh. So you should play on that." She pulls out a dress. "Wear this one."

I study it doubtfully. It's a boho maxi dress, floor length and sleeveless and with shirring from the bust to the waist, in a deep yellow with big colorful flowers. It's perfect for a late summer or early autumn evening barbecue, but it's not exactly posh evening wear.

"Trust me," she says. "You'll knock his socks off."

I do trust her, so I shower and dry my hair, then, at her urging, pin it up in a bun so loose that half of it escapes and tumbles around my neck. I add a pair of sandals with a small heel, and let her help me with my makeup—just a touch of liner and mascara to define my eyes, powder to take away the shine, and a slick of lip gloss.

"You look amazing," she says when I'm done. "You're so gorgeous." She looks at my clutch and her eyes twinkle. "You want to pack a toothbrush?"

"Ana!"

"I'm just saying."

I know Ana isn't a virgin. Despite us having the same upbringing, she's always been more rebellious than me, and I know she's had a couple of lovers. I'm not sure if she realizes I haven't. I haven't told her about what happened at the Waiora because I'm too embarrassed.

I mustn't be naive. He'll probably expect me to go to bed with him if he takes me to dinner. I should call him and tell him I've changed my mind, or at least make it perfectly clear that there will be no sex.

I look at the phone I've borrowed from the office. Then, feeling wicked, I pick it up and put it in the clutch. My heart races at the thought that I'm even contemplating having sex with Orson again.

"I don't know what I'm doing," I say, feeling a sudden surge of panic. "Shouldn't I wear something more businesslike?"

"This isn't a business meeting."

"I feel that I should think of it like that."

"Why?"

"Because it's not like we can have a relationship."

"Again, why?"

"I'm not exactly his type, and he's not mine. I don't fit in his world. And can you imagine him joining the commune?"

"Scarlett," she says patiently, "you don't have to marry every guy you have sex with." Her expression softens then, and she rubs my arm. "I know you've had it tougher than me," she says. "Dad always had higher expectations for you. Even though he treated me like the baby, he was so desperate to protect you from the world. But we are a part of it, and you shouldn't shut yourself away from it."

It's the first time she's ever said anything like that to me before, and my throat tightens. "I don't shut myself away from the world."

"Of course you do. And that's okay, because most of the time it's a difficult place. We exist in another, easier time here. But it's all right to want something more sometimes."

"I don't want more," I protest, feeling emotional as I think about our parents, and why they wanted this better life for us. "I'm happy here."

"I know, I know." She hugs me. "I'm sorry, I didn't mean to upset you on your special day. Don't listen to me. I just want you to be happy and enjoy yourself, that's all."

I hug her back. After our mother's death, several women at the commune tried to step into her role to look after us, and since Dad died, the guys have done the same, wanting to make sure Ana and I are looked after. But it's not the same as having your own parents, and so Ana and I have grown closer together and looked out for each other.

The sound of a car outside makes us pull part, and Ana rushes to peer through the net curtains. "Oh my God," she says. "He's in a fucking Aston Martin."

"Ana," I scold. "Argh, everyone is going to see it!"

"I know, they're going to be absolutely green with envy."

"It's hardly a good example to set!" I join her at the window. The car pulls up in front of the house and sits there purring before he kills the engine. "It's so extravagant."

"You can't really wish he'd turned up on a tandem?"

"Well, I..." My voice trails off as he opens the door and gets out. "Ooh."

"Wow," Ana says, eyes wide.

Orson's shirt hangs over the top of a pair of caramel-colored chinos. The shirt is black, but the placket, turned-back cuffs, and the inside of the collar are made of a paisley material the same color as his bright blue eyes. His haircut is so sharp it could cut glass, and his jaw is *smooth as*. He's wearing his fancy watch on his left wrist. He looks classy and rich and sophisticated.

What the hell does he want with me?

"I bet he smells amazing," Ana says.

"He does." I bite my lip as her eyebrows rise. "I mean I bet you're right. He looks like the kind of guy who wears expensive cologne."

Her lips curve up, but she just says, "Are you ready?"

"No."

She winks at me, then goes over to the door and answers it as he approaches.

"Hello, Ana," I hear him say.

I pick up my clutch and walk forward. It's weird; he's not six foot eight or anything, but it feels as if he fills the doorway. I guess it's his presence or his posture. He stands there as if he owns the world. As if he's a Bond villain who expects to be obeyed.

"Hello," he says. "Why are you glaring at me? I just got here." His gaze slides down me. "Wow."

"She looks good, doesn't she?" Ana says.

"She does."

"It took her half an hour to decide what to wear."

"Ana!" I push past them both and walk outside. "Come on," I say to him irritably.

"Don't do anything I wouldn't do," Ana calls.

"That doesn't leave much," I yell back and poke my tongue out at her.

Orson chuckles, then to my surprise, goes around to the passenger side and opens the door. I stare at him. He stares back, then gestures for me to get in.

"I thought you were going to ask me to drive," I say. "But I'm guessing you wouldn't let a woman behind the wheel of your baby."

"Happy to," he replies. "It has parking assistance for female drivers."

"Fucking cheek."

"You started it."

Our eyes meet, and our lips curve up.

"Are you going to be trouble tonight?" he asks softly, lifting a hand to stroke a strand of hair off my forehead.

His touch banishes all words from my brain, and I can only stare into his eyes. My God, he's so incredibly handsome. My gaze drops to his mouth, and I remember kissing him, his firm dry lips, his searching tongue.

"Don't look at me like that," he scolds, "or we won't be going anywhere. I'll drive us around the corner, and we can park for two hours and have each other for dinner."

Rolling my eyes, trying not to think how wonderful that would be, I get into the car. He closes the door, then walks around and gets in the driver's side.

I buckle myself in and look around the car's interior, stunned. It's beautiful, black and gleaming, and it smells of new carpets and polished wood and leather, as well as of Orson's distinctive cologne.

He starts the engine, and it purrs, then roars as he puts it into drive and heads out of the commune.

He glances at me as he drives and says, "Do you like the car?"

"She's beautiful."

He smiles; that's pleased him. "She is."

I inhale. "That's so good."

"New car smell. Nothing like it."

"She smells of you."

He smiles again. Oh my. If he keeps smiling like that, I'm not going to be any good to anyone.

"Of course she's far too extravagant," I say. "Mr. Ostentatious."

"That is actually my middle name."

"You know what? I wouldn't be shocked."

He just laughs.

"What restaurant are we going to?" I ask.

"It's called Tutto Bene. It's Italian."

"I kinda gathered that from the name."

"Are you going to be sassy all evening?"

"Probably. Is that a problem?"

He opens his mouth to say something, then closes it again.

"What were you going to say?" I ask.

"Nothing."

"Spit it out, Cavendish."

"I was going to say it's only a problem if you don't enjoy getting spanked."

It was so not what I thought he was going to say that I feel myself flush scarlet. He notices and laughs. "You did ask."

"Jeez."

"I'm sorry. I shouldn't tease you. I promise I'll try to rein myself in. Look, the restaurant is really nice. Tutto bene means 'Everything's fine' or 'All is well.' You like Italian?"

"I do. We had an Italian woman stay with us last year and she was a really good cook. She used to make lasagnas the size of Australia for the whole commune. And her own garlic bread."

"I love garlic bread."

"Me too."

"They do a great flatbread at the restaurant with mozzarella and rosemary. We'll have to have some of that."

I fiddle with the clutch on my lap. "Have you taken many women there?"

His eyebrows rise. "You mean girlfriends? No, none. I've been there a couple of times for business lunches." He glances at me. "I wouldn't take you to somewhere I've taken other women."

"Why?" I ask, puzzled. "I'm not your girlfriend."

His blue eyes stare into mine. "Not yet." He holds my gaze for a moment, then looks back at the road.

My heart bangs on my ribs and I feel suddenly breathless. He glances at me again, and his lips curve up as he says, "What?"

"I assumed that the point of this meeting was either to get me to lower the price for the Waiora or to get me into bed, not as a prelude to dating."

"It can't be all three?" He grins at the look on my face. "That was a joke."

"Orson, why have you asked me out tonight?"

"Because, crazy as it sounds, I like you, and I want to spend time with you."

"That does sound crazy."

"Why don't we just roll with it and see how it goes?"

I frown as he passes the turnoff for the ferry and heads for the Midnight Club. "I thought we were going into the city."

"We are."

"We're not taking the ferry?"

"No, I thought I'd fly us."

I stare at him. "Pardon?"

He gestures at the hill above the club, where a big letter H marks a flat piece of land. A helicopter sits there, bathed in the warm orange light of the evening sun.

My jaw drops. Slowly, I turn my gaze to him. He looks smug enough that I know his plan was to shock me.

"Fine," I say. "It's not like I've never taken a helicopter on a first date before."

He laughs, heads along the road that snakes up the hill behind the complex, and parks beside the helicopter pad.

"Evening, sir," says a man who's waiting by the helicopter as we get out.

"Hey, Al," Orson says. "This is Scarlett."

"Good evening, Ma'am," Al says to me.

"Hello," I say, tongue-tied at the fact that this guy obviously works for Orson. He has staff. Despite his protestation that he doesn't come from Downton Abbey, it's difficult not to have that image in my mind.

"She's all ready," Al says.

MIDNIGHT ENEMY

"Thanks." Orson opens the passenger door and brings me forward. It's not a huge step up, but he steadies me anyway, and makes sure I'm in before he shuts the door.

My heart races as I buckle myself in and look around the cabin. The dashboard in front of me is a mass of dials and screens and buttons. He gets in the other side, settles himself in the seat, and hands me a pair of headphones. "So I can talk to you," he says.

I put them on and adjust the microphone as I watch him do the same.

"Hello," he says, and a shiver runs down my spine at the sound of him inside my head.

"Do you really know how to fly this thing?" I ask as he starts the engine and the rotor blades begin to spin.

"Don't worry," he says, "I've watched a couple of YouTube videos."

"Orson..."

"Just relax. It's going to be a spectacular flight with this sunset." He starts flipping switches and pressing buttons.

Not wanting to distract him, I let him do his thing, and it's not long before I feel the helicopter lift. Seconds later, we're in the air heading across the Midnight Club, west toward the setting sun.

Orson dons a pair of sunglasses and hands me another pair, and I slide them on to guard against the sun's bright glare.

"How's your head?" I ask.

He just shrugs.

I watch him as he observes the dials and screens in front of him, secretly impressed by his competence and confidence. He has nice forearms, well-muscled and tanned with a sprinkling of brown hairs, and his hands are big and strong, with neat nails. I can remember them sliding beneath my skirt onto my bare butt, the heat from them searing into my cool skin.

Swallowing hard, I drag my gaze from him and instead look out at the view.

He was right; it turns out to be a spectacular flight. I've crossed to the city many times on the ferry and the helicopter takes a similar path, but it's very different looking down. We pass Motuihe Island with its beautiful beaches, the end of which looks like a whale's fluke from above, and then Browns Island with its preserved volcano in the center. The sun is about an hour from setting, and the sky is a fantastic palette of pinks and oranges, reflected in the Pacific Ocean, which looks like strips of iron, copper, gold, and bronze. I spot yachts and fishing boats, seagulls and albatrosses and gulls, and once even a pod of dolphins swimming alongside the ferry from the mainland, which I point out with excitement, making him smile.

He follows the northern coast of the city, past Hobson Bay, then gradually takes us lower, heading, I presume, for Mechanics Bay. He talks into his microphone, asking for clearance to land, then sets us down on top of a big yellow circle with a cross in the middle, in front of the glass heliport.

He switches everything off and the rotor blades slow to a stop, and then we remove our headphones.

"That was wonderful," I say breathlessly when he comes around to help me down.

"I'm glad you enjoyed it." He turns his attention to a guy who comes over.

"Evening, Mr. Cavendish," the guy says. "Will you be wanting her again tonight?"

"No," Orson says, but before my brain can process the implications of that, he adds, "We'll take the ferry back to Waiheke later."

"Okay, sir, I'll put her to bed."

We walk across the tarmac and into the building. Orson sees me looking at him, and says, "What?"

"For a moment I thought you were assuming I'd stay the night with you."

That earns me a frown. "I'd never assume that. Give me some credit." He takes me out the other side of the building, then pulls out his phone. "Hold on, I'll call an Uber."

I watch him bring up the app and organize a car. When he's done, he looks at me and lifts an eyebrow. "You still look baffled."

"I am."

"Why?"

"Because if you went on Tinder you'd be able to get laid every night of the week."

"Meaningless sex doesn't do a lot for me."

"Really?"

"That surprises you?"

"I thought all men liked meaningless sex."

"Wow, they really paint a good picture of us at the commune, don't they?" He tips his head to the side. "I guess working at a Women's Refuge is going to give you a skewed view of the opposite sex."

I look away, at the cars shooting past, and the shops and businesses, the buildings painted orange by the late sun. "It's nothing to do with the retreat."

"What do you mean?"

I shrug. "My father was never very complimentary about young men."

"Oh, I see. You got the 'all guys are only after one thing' speech?"

"Many, many times."

He scratches the back of his neck. "Well, I can hardly criticize him for that after my behavior at the Waiora." I look back at him, and he winces.

I study one of the buttons on his shirt. "I seem to recall that I started it."

"I didn't exactly fight you off."

Our eyes meet, and we both laugh.

"Here's the Uber," he says as a Prius draws up at the curb. We get in, and soon we're in the traffic, heading further into the city.

"It's only ten minutes away," he says.

"What time are we booked in?"

"Seven." I look at my watch, and he says, "We'll be fine, don't worry."

"I'm not worried, it's just that I'm used to being the one who organizes everything," I admit.

"You don't have to this time," he says. "Let me look after you for once."

His blue eyes look darker here in the back of the car, but they're kind, and his expression is gentle. It makes me soften inside, like a bar of chocolate left on a windowsill on a sunny day. He's so handsome. The shirt makes him look sophisticated, but the wind has ruffled his hair, and he looks young and hot.

Since my mum fell ill, I've looked after myself and Ana, run the house, and had a hand in the organization of the retreat. We're a commune, so we deal with things communally, but despite this I'm used to bearing the pressures and responsibilities of everyday life, to solving problems and dealing with the stress and upset when things go wrong. The thought of letting someone do something for me—even as small as organizing a meal specifically for me—makes me feel a mixture of bemused and touched.

I have to remind myself why I'm here, though. "Um… have you had any more thoughts on the purchase price of the Waiora?"

"Some. I'm having the land valued by another company tomorrow. And Kingi is running some figures for me. I'll have an answer for you soon."

"So there's nothing I can do to persuade you?" As soon as the words leave my lips, I realize how that sounds.

Sure enough, he frowns and says, "That's not why I asked you to dinner."

"You said, 'Come to dinner with me tonight and it'll give you the opportunity to convince me.'"

"I also said I want to see if you're going commando or not."

I nudge him with my elbow, and he chuckles. "It's a pretty dress," he says softly. "It suits you."

"I don't think it's right for the restaurant."

"You look beautiful, Scarlett. You'll draw every eye in the room."

"I don't know what to say to compliments like that."

"You must be used to them."

I laugh. "No. The guys I mix with aren't sophisticated enough to know how to flatter a girl."

"Their loss." He looks puzzled. "I know I've seen the evidence, but… you really haven't…" He glances at the driver, then back at me. "…dated anyone?"

I shake my head. "When I was younger, I spent a lot of time with the others who were my age at the commune. There was a guy, Neil, who was nice, but he ended up marrying one of my friends. They seem very happy, so I'm pleased for them. But there wasn't anyone else I could picture myself with."

"So what was your plan? How were you hoping to meet someone?"

"I wasn't. I mean… I'm not."

"You're going to become a nun?"

He's joking, but I answer seriously, "Maybe."

That makes him laugh. "Yeah, right."

"Actually, I have thought about it. Maybe not actually taking vows as I'm not Christian as such, but I have thought about dedicating my life to the commune and the retreat and to helping others. I'm sorry, that sounds very pretentious. But I know it's what my father would have wanted. And I just don't think marriage and children are on the cards for me."

His smile fades, and he mutters, "Maybe Dad was right."

"About what?"

He shakes his head. Then he says, "Your life is your own, to do with what you will. I know you believe in holistic healing and I'm sure you think that concentrating on your mental and emotional side will be fulfilling. But we're physical creatures too. I've had a taste of your passion, Scarlett. And I can tell you now that it will be an absolute crime if you don't explore that with someone. Preferably me."

Chapter Twelve

Orson

The Uber pulls up outside the restaurant, and I say, "Come on. I think you need a glass of wine."

She's been silent for a minute or two, and she doesn't say anything as we get out and head into the restaurant.

I like this place. The inside of the restaurant is neat and pleasant, but I like the garden out the back. It's surrounded by bush, kinda rustic, with unpainted floorboards, plain wooden tables, and wooden chairs with scarlet cloth back panels and scarlet umbrellas. Nearly all the tables are filled with guests, most of whom are in casual clothing, and some are even in shorts and tees, as I told her they would be.

"Oh," she says. "It's not what I expected."

"Good or bad?"

"Good," she says, looking relieved.

Secretly pleased, I smile at the owner as he spots me, and he comes over. He's in his late fifties, a suave Italian guy with gray hair I'd kill for at that age. "Mr. Cavendish! Good to see you."

"Hello, Marco. Thanks for fitting me in at such short notice."

"There is always a table for you, Mr. Cavendish. Best table in the house. Come this way."

We follow him across the garden. The fence around it is made from tiny Roman columns, which sounds naff but lends the place an elegant feel. He takes us to a table in the corner which is partly sheltered from the rest of the diners by a small fountain decorated with colorful mosaic pieces.

"Thank you," I say, and hold out Scarlett's chair for her. She lowers herself into it, and I tuck it in for her, then go around the other side and sit in mine.

"Bottled water, Mr. Cavendish?" Marco says as he lights the candle on the table between us.

"Please. Sparkling, Scarlett, or still?"

She just blinks at me.

I look back at Marco, who smiles. "I will bring you both," he says. "And some flatbread and olive oil while you look at the menu."

"Thank you."

He gives me the wine menu, then goes off to get our water.

"What kind of wine do you like?" I ask her.

She just stares at me.

"Scarlett?" I frown. "You look as if someone's switched you off."

She tears her gaze from me and looks around the restaurant. "That waiter knew you."

"Marco? He's not a waiter; he's the owner."

"The owner?"

"Yeah. I told you, I come here on business. Kingi and I bring clients here. Marco looks after us. What kind of wine do you like?"

"Um, white."

"Okay. What type?" I pass her the menu. "Take a look, see if anything jumps out at you."

She stares at it. She's still staring at it when Marco comes back with a tray containing two bottles of water, glasses, a plate of their delicious flatbread, and two small dishes of olive oil and salt. He places it all before us, then says, "Can I get you a drink?"

I gesture to Scarlett. She sucks her bottom lip as she studies the menu, then says, "Um… what about the house Sauvignon?"

I roll my eyes, take the menu from her, and hand it to Marco. "We'll have a bottle of the Louis Roederer please."

He winks at me. "Yes, sir." He goes off to get it.

"That's champagne," she says. "I saw it on the menu."

"It is."

"It was over five hundred dollars a bottle."

"Cheap at twice the price."

"Orson!"

"What?"

"You can't just order the most expensive thing on the menu to impress me!"

"What's the point in having money and not using it to impress the girl of your dreams?"

She stares at me.

"It's just a phrase," I say. "Don't go running for the hills." I point at her menu. "Anything there you like?"

"You're seriously going to spend five hundred dollars on a bottle of champagne?" She glares at me. "Imagine the good you could do with that money."

"I do plenty for charity. I work hard for my money. And tonight I want to spend it on you, so stop complaining. Most girls would be thrilled to be spoiled like this."

"I'm not most girls."

"I'm getting that."

Muttering to herself, she opens the menu and starts reading. Lips curving up a little, I do the same.

"I don't know what to choose," she says eventually. "I'm too nervous."

I frown. "Why are you nervous?"

"A billion reasons." She gives me a wry look.

"I'm sorry. I don't want you to feel intimidated. I thought this place was nice and relaxed."

"It is. It's me." She glances around at the other diners, who are all talking and laughing and obviously relaxed. Then she looks back at me. Oh no, she's actually trembling a little.

"Would you like me to order?" I ask gently.

She nods.

"Would you like a starter?"

A shake of her head.

"All right." I study the options until Marco comes back with the champagne and asks if we're ready to order.

"Vegetable risotto for the lady," I tell him, closing the menu, "and Chicken Parmigiano for me, please."

"No starters or pasta or side dishes?" he asks as he pours the champagne into two tall glasses.

"It's all I could do to get her to choose one dish," I reply. "Maybe if the wind's in the right direction I'll be able to talk her into a dessert."

He chuckles, leaves the bottle in the bucket, and goes off to place our order.

"I'm sorry," she says. Her eyes glisten. "I don't know what I'm doing here."

"You're going to have a great meal, that's all, and sit and talk to me. Don't pay any attention to anyone else." I tear off a piece of the flatbread and dip it in the olive oil, then the salt before eating it. Then I gesture to her to do the same.

She copies me and eats a tiny piece. "Mmm. That's good."

"Eat a bit before you have any champagne or you'll fall off your chair with all the adrenaline running through you right now."

She does as she's told and eats half the flatbread with me before finally taking a sip of the champagne. She laughs. "The bubbles go up my nose."

I smile. "Do you like it?"

"Mmm. It tastes of almonds. And citrus."

"It does. Well spotted. I forgot that the commune has vineyards. Do you make your own wine there?"

"No, we don't have those facilities. We have a long-standing partnership with a local winemaker, and we sell the grapes to him to process. He always gives us a case or two of the wine when it's ready."

"Do you drink spirits? Whiskey, vodka?"

She shakes her head. "Dad preferred not to have them anywhere on the commune. Alcohol has often played a part in the lives of the women who come to us, and so it's best if it's not readily available. We offer them a glass of wine with Sunday lunch and that's about it."

"We've led very different lives."

"Just a bit." She smiles.

She looks amazing tonight. The long dress clings to her figure when she moves, and I'm pretty sure she's not wearing a bra, and maybe no underwear either. I'm trying not to think about it because I don't want a hard-on at the table, but it's difficult when she's sitting in front of me, all soft and sexy.

"I have something for you," I tell her. I slide my hand into my trouser pocket, extract the item, and place it on the table. It's a small soft bear with a heart in its hands that says 'I love you more than chocolate.'

"His name is Bearcub," I say. "That's what my name means—bearcub."

She stares at the bear. Then her expression softens, and she picks it up. "For me?"

"Yeah."

"I wondered what that lump was in your trousers. I thought you were pleased to see me."

We both laugh.

"Thank you," she says graciously. "I love it." She places it on the table to her side, then returns her gaze to me and studies me with interest. "You look a lot like your father."

I scowl. "I don't want to talk about him."

"Why not?"

"He's not my favorite person at the moment."

"Why? What has he done?"

I lean back in my chair and turn my fork over in my fingers. "It doesn't matter."

"He doesn't approve of you having dinner with me." It's a statement. She's obviously guessed from the way he was so rude to her in my office.

"No."

She doesn't look upset, just curious. "He seems young to have a son your age."

"He was only nineteen when I was born. I think I was an accident." My lips twist.

Her brown eyes survey me thoughtfully. "Tell me about your mum."

"What do you want to know?"

"Were they happy together?"

"They had two kids."

"That's not an answer."

I shrug. "I guess they were. He never cheated, as far as I know."

"So that's your definition of happiness—whether the guy cheats or not?"

I just give her a sardonic look.

"What was your mum like?" she asks.

I look away then, picturing my mother. "Tall. Blonde. Beautiful. Elegant. Reserved. In control. Some would say cold. I don't remember her ever giving me a hug. I was closer to the nanny than I was to either of my parents." My feelings about my mother confuse me. Her death hit me hard, even though I wouldn't have said we were close. "I want to say I don't miss her, but I do, and that frustrates me." I stop talking then, feeling as if I've said too much. Scarlett's brows have drawn together. "What was your mum like?" I ask, wanting to draw the attention away from myself.

"The complete opposite. Māori. Curvy. Warm. Friendly. She belonged to everyone, in a way, not just to me." She sips her champagne. "Do you know why our fathers were such bitter enemies?"

"No. He won't tell me. I know they went to school together. But something happened when they were about eighteen, I think. I know they had a physical fight and had to be broken up by a teacher. Both of them were suspended for it."

"I didn't know that," she says softly.

"That's about all I know. Kingi's dad, Rangi, joked about it once. He was a couple of years above them. Dad got angry and told him to shut the fuck up, which was weird in itself because he never spoke like that to his friends."

"Strange." She looks down at her dinner.

For some reason, something to do with her expression, I get a prickle of warning. "Do you know something about their relationship?"

She scoops up a forkful of risotto. "No." She eats it, her gaze flicking up to mine. I don't think she's telling the truth, but I can't just accuse her of lying. "So," she says, "when's your birthday?"

"Fourteenth of October."

"So you're a Libra."

That makes me laugh as I cut into my chicken. "I thought you weren't into astrology?"

"Only for fun."

"What does it tell you about me?"

She thinks as she chews. "Mmm." She swallows. "You're charming. Intellectual."

"You needed to know my star sign to figure that out?"

"You're a peacemaker. A natural mediator. You're just and fair."

I shrug. "I guess that's true."

"You like beautiful things."

"Well, duh."

"I don't mean women. Well, women as well, probably, but I'm guessing you enjoy fine art, music, good food, the sensual things in life. You like thoughtful discussions, and you're adaptable and flexible. But sometimes you have trouble making a decision. You procrastinate.

You overanalyze. And you're a people pleaser. You care what others think about you."

"Wow."

"Was that accurate?"

"Oddly, yes, very."

She just smiles.

"When's your birthday?" I ask, intrigued.

"I... don't want to tell you."

"Why?" I ask, amused. When she doesn't reply, my eyebrows slowly rise. "It's not today, surely?" When her lips twist, I lean back and give a short laugh. "You should have told me."

"I knew you'd make a fuss." She eats some more risotto. "This is wonderful, by the way."

I watch her, realizing that this must be her first birthday without either of her parents present. If she'd been in the commune, maybe they'd have thrown her a party—I've read that communities like hers make a big thing out of personal celebrations. But instead she agreed to come out with me. I'm oddly touched.

I wish I'd known; I'd have bought her a present, something more than the bear. But maybe she wouldn't have accepted it.

I start eating again, tucking into the sauteed new potatoes. "So you're a Pisces?"

She laughs. "How did you know that?"

"I'm not completely hopeless." I take out my phone, Google it with one hand, and lay it on the table so I can read out the character traits while I eat. "You're compassionate and empathetic. Well, I knew that. Creative and intuitive. That makes sense. Idealistic. Well, that goes without saying."

She gives me a sarcastic look, but I choose to ignore it.

"You're romantic and spiritual. But you can be overly sensitive, easily influenced, and have trouble dealing with the practical matters of life, to the point of neglecting your own needs at the expense of looking after others. I think that pretty much sums you up."

"See? There is some truth in it."

I smile and turn off my phone, then pick up my champagne glass. "Do you neglect your own needs?"

She opens her mouth to respond, and then closes it, her expression turning suspicious. "Are you asking whether I masturbate?"

I cough into my champagne, then have to spend a few moments dabbing my face, hand, and glass with a serviette to mop up what I've spilled. "Jesus," I say, "don't do that to me."

"What?" She starts laughing.

I glare at her. "You can't talk about that at the dinner table and not expect it to have an effect."

She has another forkful of risotto, her eyes dancing. "It's perfectly natural."

"I know that…"

"I mean, you're not going to tell me that you don't do it."

I concentrate on cutting up my chicken. "This is not an appropriate conversation for the dinner table."

"That's your father talking."

"Please don't talk about my father and sex in the same sentence."

"Well, aren't you being all prim and proper," she says, amused. "Do they not talk about masturbation in your family?"

"Scarlett! For fuck's sake."

She giggles, which is such a delightful sound that it makes me smile.

"And no, we don't talk about it in our family," I reply. "And certainly not at dinner."

She eats her risotto, her big brown eyes wide as she watches me.

"Stop it," I scold, cutting another piece of chicken.

"What?"

"You know what. I can tell what you're thinking."

"I can't help it. It's just the thought of you… you know…"

I blow out a breath and try to concentrate on finishing off the potatoes. "I'm not listening."

She continues to watch me curiously. "So you wouldn't say you were close to your father?"

I shrug. "We're not *not* close. He's just not touchy feely. He told me when I was in my early twenties that I needed to be careful with relationships because of our wealth, and that I must never give in to my feelings."

"He must think I'm after your money."

"Well, you are," I point out. "But at least you're honest about it."

She studies her plate. Then she lowers her fork onto it.

"Shit," I say hastily, "I'm sorry. It was a bad joke."

"No, you're right." She sits with her hands in her lap. She hesitates, then says, "George and Richard want me to get to know you better so

I can try to convince you to pay the extra two and a half million. It's why I agreed to come to dinner with you."

"I know."

She looks puzzled. "You know?"

"Of course I know."

"Then… why did you ask me?"

I finish the last mouthful and put my cutlery down. I have a mouthful of champagne, then wipe my mouth with the serviette. Finally, I lean on the table, look into her eyes, and hold her gaze. She's so fucking beautiful. I think about undressing her, about kissing her all over, and about sliding inside her and making her mine, and I know my thoughts are going to show in my eyes.

Slowly, her cheeks stain red.

"That's why," I say.

Somewhat smugly, I lean back and gesture at the waiter. "Let's have a dessert," I say to her. "They do a really nice Tiramisu here."

Chapter Thirteen

Scarlett

When I don't express a preference for dessert—because my brain has turned to the consistency of melted caramel—Orson orders a Tiramisu for two. The waiter tops our glasses with the last of the champagne, then goes away.

"Excuse me a moment," Orson says, and he rises from the table and goes inside.

I watch him go, then turn back to my glass and let out a shaky sigh before sipping the champagne. The magical bubbles are starting to have an effect, and I can feel my nuts and bolts loosening, releasing the tension in the tendons and ligaments between my joints that feel so tightly strung.

I don't know quite what it is that I'm so tense about—is it the environment? The food? The champagne? Not really, because it's very relaxed here, and the food and drink are delicious.

It is, of course, the man who's been sitting opposite me. If you look up the phrase 'larger than life' in the dictionary, I'm sure you'd find a photo of Orson. He's like a strawberry whose taste is so intense, so strawberry-like, that it's more strawberry tasting than any other strawberry in the whole history of strawberry-osity.

I think I might be a little bit tipsy.

I pick up the bear and stroke a thumb across its soft fur. Maybe it's the adrenaline, like he said. After all, I've only had two glasses of champagne, but I know that alcohol can increase epinephrine levels, which would explain my racing heart and the feeling of excitement rising through me like the bubbles in the champagne.

I think about the way he leaned forward on the table and stared into my eyes, like a black panther who'd spotted a deer with a particularly juicy haunch. He did everything but lick his lips. He wants to sink his teeth into me.

And oh my God, I want him to… so, so much…

He exits the restaurant and walks across the garden, and I watch him, my pulse picking up again. He walks so confidently, as if he owns the place, and as if he expects everyone in the restaurant to be looking at him, which I think they are, because he's the most gorgeous guy here. And he's with me. I can't help but feel flattered at that.

He sits back down, his lips curving up. "What?" he says. "Your eyes are like saucers."

I shake my head. I have to bear in mind the effect of the champagne and adrenaline mix and ensure I don't make any hasty decisions.

"Aren't you cross with me?" I ask.

He blinks. "About what?"

"The fact that I've been sent here to seduce you into accepting the increased price."

He leans back, one arm over the back of the chair, playing with his spoon with the other hand. "Firstly, I don't get cross with women. And secondly, *is* that why you're here?"

I moisten my lips with the tip of my tongue. "No."

He gives a small smile.

I hum along to the song playing in the restaurant, and his eyebrows rise. "You like Billie Eilish?" he asks.

"Yeah. You?"

"She's all right. I'm just surprised you know her stuff."

"I don't just listen to Bob Dylan and burn incense, you know. I also listen to Van Morrison and Neil Young and… brace yourself… modern music."

He chuckles. "What else do you like to do in your spare time?"

I tell him a bit about my painting and creative writing. When I mention I play acoustic guitar, he laughs and says, "That was a dot on the cards."

"So what do you do?" I ask sarcastically. "Apart from putting your gold coins in piles?"

He grins. "I don't get a lot of free time. Sometimes…" He stops though as the waiter arrives with our dish of Tiramisu. To my shock, two sparklers are sticking out of it, and the waiter sings 'Happy Birthday' as he places the dish before me.

MIDNIGHT ENEMY

Orson joins in with the words, laughing at the expression on my face, then thanks the waiter, who withdraws with a smile.

"Naughty boy," I scold, semi-embarrassed at the smiles of the other diners.

"Least I could do," he says, removing the sparklers once they're finished and dropping them into the tumbler of water the waiter has left for that purpose.

"Wow." I take one of the spoons and stare at the concoction in front of me. Layers of sponge mingle with mascarpone cream and a dusting of cocoa powder.

"Dive in," Orson says, and he dips his spoon into his side of the dish, then has a mouthful.

I do the same, close my lips around the spoon, and taste the dessert. My eyelids flutter shut. Oh my God, it's amazing—rich, creamy, and sweet, with the taste of coffee and, I think, a touch of brandy.

"Damn," Orson says.

I open my eyes to see him watching me, his brows drawing together. I lick my lips and swallow. "What?"

"It's backfiring on me," he mumbles, helping himself to another spoonful.

I blink at him. Then, slowly, I dip my spoon in and eat another mouthful, keeping my eyes on him as I eat the creamy mixture, then turn the spoon over and suck it clean.

He gives a short laugh, and I chuckle too.

"Minx," he says, his eyelids dropping to half-mast.

I have another spoonful, my heart racing. I've never felt that I've had power over a guy like this before. All the guys my age in the commune are like kids compared to him. He's so... capable, and confident, and in control. I've never met anyone like him. He fascinates me.

"You were about to tell me what you do in your spare time," I say. "I know you like motorbikes."

"Not for a while," he says ruefully.

"No, of course not, I'm sorry."

"Ah, it's okay. I shouldn't really be tearing around the city at my age anyway."

"You're only twenty-seven," I say, amused. "You're hardly drawing your pension."

"I'm a respectable businessman."

"That sounds like your father talking."

He just gives a wry smile, so I know I'm right.

"So come on," I tease, having another spoonful of Tiramisu, "you must do something other than business from time to time."

"I'm at the club past midnight several nights a week."

"Socializing?"

"Networking mainly. And I meet with the other members of the Midnight Circle to talk business."

"And when you're not at the club?"

"I work out at the gym. Read a bit. Play PS5 games. Watch TV. The usual."

"Nothing creative?"

"I'm a left brain kinda guy." He smiles. "You look puzzled."

"I can't imagine not being creative. Barely a day goes by when I'm not making something. Music, art, stories."

"Love?" His eyes crinkle at the edges.

"You know the answer to that," I tell him wryly, having a sip of my champagne.

He finishes his half of the Tiramisu and pushes the dish toward me. I have the last few spoonfuls, then lean back with a sigh. "That was delicious."

"The best in the city."

"I'm guessing you have the best of everything?"

"No point in having money if you don't."

I smile. "I guess."

We both finish off our champagne. "Would you like coffee?" he asks.

"No thank you. I'm full."

"Happy birthday."

"Thank you. I've had a lovely time."

He sighs. "It's a shame it's over. I'm guessing you wouldn't like to go for a drink at a bar?"

"Um, not really. I think I've had enough alcohol."

"Fair enough. You want me to call an Uber back to the ferry?"

I meet his eyes. My heart—which has been going faster than normal all night—picks up speed.

I moisten my lips with the tip of my tongue. "Aren't you going to ask me?"

His blue eyes are intense, flickering with flame from the candle on the table between us. But he hesitates, and I suddenly realize what an idiot I've been.

"You're worried I only want to go with you because of George and Richard," I whisper. "That I'm trying to seduce you." Oh, I'm such an idiot…

But his brow creases. "No. I hadn't even thought of that." He gives me an impatient look. "Scarlett, I'll pay the seventeen and a half million for the Waiora. Of course I will. I was always going to."

My eyebrows shoot up and my jaw drops. "Really?"

"Yes."

"When did you decide that?"

"The moment you told me what they wanted."

I stare at him, confused. "So why did you ask me to dinner?"

He just laughs. Then he tips his head to the side. "Anyway, it's not why I hesitated to ask you back to my place. I hurt you last time, and I don't want to do it again."

"I'm no expert, but as I understand it, once it's done, it's done…"

"I'm no expert either. I think you're right. But being someone's first is kind of a responsibility, and down the line I don't want you to regret that it was me."

"I wouldn't," I whisper.

We study each other for a moment.

"So…" he says eventually, "if you know I'm going to buy the pool at the full amount… and you don't have to seduce me… would you still like to come back to my place?"

I suck my bottom lip. Then I nod.

His eyes light up, and his lips curve into a smile. "Come on," he murmurs.

He rises and holds out a hand, and I get up, pick up Bearcub, and slide my hand into Orson's. His warm fingers close around mine, and he leads me into the restaurant, where he pays for dinner and orders an Uber. Then he takes me outside, and we wait for it to arrive.

"Thank you for dinner," I say. "I should have offered to pay half."

He just laughs. Then he turns to face me, slides a hand around my waist to the small of my back, and moves close to me.

His gaze scans me, desire in his eyes. "You're so fucking beautiful," he murmurs. Then he dips his head and lowers his lips to mine.

His hand splays in the middle of my back, holding me there, showing me he's not going to let me go until he's kissed me. Powerless to resist, I reach up onto my tiptoes and rest my hands on his chest, leaning into the kiss. My fingers pluck at his cotton shirt, and I give a soft moan in my throat as his lips move across mine. It's a public kiss, no tongues, but my heart bangs anyway, my insides turning molten as my blood heats up like mercury in a thermometer.

When he eventually lifts his head, his pupils have dilated, and we're both breathing fast. "Uber's here," he says, his voice husky.

I detach myself and get in, hoping I don't faint, because I feel a bit dizzy. Maybe it's the champagne. Or the adrenaline. Or maybe I'm hyperventilating. I should have brought a brown paper bag with me.

Orson gets in the other side, and the car slides into the traffic.

He picks up my hand and kisses my fingertips. "Are you sure about this?" he murmurs. "I'm not expecting anything. If you'd rather go home, that's fine."

I shake my head. "I'd like to see where you live."

His lips curve up. "Okay."

"Where *do* you live, actually?"

"I have an apartment overlooking the harbor."

"Don't tell me—the penthouse?"

He just smiles, so I know I'm right.

"But you stay at the club sometimes?" I ask.

He nods. "I have a suite in the hotel."

"So you have two houses?"

"I also have a bach up in the Bay of Islands."

My jaw drops at his mention of a beach house in what many call the most beautiful part of New Zealand. "Seriously?"

"Yeah. And I have a townhouse in Wellington, another in Christchurch, and one in Dunedin."

"Wow."

He grins. "I go to a lot of meetings and conferences across the country."

"It's impressive. Do you ever look forward to settling down, though? Putting down roots?"

He looks surprised. "I haven't thought about it."

"What about when you have a family? A wife and kids."

He looks genuinely puzzled, and I can see he really hasn't considered it. "I guess," he says.

"You've never considered asking any of your girlfriends to marry you?" I ask. The words sound funny as they leave my mouth, as if I'm trying to force apples through small square holes in a wire fence. The thought of him being with other women, being intimate with them, twists me up inside.

"No," he says.

"Why not?"

"Dunno. Never been in love."

I stare at him. "Never?"

"Have you?"

"No."

"Then why is it so surprising?"

"Well, you're an old man for a start…"

He gives a short laugh. "Thanks."

I feel oddly breathless. "But you've lived with someone?"

"No. Not permanently."

"They've stayed over at your apartment though?"

His lips slowly curve up. "Scarlett…" he says, drawing the word out, "are you jealous?"

"No. Not at all. I wouldn't… I'd never… Goodness. How can you even say that?"

He chuckles. "No other woman has been to my current apartment."

"Really?"

"I've only been there six months."

"You haven't dated for six months?"

"I haven't dated for nearly a year."

"Why not?"

He just shrugs. "Been busy."

"You really don't go on Tinder or have one-night stands?"

He shakes his head. Then he slowly smiles. "You like that?"

I shrug, but I have a warm feeling inside.

He looks out of the window, then says, "Here we are."

We're right on the waterfront, not far from busy Queen Street, with Queens Wharf on our right and towering buildings on our left. We get out and he takes my hand again, then leads me past a hotel to an apartment block that glows like a jewel in the dusky evening. I look up, and up, and up. It's cube-shaped, but the bottom half has an interesting twisted façade.

"It's inspired by the Māori Pikorua motif," he says.

"Oh…"

"It's New Zealand's tallest residential tower. There's a gym, a pool, a library, resident lounges, an entertainment hub with a small cinema, and a restaurant with a twenty-four-hour kitchen for room service."

"Wow." I can't think of anything else to say. It's like an extremely exclusive hotel. He actually lives here?

Glass double doors slide open as we approach, and we enter a large lobby. Wood-paneled walls and a natural stone floor make it look classy and spacious, while green plants in white pots give it a natural touch. A couple of young businessmen sit on a leather suite in a small lounge near to the front desk, presumably waiting for a friend. Orson nods at them and says, "Evening," as we pass, and they smile back.

"*Ahiahi mārie*, Mr. Cavendish," says the Māori guy standing behind the reception desk. It means good evening.

"*Kei te pēhea koe*, Rawiri?" Orson asks, surprising me with the way it rolls off his tongue. It means 'how are you?'

"*Kei te pai ahau*," Rawiri replies, meaning I'm good.

"This is Mahuika Stone," Orson says.

"Everyone calls me Scarlett," I add, flushing at the sound of him using my full name.

"Kia ora Scarlett." Rawiri smiles. "Anything I can do for you, Mr. Cavendish?"

"No thanks, all good."

"Have a great evening."

Orson nods and leads me over to the elevators. He pushes the button, the doors open, and we go into the carriage.

He takes a key card out of his pocket and touches it to the pad. There are fifty-seven floors, and he presses the button for fifty-four.

"Not the top floor?" I tease. "Thought you'd have the biggest and the best."

"The top three levels are for services," he says as the doors close and the elevator starts to rise.

"Oh."

He chuckles.

"I didn't realize you could speak Māori," I say.

"Everyone learned Māori at my school. Kingi always says I have terrible pronunciation."

I lean back against the wall of the carriage. "You speak it just fine. Was it a posh school?"

"Somerset College."

"Private, I'm guessing." I can't keep a sarcastic tone out of my voice.

"Yes." His lips curve up. "You disapprove."

"Of course I disapprove. Decent education and medical care should be available to everyone, not just those who can afford it."

He tips his head to the side, his eyelids lowering to half mast, looking so sexy that it makes my mouth water.

"You're so privileged and elitist," I say breathlessly. "So confident and arrogant."

"Yep. I always get what I want."

"And what do you want right now?"

He laughs, walks toward me, and takes my face in his hands. "I fucking adore you."

"Oh! I—"

I have no chance to say anything else, because he crushes his lips to mine, presses me up hard against the wall, and kisses the living daylights out of me.

Oh my God, I've never been kissed like it, not even remotely. There's enough heat in his lips to brand me, and when I gasp, my mouth opening, he plunges his tongue inside and deepens the kiss until I'm breathless and aching with longing.

Only when the lift pings and the doors open does he move back. His blue eyes blaze as they search mine, and then he takes my hand and leads me out and along a quiet corridor. It's thickly carpeted so our feet make no sound. There are four doors, two to the left and two to the right, and he walks to the furthest door on the left.

He stops before it, then to my surprise turns to me. He takes my face in his hands again.

"Are you sure about this?" he asks gently.

I nod.

He strokes my cheeks with his thumbs. "I don't want to keep asking, but I need you to know that if you want me to stop at any time, just say so, and I will, okay? I won't be angry."

This guy makes me melt. "I know," I whisper, because even though I've just called him arrogant and privileged and he's told me he always gets what he wants, I believe him. He hasn't forced me to come here. It's entirely my choice, and I know if I said I wanted to leave, he wouldn't stop me.

I have no intention of doing that, though. Not in a million billion years.

"You going to give me a safe word?" I ask, trying to be sassy.

He chuckles. "You won't need one." He lowers his head and kisses me, this time so gently it's as if a butterfly has landed on my lips. Then he lifts his head, touches his key card to the door, and we go inside.

Chapter Fourteen

Orson

"Jesus," she says. "It's enormous."

"Thank you," I reply, amused.

She sends me a wry look. "The apartment, I mean."

I grin, take my Converses off, and leave them by the door, and she does the same with her sandals, leaving Bearcub sitting on them. Then I watch her walk forward and stand in the center of the living area. I move next to her, trying to see it through her eyes. The apartment takes up a corner of the entire floor. One side faces the harbor. The glittering lights of the Harbour Bridge across to the North Shore are reflected in the water, making it seem as if the city is strung with Christmas lights. The other window looks across the gleaming lights of the city with the Sky Tower just visible to the right, only a few hundred yards away. The view is magnificent in the daytime.

In the lounge, a plush light-gray carpet covers the wooden floors, and a light-gray suite with scattered fawn and navy-blue cushions faces a widescreen TV. A round dining table with four chairs sits to one side, not far from the kitchen. My housekeeper was in this morning, so the gray marble work surfaces and all the mod cons gleam when I switch the lamps on. The art on the walls is abstract and tasteful. I didn't pick it—the decorators did, but I like it. My PlayStation sits next to the TV.

"It's… beautiful," Scarlett says.

I toss my wallet and keys on the counter, noticing her cautious tone. "You can say if you don't like it. I won't be offended."

"No, I mean it, it's beautiful, it just doesn't look… lived in. It's like a show home."

"I don't spend a lot of time here, it's true. When I am here, I tend to go in the study."

"Can I see that?"

Surprised, I say, "Of course. Would you like a drink first?"

"No, thank you."

I walk across the room, and she follows me down the corridor, then into another room on the left.

"Wow," she says. "Yes, okay, this is more you."

Here, bookshelves line two walls, filled with books, magazines, and journals. There's an old oak desk and a leather office chair at one end, and a very soft black leather sofa at the other, both facing the view of the city. The coffee table in front of the sofa is scattered with more books and journals, my Kindle, and my iPad. An open drinks cabinet holds a dozen different bottles of alcohol—mostly whiskey and bourbon, and a row of crystal tumblers.

"My den," I say.

She smiles. "It smells of you. I love it. It's much nicer than the lounge." She glances at the books. "Can I look around?"

"Of course. I don't have anything to hide."

She walks around the room slowly.

"Are you looking for something?" I ask, perching on the edge of the desk.

"You've told me a little about your business. That you go to the gym and play video games sometimes. But that's all. I want to find out what makes you tick."

"Apart from you?"

She just laughs, stops by the first bookcase, and starts looking at the titles. She reads some of them out. "Profitable Properties, Property Management Excellence, The Psychology of Money, The Intelligent Investor." She pulls a face. "They're all business books. Very dry."

"They are, rather. I don't read them all cover to cover. I tend to dip into them for reference or to check facts."

She continues walking, past another bookcase of finance, property, investment, and management books. "The Five Dysfunctions of a Team, The Making of a Manager, How to Deal with Difficult People. Like me?"

I just smile.

She carries on to the next bookcase. "Oh… these ones are different. Teach Students How to Learn, McKeachie's Teaching Tips, Everyday Lessons from the Science of Learning. Do you teach?"

I nod. "At the university. One afternoon a week."

MIDNIGHT ENEMY

Beneath it is a shelf containing books on coaching rugby. "Rugby Drills, Rugby Skills, Tactics and Rules, Confessions of a Rugby Mercenary. You coach rugby?"

I nod again. "At the local high school with a friend who's a teacher."

"Hmm." She moves on to the next shelf. "Lots on space," she says. "Astronomy, the solar system, the International Space Station. Sports. And… oh my God…" She stops by the numerous shelves of biographies. "Steve Jobs, Carrie Fisher, Oscar Wilde, Sylvia Plath, Buster Keaton, Pontius Pilate, Thelonious Monk…"

"I'm interested in people," I say with a shrug.

"I saw a Kindle on the table. Do you use it?"

"I do. I read a lot. Fiction on the Kindle. I tend to buy non-fiction as hardbacks."

She stares at the next shelves and gives me an interested look. "Poetry?"

I don't say anything.

She looks back and runs a finger along them. "Amanda Lovelace, Shel Silverstein, Rupi Kaur, John Milton, Emily Dickinson, Walt Whitman, Homer, Coleridge, Robert Frost… Wow, lots of collections… Every poet I can think of is here. And books on writing poetry! A Poetry Handbook. Poemcrazy. A Little Book on Form. Writing Haiku. The Sounds of Poetry." She looks at me. "Do you write poetry?"

I've never told a soul about the poems I write. I slide my hands into the pockets of my trousers and study my bare feet.

She comes up to me. "Do you think I'm going to mock you for it?"

I shrug. "I'm not showing you any."

"Okay."

"I only do it for fun and it's terrible."

She tips her head to the side to look at my face. "I'm not a literary snob, Orson. Poetry should be for everyone to both read and write, just like art. It's not about creating a masterpiece. It's about expressing yourself." She lifts a hand to my face. "Your father has really done a number on you, hasn't he?"

"Actually, it wasn't him."

"Oh?"

I frown. "It doesn't feel right to speak ill of the dead."

She strokes my face. "It's not speaking ill if it's stating a fact."

I suppose that's true. I huff a sigh. "My mother found a folder of poems I'd written once. She threw them away and told me to stop being childish."

Her jaw drops. "Seriously?"

"She didn't agree with pastimes that were 'unproductive'. Her word."

She looks genuinely puzzled. Then she says, "Do you write anything else?"

Man, this girl is astute. "Ah… some bits and pieces."

"Like…"

I purse my lips. Then I walk around the desk and open the large drawer at the bottom. She joins me and bends down to look into it. Lightly, she runs her fingers over my twenty or so poetry journals, and then examines the folders beside them. Three of them—printed copies of the manuscripts I've written.

"Orson," she says softly, "you've written three books?"

"Yeah."

"What kind of stories?"

She sounds so fascinated and impressed that it unlocks the heart I keep tightly padlocked. "Sad books," I say, my lips quirking up.

She stands and closes the drawer, not asking to see them, which I appreciate, then rests her butt on the table. "Sad in what way?"

"I don't know. They always seem to end up melancholy. Stories about loss. I don't know why, I don't think I'm a melancholy person."

She thinks about that while she studies me. Her brown eyes are very dark and passionate. "Have you read Harry Potter?" she asks.

"Yeah, many years ago."

"You know how Voldemort stored parts of his soul in objects called Horcruxes?"

"Yeah."

"I feel that's what happens when we're creative. The more soul we have, the more we need to store it in creative projects—writing and making art and music. I'm relieved you feel you have a soul to store. I was beginning to think you were a robot."

I give her a wry look, but the sentiment warms me through.

She giggles, walks over to the leather sofa, and lowers onto it. "Do you sit here in the evenings and look out over the city?"

"Yeah. And think about you."

She rolls her eyes. "You do not."

"I do. I imagine doing this." I sit next to her, then, before she can say anything, I pull her onto my lap, turn, and lie back with her on top of me.

She squeals, and I laugh and release her, but she doesn't get up. Instead, she looks down at me with eyes filled with wonder.

"I can't believe I'm here," she says, looking puzzled again. "You're one of the richest men in the city, if not the whole country, and you're young and gorgeous and fit and extremely sexy. And you write poetry, which I adore, even if it's bad. And… you want me. I don't get it."

I tuck a strand of her hair behind her ear. "Get what?"

"Why you want me?"

The city lights behind her make her look as if she has a halo. "Because I feel as if I've been living in a city filled with smog, and now I'm standing on top of a hillside in the middle of the country. You're a breath of fresh air, Scarlett. Completely natural."

"I don't know what to say to your compliments," she says, frowning.

"You don't have to say anything."

"Are you trying to get around me?"

I run my fingers down her back, following her curves beneath the soft dress. "In what way?"

"To get a better price for the Waiora?"

"I've already told you, I'm willing to pay full price. Let's not talk business. Business is dull."

"I thought you loved business."

"Not right now. I have other things on my mind."

She moves her hips against mine, obviously feeling my erection. "So I see."

I roll my eyes. "I have a beautiful, soft woman lying on top of me, who's almost certainly going commando. What did you expect?"

She rocks her hips this time, stroking up my length. My lips slowly curve up.

"You're a big man," she comments.

"Six foot two."

"I wasn't talking about your height."

"Really?"

"I was talking about your feet."

I chuckle and lift a hand to run a strand of her hair between my fingers.

"And your hands," she says, turning her head to kiss my palm. She takes my hand in hers and studies my fingers, my wide palm, the broad back, looking thoughtful.

"Penny for them?" I ask.

"I was thinking that your skin has warm, reddish-brown tones. Mine has cool brown tones. They'll look good together. When we're naked, I mean."

My eyebrows lift as heat shoots through me.

"Sorry," she says, "was that too presumptuous?"

I just laugh, hold her tightly, and twist on the sofa so she's beneath me. The skirt of her dress is now wrapped around us both, binding us together.

I kiss her, and she opens her mouth to accept my tongue, wrapping her arms around me. She strokes down my back, her fingers feeling my muscles through the cotton. I let my lips move across hers, content to kiss her while she explores.

"Can I undo your buttons?" she whispers when I eventually lift my head.

Amused that she felt she had to ask, I say, "Of course." I kiss her nose, her cheeks, her eyebrows, and back to her mouth, while she pushes the buttons through the holes until they're all undone. She moves the two sides of my shirt apart and rests her hands on my skin. "Mmm," she murmurs, exhaling against my lips. "You're hot."

"Sorry, I forgot to put the aircon on." I know my skin must be slightly damp.

"It wasn't a complaint." She strokes down over my pecs to my abs, then traces her fingers around to my ribs. I shiver, and her eyes light up.

Turned on now, I delve my tongue into her mouth, and she moans, stroking up my back, then down my spine. My trousers are still done up, but she sneaks her fingers beneath the waistband, reaching down to feel the top of my butt.

"Maybe we should take our clothes off," she says breathlessly as I kiss down her neck.

I lift my head and give her an amused look. "Do you have somewhere you need to be?"

"No…"

"Then why rush?"

In between a series of light butterfly kisses, she says, "You're very bossy."

"You think?" I kiss up her jawline to her ear.

"Are you a Dom?"

That makes me laugh. I push up and give her an amused look. "Where did you hear that term?"

She gives me a sarcastic look. "I'm not completely naive. I've read romance novels."

"Okay, well, maybe it's a bit early to be talking about BDSM and stuff like that."

"Are you, though? Have you had subs?"

"No."

"But you are bossy."

"That doesn't mean I'm a Dom."

"I've read Fifty Shades. You seem quite like Christian."

"I'm really not. That's not my thing. If I were to be a Dom, I'd be a soft one."

"What does that mean?"

"Someone who's into praise and reassurance and communication. And pleasure."

"Isn't all sex about pleasure?"

Her brown eyes are nearly black in the semi-darkness of the room. "For some people it's more about the other person's pleasure than their own."

She doesn't say anything, although her breasts rise and fall quickly with her fast breaths.

"I'm not a pillow princess," she informs me.

I laugh again. "Okay."

"I'm just saying, I don't expect to lie there and be pleasured. I want to take part."

"Noted."

"Are you teasing me?"

"A little." I kiss her. "You're adorable." Then I kiss her again, longer this time.

She murmurs something that ends up muffled against my lips, then wraps her arms around me and kisses me back.

We kiss for a long, long time. Gradually, she relaxes, sinking back into the cushions, while I move my lips across hers, gentle and sensual, pressing lightly from one corner of her mouth to the other. I trace the tip of my tongue across her bottom lip until her lips part, then slowly slide my tongue into her mouth, a sexy invasion, mirroring what I hope is going to happen elsewhere soon. A soft moan escapes her, and in response I growl deep in my throat, causing her to tighten her fingers on my back and dig her nails in.

I lift my head. "I think maybe we should move this to the bedroom."

"I don't mind staying here."

"I want us both to be comfortable." I push up, and I'm unable to stop myself wincing as a sharp pain tears through my shoulder.

"I'm sorry," she says, sitting up, "I forgot about your injury. Is it sore?"

I get up off the sofa. "I'm fine."

"Is your head okay?"

I don't answer and extend a hand to help her up.

She ignores it, though. "You should take some painkillers."

"Later."

"No, now."

"I'm okay."

"I don't want you to be in pain. Orson, do you feel guilty about what we're doing?"

I stare at her. "Why do you say that?"

She goes over to the coffee table, picks up the pack of Panadol that was half hidden beneath a journal, pops two, and picks up the water bottle standing next to them. Then she turns and holds them out to me.

"Take these," she says.

My head does hurt, so I take them from her and knock them back with the water. Then, as I screw the top back on the bottle, I say, "Why did you ask if I feel guilty?"

"Because how we feel has a direct effect on pain."

"I don't feel guilty."

"Are you sure about that?"

I frown at her.

"You're not corrupting me or leading me astray," she tells me. "And you're not seducing me. I went to dinner knowing where it was likely to lead."

I'm momentarily speechless. The truth is that she's right. Although I asked her back, it's impossible not to wonder whether she's only here because the two guys at the commune have told her to do her best to get the full price for the Waiora. I told her I'd pay it anyway because I'd hoped it would banish that feeling, but it hasn't.

"You don't believe me," she says, and her eyes flare. "I do have a mind of my own."

"I know."

"Doesn't sound like it. You really think I'd go to bed with you because George asked me to? That I'd prostitute myself for the pool?"

"No…"

"I don't believe you."

"Scarlett…"

She's gradually growing more irate. "I accept that I initially agreed to go to dinner with you to discuss business. But that wasn't the only reason. I didn't kiss you in the gazebo because of the pool. And I'm not here because of it."

"I know."

Her eyes blaze. "I don't know how you could think that of me."

My God, she's sexy when she's irate. I'm turned on even though I'm annoyed. "I don't."

"I was a virgin when we met at the gazebo!"

"I know, I was there, remember?"

"Are you being sarcastic with me now? God, you're arrogant, and condescending, and patronizing. You're everything I've been brought up to believe."

"Probably." I glare at her. "And you drive me crazy with your hippy-dippy, muesli-eating, let's-all-hold-hands-and-sing-Hosanna bullshit." I move closer to her. "I don't know why I want you as much as I do."

Her eyes widen. She backs away and holds up a hand. "Don't you dare turn on the charm."

"I'm not." I continue to walk forward.

She backs up and meets the wall with a bump, and raises both hands to rest them on my chest. I move closer, until I'm pressed up against her. "You're so fucking beautiful," I say, my voice husky with desire. "Even though you drive me nuts."

"You said if I wanted you to stop, you'd stop," she says tartly.

I lower my head to brush my lips against hers. "I will." I kiss her, very lightly. "Do you want me to stop, Scarlett?"

She doesn't reply.

I kiss her again. "Just tell me to stop."

She doesn't.

I kiss her a third time. "Push me away."

Her fingers clutch at the two sides of my shirt. "I can't," she says hoarsely.

Heat surges through me. "Do you want me, baby girl?"

Her answer is just a whisper across my lips. "Yes…"

"Because I want you, so bad…" I give her a few more seconds to complain, and when she doesn't, I take her hands in mine, pin them to the wall, and pour all my desire into a kiss that sends my heart banging and makes me as hard as iron.

Chapter Fifteen

Scarlett

I gasp, but all that does is let him plunge his tongue into my mouth and kiss me so deeply I feel as if I'm losing all sense of time and place.

I can't move because he's pinned my hands, and his whole body is pressed up against mine. I can feel his hard erection against my belly. He's so tall, and big, and strong, I feel helpless. Oh my God, why does that turn me on so much? I should be outraged. I should be giving him a knee in the groin and telling him he's acting inappropriately, and I should walk straight out of here.

I don't, though. Instead, I flex my hands where he's holding my wrists, and a small moan escapes me.

He moves back, looking at me with those fierce blue eyes. Then he bends and, without warning, lifts me up and holds me beneath my butt, so I have to wrap my legs around his waist.

I hold his face with my hands and kiss him, tilting my head to the side, while he carries me through to the bedroom. I have a brief glimpse of a large room, one wall of which is all windows, with a gigantic bed that faces out over the city, before he crosses the room, climbs onto the bed, and lowers me onto my back so my head is on the pillows.

He sits back and takes off his shirt, revealing his glorious body, then leans over me, a hand on either side of my shoulders. My jaw drops. Oh my God, the muscles. I lift my hands and rest them on his pecs, then brush them across to his shoulders, down his biceps, back up, and down his chest. He has a delicious scattering of hair, and I follow it down to where it narrows into a thin trail that disappears into the waistband of his trousers. I've seen this on other men when they've worn shorts but gone topless down by the pool, but this is the first time I've examined it. I follow it down to the waistband, then stop, conscious of his erection just beneath it.

Without asking, he lifts up, undoes the button, and slides down the zipper. Then he leans over me again. I stare, fascinated, at the way his erection juts out, straining at the black cotton of his boxer briefs.

I look up into his eyes. He hasn't put the lamp on. The colored lights of the city and the light from the rising moon fall onto his back and hair, but his eyes look midnight-blue in the semi-darkness.

"Can I touch you?" I whisper.

"Yeah." His voice is little more than a husky growl. He wants me. It makes my heart race.

I touch a finger to the tip of his erection and circle it, feeling the head. Then I turn my hand palm up, slide it down the shaft, and slip it beneath the seam of his trousers, all the way down to cup his balls. It's the first time I've felt this part of a man, and I explore shyly, enjoying this adventure. His cock twitches in response, making me catch my breath.

He lowers down to kiss me, then stretches out beside me, half on me, heavy, pressing me into the mattress. Sliding a hand up my skirt, he lifts my leg up, cups my ass, and pulls me against him. Now his erection nestles against my mound, and when I rock my hips it slides through my sensitive skin and arouses my clit.

"Mmm..." I close my eyes, lost in bliss as he rocks slowly against me while he kisses me. My heart races, and when I place my hand on his chest I can feel his heart doing the same, but he kisses me slowly, apparently still keen to keep the pace slow.

We kiss for a long time, the room slowly growing warmer. I slip my hand to the back of his neck and feel the short hair there, then cup his face, my thumb brushing his smooth jaw. No sign of bristle, so he must have showered before he met me. The thought of him in the shower, naked, preparing himself for me only serves to make my heart beat faster.

Eventually, he moves back and says, "Can I take off your dress?"

I nod, and he helps me pull it up my legs, over my hips, then peel it up my body and over my head. He tosses it aside without looking, his gaze fixed on me.

"I knew it," he says.

I glance down—I'm completely naked now. I look back up at him. "Is it a problem?"

He just laughs and kisses me, his mouth hot and hungry. He rests a hand on my collarbone, just below my throat, then draws a finger down between my breasts to my belly. Finally, he cups my breast and brushes his thumb over the nipple, then lowers his head and covers it with his mouth.

I close my eyes, my mouth opening in a gasp at the feel of his warm, wet mouth fastening on me. Oh God… I clench inside as he circles the areola with his tongue, then teases the tip. When he sucks, I can't stop a long moan escaping my lips.

"Jesus," he mumbles, and he lifts up and moves over me. He kisses my other breast, and I watch, puzzled, as he kisses down to my belly… and then lowers down between my legs.

Oh shit. Seriously? I knew men did this, but on the first date? Is this normal?

He pushes my legs up as he kisses over my mound, and I stare up at the ceiling, my heart banging on my ribs, fighting the urge to cover myself up. He rests a hand on my thigh, and then I feel him slide his thumb down into the heart of me.

"Fuck," he says. "You're so wet."

I close my eyes and rest my hands over them as he strokes his thumb back up to my clit and circles the pad over it. Oh God, I'm so turned on that it throbs at his touch. He does it again, spreading my moisture over my sensitive skin, then lowers his head and does the same with his tongue.

I let out a long, uncontrolled moan at the intense sensation of his mouth on me. His other hand is resting on my thigh, and his fingers tighten on it, while he groans and covers my clit with his mouth. He sucks, and I gasp at the intense sensation. *Fuuuuuuck…*

He continues licking and sucking, teasing my entrance with his thumb, but not penetrating, and I'm so keyed up that it's literally about two minutes before I feel my muscles start to tense inside.

"Oh no," I say, embarrassed that it's happening so quickly.

"Mm," is all he says, and he continues to swirl his tongue over my clit with the same rhythm… oh God he knows that's exactly what a girl needs… and it's so amazing that my orgasm sweeps over me… a swift tightening inside… so intense it almost hurts, argh… and then the incredible pulses… I gasp with each one, screwing up my nose, my body jerking with uncontrollable pleasure…

He keeps going until I finally fall back onto the bed, limp and exhausted, at which point he releases me and starts kissing his way back up my body. Over my belly, up my ribs, my breasts, my neck, and back to my mouth. Then he lies on top of me and kisses me until I'm breathless again, and the nice, relaxed feeling fades slowly, and need begins to build up inside me once again.

He lifts up then, gets off the bed, and rids himself of his trousers, tossing them away on the floor. Then, while I watch with wide eyes, he removes his boxer-briefs and throws them away, too. His erection looks enormous to my innocent eyes, long and thick and hard.

"Jesus," I say. "That won't fit."

That makes him laugh as he opens his wallet and takes out a condom. "I'm not that big. You just don't have anything to compare it to."

He climbs back on and kneels between my legs, rolls the condom on, and leans over me again. Lowering a hand, he strokes his thumb down through my sensitive skin, and groans as he obviously finds me still wet and swollen.

He bends and kisses me, then looks me in the eyes. "Are you sure about this?"

"I thought you weren't going to ask me again."

"I want you to be sure."

"I'm sure."

"Even though I'm the enemy?"

We study each other for a moment.

"You're not my enemy," I whisper.

He pauses. Then, his lips curving up a little, he moves his erection down with a hand until the tip presses against my entrance.

Leaning a hand either side of my shoulders, he looks me in the eye as he pushes his hips forward.

My mouth opens in a gasp as he penetrates me. I feel myself stretch to accommodate him, but it doesn't hurt. He pauses and waits for me to adjust, then says, "Okay?" When I nod, he moves back, then pushes forward again. I realize he's easing his way inside me, pausing until I get used to him before gradually sinking further in.

"That must be all of it," I say on the fifth or sixth thrust.

"Not quite. You're very tight. Just relax."

I inhale and let out a shaky breath, trying my best.

"Well done," he murmurs, pushing forward again. "Almost there."

Jesus, there's more? I moan, and he lowers down and kisses me. "You feel amazing," he whispers, teasing my lips with his tongue. "You're doing so well, taking all of me like this."

"Ahhh… please say that's it…"

"One more inch…" He withdraws, then moves forward with a groan as he sinks into me. "Fuck me, you're tight…" Finally, he stops, his hips flush with mine. "That's it, baby girl. That's all of me. Good girl." I open my eyes and look up at him. His eyes catch the moonlight, blazing with desire. "This is where the fun starts," he says, and begins to move.

He lowers down and kisses me, and I wrap myself around him, enjoying being so close to him, and having him inside me in the most intimate way a woman can have a man. My hands roam over him almost of their own accord, feeling the way his muscles move, the smoothness of his skin. I brush my thumb over his Adam's apple, then draw my hands across his broad shoulders and down his chest, feeling the hairs there beneath my fingers before circling around to his back and down to his butt. His muscles tighten as he thrusts, and he grunts when I dig my fingers into them.

Sometimes I've wondered why people seem so obsessed with sex, but I can totally understand now. If I was married to a guy like this, I'd want to do it all day every day.

"You feel amazing," he murmurs, cupping my breast and lowering his head to suck my nipple. "You're so soft all over, so incredibly beautiful."

Flattered, I sink my hand into his hair, then clutch my fingers and gasp as he sucks extra hard. He laughs and, lifting up, withdraws, holding onto the condom.

I'm disappointed and go to complain, but he rolls onto his back, then pulls me on top of him. "Sit up," he says. "You do it this time."

Ooh, he wants me on top. I straddle him, move a hand down, and guide him to my entrance. Then I push down a little. Mmm… I tip my head back and close my eyes, loving the sensation of him entering me so slowly. I let out a breath, trying to relax, and this time it's easier, taking only a couple of thrusts for him to slide all the way in.

He rests his hands on my hips and watches me, his eyelids falling to half-mast. "That feels so fucking good."

I slide my hand beneath me, feeling where our bodies are flush. "Mmm."

"Can you take your hair down?" he asks softly.

Surprised, I lift my hands to my bun, release the clips holding it in place, and lean over to put them on the bedside table. When I sit back up, I watch him observing me as I unravel the strands and let them tumble around my shoulders. He cups my breasts, his gaze drifting to them. Ohhh… He likes watching me. Keeping my hands on my hair, I start to move, learning how to rock my hips to drive him in and out of me. He watches, teasing my nipples with his thumbs and forefingers, and I close my eyes and tip my head back again, liking the sensual feel of my hair tumbling down my back.

"Do you like being on top?" he asks, tugging my nipples once, twice, then a harder third time.

"Ooh." I clench around him and he laughs, so I take his hands in mine and pin them above his head. "It has its advantages."

He flexes his fingers in mine, his lust-filled gaze watching me as I move. I like this, being able to set the pace. I love the way his biceps bulge, and how strong the muscles in his shoulders and chest look. And I was right—the cool tones of my light-brown skin looking amazing against the warm tones of his tanned body.

Without warning, he lifts up, surprising me, making it quite clear that he was only playing at being restrained. Still holding my hands, he moves my arms behind my back and holds them with one hand, then cups a breast and lowers his mouth to it. I arch my back, shocked at the ease of his movements, and unable to catch my breath as he sucks. My head tips back, and I move my hips, moaning at the feel of him so big inside me.

"Scarlett," he murmurs, kissing up my neck, then bringing my head down to kiss me. His mouth slants across mine, hot and demanding, his tongue tangling with mine, and I feel myself begin to spiral out of control.

"Not enough," he says mysteriously and, holding me around the waist, he somehow turns, flipping me onto my back again. He kisses me again, lifting my legs to wrap them around his waist, and I realize it enables him to go deeper inside me. He pushes his hips forward, stretching me, and I groan at the sensation of being speared to the mattress.

"Too much?" he says, easing back.

"I'm never going to be able to walk again."

He just laughs and kisses my throat hungrily, big wet kisses, sucking slightly at the point where my pulse beats, as if he wants to feel the way my heart's pounding.

I moan, and he groans and thrusts harder. "You're driving me crazy," he says in my ear, his voice husky with desire.

"Mmm…"

He lifts up, still moving inside me, leaning on one hand, and brushing his other hand up my thigh, up my body, over my breast, and down my arm, before taking my hand in his. He links our fingers, and for some bizarre reason that feels even more intimate than everything else that's happening. I look at our joined hands, then up into his eyes, and experience the electric jolt I often get with him, a zap to my nerve endings all the way through my body that makes my lips part as I inhale sharply.

Moving my hands above my head, he holds them there by my wrists and kisses me hard as he thrusts. Oh my… He must have changed the angle somehow because he's grinding against my clit now, arousing me with every rock of his hips… Being held like this makes me feel as if I have no say in my own pleasure—he's going to drive me to the edge regardless of whether I want to go there or not…

I moan against his lips, and he says, "I love the way you tell me what you like," as he kisses down my neck.

"Oh that's so good," I whisper, feeling the first tingling of an orgasm way off in the distance. "Don't stop…"

"No problem there," he mutters, thrusting hard. "Fuck. You feel amazing."

"Mmm… Orson…"

"Ahhh, baby girl… you're so soft… and wet for me. Are you going to come?"

"Yes…"

He slows and presses gentle kisses over my face. "Good girl… you're doing so well taking me like this your first time."

"Ohhh…"

"Just relax… let me take you there. You don't have to do anything."

"Mmm…"

He rocks slowly, long slow thrusts, and it's only another twenty seconds or so before I feel my orgasm approaching, the curious tightening of the muscles deep inside.

"Yeah," he says, obviously sensing something, "beautiful girl, come for me…"

My toes curl, and my mouth opens, but no words come out as I clench around him and the amazing pulses start. Only then do little *Oh-oh-ohs* tumble from my lips, and he kisses me as if he wants to capture them like butterflies, murmuring words of encouragement all the way through it, although my brain is spinning too fast for me to make sense of them.

When they finally fade away, I open my eyes and look straight into his.

"You're so beautiful," he murmurs, still moving inside me.

"Mmmm…"

He lifts up, supporting himself on his hands, either side of my shoulders, and begins to move faster. I tighten my legs around him, thrilled at the thought of him taking his pleasure from me, and watch with awe, moving with him and doing my best to drive him to the edge.

It only takes a minute or two before I feel him change… his thrusts become faster, his mouth more demanding, his groans louder. I scrape my nails down his chest and then try squeezing his nipples to see what it does to him. He growls, pins my hands above my head again, and thrusts harder, and I can only lie there and watch this magnificent man as he takes himself to the edge and tumbles off into the abyss.

Mmm… the beauty of a man's climax… my first experience of it, and hopefully not my last. He groans, shudders, and then stills, tensing, and I feel him twitch and jerk inside me. He pushes his hips forward, burying himself inside me—ooh, ow, I'm a little tender there now—but I don't say anything, and just stare up in wonder as he comes. I did that. I gave this guy the ultimate pleasure.

Wow, I love sex so much.

Chapter Sixteen

Orson

Scarlett is wrapped around me completely, and I'm buried deep inside her. Oh man. That was amazing. She stares up at me, and I sigh. I don't know what this girl does to me, but every time she looks into my eyes I feel as if I've stuck my fingers in a socket.

I lower my head and kiss her gently. "Are you okay? Sorry, I got carried away. I didn't hurt you?"

"No," she says. But when I withdraw, she winces, so I know she must be tender.

"I'm so sorry." I move off her and dispose of the condom. "Poor baby girl." I get up and pull the duvet over her as she curls onto her side. "Hold on." I go through to the ensuite bathroom, retrieve a clean facecloth, run it under the cold tap and wring it out tightly, then take it out to her. "Here, this might help. Open your legs."

Shyly, she does so, and I press it to where she's sore, then close her legs gently.

"Thought you hadn't been with a virgin before," she says tartly.

"I haven't. It's standard sports practice. Cold compress for soreness. I'll be back in a minute."

I walk along the corridor and cross the living room to the kitchen. After retrieving a couple bottles of water from the fridge and a box of chocolates, I take them back to the bedroom. Then I climb onto the bed beside her.

I unscrew the top of one of the bottles and hand it to her. "Drink," I instruct.

"Yes sir," she says saucily.

I chuckle and watch as she downs a few mouthfuls while I unscrew my bottle. I drink a quarter of it in one go, then leave it on the bedside table and take the wrapper off the box of chocolates.

"Treats to Tempt You," she says, reading the name of the shop on the box.

"I got them from Doubtless Bay. Best chocolates in the country." I open the box and offer them to her. She chooses a kiwifruit truffle. I pop a caramel truffle in my mouth, then leave the box on the bed behind me and pull her into my arms. She snuggles up to me, and I hold her while I stroke her back.

"Mmm." She nuzzles my neck. "You smell so good."

"So do you."

"I didn't expect this."

"What do you mean?"

She shrugs. "I thought you'd get up and call me an Uber afterward."

"Jesus. You really don't have a very good view of men, do you? Or is it just me you think of as a Neanderthal?"

"Kinda just you."

"Well, thanks for being honest."

She giggles. Then she kisses my chest. "I was wrong, Orson. I'm happy to admit it."

I tuck a finger under her chin and lift it. "Me too."

She looks into my eyes. "Don't do that."

"Do what?"

"Whatever you're doing. You make my stomach flip."

So she feels it, too? We study each other for a moment, lit by the light of the city and the soft silver glow of the rising moon.

She leans her chin on her hand, resting on my chest. "Tell me one line of your poetry."

I narrow my eyes. "I told you, I don't share."

"Not even one line? For me?"

I purse my lips, thinking. I don't want her to make fun of me. But equally she's asked, which no other girl has done.

"Okay, I wrote this last June.

A midwinter toast
To the return of the sun
Marks lengthening days
And the first, sweet, fleeting glimpse
Of summer in my cold heart."

She surveys me with wide eyes. "You wrote that?"

"I did. It's a tanka—an extended version of the Japanese haiku."

"What were you feeling when you wrote it?"

I play with a strand of her hair. "I'd broken up with my girlfriend a month before."

"You were sad?"

"A little. The winter solstice felt like a turning point."

She trails a finger through my chest hairs. "Do you see her much?"

"No. She moved to Dunedin."

"Do you miss her?"

"No. Not now."

She scowls. "I don't like thinking about you with other women."

"There are no other women, Scarlett. Every girl pales into insignificance next to you."

She looks a little mollified—she likes that. I kiss her hair, and she smiles.

"Can I have another chocolate?" she asks.

"Of course." I retrieve the box for her.

"I don't know why I'm hungry," she says, choosing one.

I pick a chocolate-covered cherry and hold it for a moment. "Don't worry, it's the sex. I could eat a whole box of fried chicken."

"That's terrible for your arteries."

"I'll get a side of kale for you."

"Jeez, what is it with you and kale? That's not all I eat."

I chuckle and pop the truffle into my mouth. It's left a circle of chocolate on my thumb and forefinger. I lower a hand to her breast and tease the end of her nipple, smearing it with chocolate.

"Hey," she says, but before she can protest further, I push her onto her back, cover the nipple with my mouth, and suck the chocolate off.

"Ooh." She tries to push me away, and then her fingers curl and clutch at my shoulders as she moans.

After making sure I've removed all the chocolate, I lift my head and kiss her, delving my tongue into her mouth. She tastes sweet, and I feel myself stir again, even though I'm pleasantly sated.

"Mmm." She presses her lips together, her eyes flaring. "Naughty boy."

"I haven't been called a boy for about fifteen years."

"Then I'm definitely going to call you that." She rolls over. "Back in a sec." She removes the cloth from between her legs, hesitates, then says, "thank you for this."

"I hope you're not too sore."

"I'm okay." Giving me a shy smile, she goes into the bathroom.

SERENITY WOODS

I lean back on the pillows, stretching out, and yawn. Then I look up at the ceiling. Will she want to stay the night? Maybe her sister will worry if she doesn't go back this evening. I wonder whether the Elders are keeping tabs on her, too.

That makes me think of my father. He knows I'm out with Scarlett this evening. Frowning, I reach for my phone on the bedside table and touch the screen. Sure enough, there's a message from him. *Hope you're being sensible.*

I toss the phone onto the table crossly. Fucking hell. Sometimes I hate my father.

Scarlett comes out of the bathroom and gets back on the mattress. She pulls the duvet up to her waist, rolls onto her front, tugs a pillow down, and rests her head on it. "Tell me about your school and what it was like growing up for you."

Surprised, because no girl has ever asked me that before, I stretch out beside her and offer her the chocolates again, me stretched out on my side, head propped on a hand, her on her stomach, hugging the pillow.

I tell her about going to boarding school. How I hated the first few weeks. I refused to cry like some of the boys in the dorm, but I lay awake for hours, eyes burning, hating my parents for sending me away when my sister was still at home in her bed. Then I describe how I met Kingi. We were in different classes but were brought together for a rugby match. At the time we were the same height and build and we played inside and outside center. We were both sprinters, and for some reason, even at that age, we were able to read each other, and we made enough good passes that we were chosen for the rugby team that year. Like me, he also excelled at mathematics, which meant we were put in the top class together, and I quickly grew to like the kind, funny, matter-of-fact Māori boy. We formed a firm friendship, decided to both take finance at the University of Auckland, and ended up going into business.

"His sporting career far surpassed mine," I say. "He was so fast—he could easily have been an Olympic sprinter. But his first love was hiking, and he still loves taking off into the bush with a backpack and disappearing for days. He likes rock climbing, white-water rafting, spelunking, anything where he can grow a scruffy beard and not have to wash for days."

"I'm guessing he does this activity by himself."

"He doesn't take girls with him, if that's what you're asking. He's six four with a thick beard. Sightings of Bigfoot rise monumentally every time he goes on a trek."

She giggles and studies the truffles. "What's he like? As a person, I mean? I've spoken to him briefly and he sounds nice."

"He's a great guy. Good sense of humor. Down to earth. Doesn't take any nonsense."

"Who's the smartest?"

"His IQ is one above mine, and he never lets me forget it."

She grins. "What is yours?"

"My IQ? One-six-one."

Her eyes widen. "One hundred and sixty-one?"

"No. Sixteen-point-one."

She doesn't laugh. "That's higher than Einstein's."

"Only just."

"Orson, that puts you in the genius category."

I put a dot of chocolate on her nose, then lean forward and lick it off.

"Maybe not," she says, rolling her eyes. "Seriously, though. You said you weren't as smart as your friends!"

"I'm not. I told you, his IQ is one point higher." I grin at her huff. "Yeah okay, I know I'm pretty smart, and figures came easily, but I did have to work hard at all my other subjects."

"So is Kingi married?"

"Nah. He lived with a girl for a few years. She cheated on him, and it broke his heart. Since then he's not dated much, and nothing serious."

She frowns. "Why did his girlfriend cheat on him?"

"Who knows why people do that?"

"Have you ever cheated on a girl?"

"Of course not."

"Has Kingi?"

"No, and he never would."

She pops a truffle in her mouth. "Okay," she says softly.

I have a mouthful of water. "So you went to school in Kahukura?"

She nods. "Dani is our main teacher. She'll probably retire soon."

"She teaches all the kids at the commune?"

"Yes. There are about twenty-two kids now, I think. We have the Te Whare Ako—it's a small schoolhouse. It's a beautiful little place, and it has a great vibe."

"That's quite a task, to be able to cater for all educational ages and levels."

"Oh, other adults help out and teach practical skills like gardening and herbal medicine alongside the traditional subjects." She stops at the look on my face, and her lips curve up. "Go on. Mock me if you want."

"I wouldn't dream of it." I purse my lips. "All right, I can't resist. Is it called the Waiora School of Forest Bathing and Fern Identification?"

"Yeah. We offer a major in Vegan Cheese Making with a minor in Moon Phases."

We both laugh.

I reach out and take a strand of hair and play with it.

"You can ask," she says.

"Ask what?"

"Whatever you want. About the commune. I know you're puzzled. I won't take it as a personal insult."

I run the strand of hair through my fingers, thinking about it. "I think it's idealistic, that's all. It's all well and good treating everyone as equals, having higher ideals, and using trust as a governing principle. But you must have seen what happened during COVID—people emptying the shelves of essentials even though the government had begged everyone not to stockpile. At heart, people are selfish."

"I don't believe that would happen in a tight community where everyone depended on everyone else. It happens where people are strangers. At Kahukura nobody would dream of taking something that belonged to another person."

I let the strand of hair curl around my finger. Her eyes are wide and open, as innocent as a newborn baby's.

I reach out and pretend to remove a pair of spectacles from her.

"What are you doing?" she asks, puzzled.

"Taking off your rose-tinted glasses."

Her expression turns wry. Then she lifts a hand in the air and mimes moving something from left to right in front of me. When I lift my eyebrows, she says, "Just letting in some sunlight. It must be pretty dark in that hermit cave you live in. Why don't you come out and join the rest of humanity?"

"No thank you. I despise the rest of humanity."

A frown flickers on her brow. "You might have nine zeroes in your bank account, but out of the two of us, I consider myself the wealthiest."

"Is this where you give me a speech about love and not money filling the human heart? Because mine isn't empty. I have family, and friends. I just happen to be rich as well."

"Money is the root of all evil."

"Actually, if we're going to quote the Bible, Timothy says 'For the love of money is a root of all sorts of evils.' It's a love of money that's the problem, not the money itself. Money is like electricity—it's a tool. Electricity can be used to power a respirator or an electric chair. Money is the same. It can be used to buy drugs or pay for hospitals. It's the unhealthy pursuit of and craving for it that can lead to evil."

She chews her bottom lip. "I suppose that's true."

"It's why we formed the Midnight Circle. It's a way for us to help those in need."

"To make yourselves feel better about having more than everyone else?"

I look away, out of the window at the view of the city. If I'm honest with myself, she's right, and that stings a bit.

"I'm sorry," she says. "That was uncalled for. You've been so nice to me, taken me out for dinner, brought me here, made love to me in the gentlest way possible. I didn't mean to sound ungrateful."

"It's okay."

"It's not." She moves toward me, slides her arm around my waist, and snuggles up to me. "I apologize."

"Honestly, it's okay. You were right. Part of the reason for setting up the Circle was to make ourselves feel better, even if it was unspoken."

She kisses my chest, then my neck. "Don't let's talk about it anymore."

My lips curve up. "All right." I turn and put the almost-empty box of truffles on the bedside table, then come back and cuddle up to her, drawing the duvet over us. "Will you stay the night?" I murmur, nuzzling her hair.

"Would you like me to?"

"Yes."

She nods. "Okay."

I stroke her back. "Do you think the Elders will be okay with it?"

"It's none of their business."

"No, I don't think it is, but I don't want you to get into trouble."

"I won't. Will you get in trouble with your father?"

"What he doesn't know won't hurt him."

She gives a short laugh.

We lie there like that for a while, wrapped around each other, and it's not long before her breathing deepens, her body releasing its tension, relaxing against me.

Tomorrow we'll both have to face the music. My father will assume that I asked Scarlett back here, and he'll be angry about it. He'll say she only came here because the Elders asked her to seduce me for the extra two and a half million. And I'll have to admit I've promised her I'll pay it.

I wince. There was no other way to prove to her—or, rather, to myself—that she was sleeping with me because she wanted to. Even so, it makes me uncomfortable. I can find two and a half million down the back of the sofa. Kingi will say I've been an idiot, but he'll sort it out for me. The money isn't the issue.

The problem is that we come from worlds that are so far apart, we can't even see the other from where we are. It's as if she lives in the Arctic Circle and I live in Antarctica, and we're separated by the curvature of the globe. She doesn't even have penguins. Or is it me that doesn't have penguins? I can't remember—I'm getting tired. The point is that one of us doesn't have penguins, and… fuck me, I can't remember the point.

Right now, all that matters is that Scarlett's hair smells of strawberries, and her breath is warm on my chest, and her skin is soft beneath my fingers. I'd like to make love to her again, but I don't want to make her sore. And anyway, I need some sleep.

I close my eyes and let myself sink into darkness.

*

When I wake, the sun is just peeking above the horizon. I've slept right through—something I haven't done in years. I usually wake around two or three, and sometimes I even get up and do some work. So to discover it's morning is a pleasant surprise.

I yawn and blink, then focus on the person in the bed next to me. She's lying on her stomach, hugging the pillow again, face turned away from me.

I move a little closer.

She smells warm and sweet. Her hair spills across the pillow like chocolate ribbons. I press my nose to it, then kiss her light-brown skin in the crook of her neck. She doesn't stir, so I continue. I kiss her shoulder. Then duck under the covers and kiss down her arm. She moves then, bringing her arm forward, which leaves her ribs and waist exposed for me, so I continue to kiss down, shifting on the bed. I kiss over her hip, then press my lips to her beautiful ass, at which point she stirs and murmurs, "What are you doing?"

Without answering, I roll her onto her back and open her legs.

"Oh my God, Orson!"

"Just relax."

"Oh... let me have a shower first..."

"Nope." I move between her legs and lower down, and before she can complain or get up, I bury my mouth in her.

"Argh! Oh my God. You wicked man..." She covers her face with her hands.

She smells warm and intoxicating, and I slide my tongue down from her clit and tease her entrance gently. She moans and tilts her hips up, and so I stay there for a while, adding a couple of fingers, playing with her gently so she doesn't get too sore. It doesn't take long before she's swollen, and we're both covered in her moisture, my fingers sliding slickly through her, into her, while I tease her sensitive little button with my tongue.

"Aaahhh..." She begins to move her hips, so I know she's close to coming. "Mmm... please..."

"Just relax," I tell her, replacing my tongue with my fingers for a moment, not letting up the pace. "There's a good girl."

"Oh my God, don't start."

I stifle a laugh. "You're doing so well, even though I know you must be sore. I don't want to hurt you. So relax and let me take charge."

"Mmm..."

"I just want to make you feel good." I kiss around where my finger is circling over her clit. "I want to give you pleasure, Mahuika. My little fire goddess. My beautiful Scarlett woman. Open up for me. Give yourself to me."

"Oh... Orson..."

I replace my finger with my mouth, cover her clit, and suck gently. At the same time, very carefully, I slide two fingers inside her. She moans and tightens around them, and I murmur my approval as I stroke in and out of her.

"I'm so close," she whispers, sliding a hand into my hair. "Aaahhh... Mmm... Don't stop..."

I have no intention of stopping, and I suck a little harder, pushing her thighs open wider with my other hand to expose her completely to my mouth. Fuck, she's so wet, and so smooth, and I'm so hard... I want to plunge my cock into her and ride her all the way to next week, but I have to restrain myself today.

Instead, I concentrate on her, and it's not long before her chest is heaving with ragged breaths, and her fingers are tightening in my hair. I suck harder, and then she comes, clenching around my fingers, gasping with every pulse. I hold her tightly all the way through it, groaning at the thought of what she must be feeling, imagining that blissful sensation deep inside her.

And then she collapses back, and I withdraw my fingers, give her a last kiss, and move up to lie beside her.

"Mmm." She gives me a lazy smile. "That was a nice way to wake up."

I prop my head on a hand. "Better than an alarm clock."

"Mmm, I'll say." She lifts the duvet and looks down, then gives me a mischievous smile. "Are you going to do anything with that?"

"Nope. Not today."

She frowns. "Why?"

"I'm not going to make you sore."

"I'm okay."

"No, and you can't talk me into it."

She pouts. Then she lifts the duvet again and studies my erection. It gives an involuntary twitch, and her lips curve up.

She looks up at me. Then she lifts up and ducks beneath the covers.

"Ahhh... Scarlett..."

"Just relax."

"You don't have to do that..."

"I want to see what you taste like."

"Let me have a shower first."

"No. Lie down."

I flop onto my back and cover my face with my hands. I feel her move over me, then between my legs. She tosses the duvet back, and then she's still for a moment. I think she's studying it. Jesus.

"Mmm," she says. "Anything I should know?"

"Just watch your teeth."

She laughs. Then she takes me in her hand and lowers her mouth.

I groan as she kisses me. I'm a little tense at first, after all it's not every day you loan your family jewels to someone who's never seen them before. But she's gentle, exploring me with her tongue, tracing the tip around the head and down the shaft. Then she says, "Show me how to touch you."

I take her hand in mine, close it around my cock, and show her how to stroke me, and then I remove my hand and she continues, accompanying it with kisses, and then finally closing her mouth over the head. I hold my breath, then let out a long sigh as she brushes her tongue across me and sucks. Ahhh… fuck…

She carries on, and I let her know when I like what she's doing with heartfelt sighs and grunts. She looks up at me with her big dark eyes, which is so sexy that it doesn't take long before I feel my climax approaching like a bullet train.

"Ah, baby girl…" I do the same as she did and slide my hand into her hair. "I'm going to come…" I don't want to do that when she's never done it before—I'm sure that can put a girl off for life.

She doesn't move, though, and it occurs to me that maybe she really is innocent and doesn't understand what's going to happen. "Honey…" I implore, "you need to stop, or I'll come in your mouth…"

Instead, she slides her lips further down the shaft… oh fuck… there's no coming back from that, I couldn't stop if she begged me now. Heat rushes through me, everything contracts, and my climax washes over me like a tsunami. Aaahhh… I groan, long and loud as she strokes me, and feel her throat tighten as she swallows.

Holy fuck…

When I'm done, I lie there and press the heels of my hands into my eyeballs as she kisses up my chest and lies on top of me.

I move my hands and glare at her. "I tried to warn you."

"Nom nom nom," she says. She licks her lips. "Want a taste?"

SERENITY WOODS

"Jesus…" There's no time to protest as she crushes her lips to mine and delves her tongue into my mouth, so I go limp and let her, while the rising sun drapes gold blankets over us, warming us through.

Chapter Seventeen

Scarlett

"I should get up. I've got a class at ten." My words are reluctant. It's warm in the room, and Orson is stroking my back, his fingers moving seductively up and down my spine. But I need to get back, shower, and prepare myself for the inevitable questions that are going to come my way.

"Yeah," he says, although he doesn't move.

I rest my chin on his chest and look up at him. His eyes are closed, his face relaxed. He has a touch of stubble this morning. Fascinated, I lift a hand and trace a finger along his jaw, feeling the scrape of the hairs beneath my fingernail. He opens one eye to look at me, and the corner of his mouth quirks up.

It was a fantastic meal and an amazing evening. And it was super to go to sleep with him and be woken up by the touch of his fingers and the feel of his mouth on me. Mmm.

But nothing lasts forever. Buddhists say that pain comes from trying to resist suffering, and suffering happens when we become attached to things that are fleeting. So if we can detach from our attachments and cravings, we are able to reduce our suffering.

This thing with Orson is fleeting. I know that. Even though I told him *I'm not your girlfriend*, and he replied *Not yet*, I refuse to think of this as anything other than a bubble floating on the wind. I'm going to accept it for what it is, and go back to my life a better person for the experience.

I wonder whether he has time for breakfast, and I'm just about to ask when I hear a sound somewhere in the apartment.

I sit up, clutching the duvet to my breasts.

"What?" he asks.

"There's someone outside." For a moment I have the horrific thought that it's an old girlfriend who's let herself in. She's going to come into the bedroom with an axe and chop me up into a black bin bag when she finds out he's with me.

But he just yawns, stretches, and says, "It's okay, it's only Gina."

"Gina?"

"My housekeeper."

My eyebrows shoot up. "You have a housekeeper?"

"Well, yeah. I'm not going to pick up my own socks." He grins at the look on my face. "I'm joking."

"I don't think you are."

He tips his head to the side. "Why are you shocked?"

"I don't know. How many other people work for you?"

"Well, I might not be Scrooge McDuck, but Kingi and I run quite an empire. We know a lot about finances, but we still have financial advisors, bankers, and tax advisers. Twenty or so other staff at Te Aranui, including security, secretarial, HR, that kind of thing. A hundred staff at the Midnight Club and the resort, but they don't work directly for me—secretarial again, waiters, maintenance, cleaning, gardeners. I had an interior designer when I first moved in here who decorated it for me. I have a chauffeur sometimes."

My eyebrows shoot up. "Seriously?"

"Yeah, on longer journeys when I'm not flying, so I can work rather than have to concentrate on the road." He smiles. "It's not unusual in the world I come from."

"It is in mine."

"I can see that." He rolls over and gets up. "Come on. We'll ask Gina to make us some breakfast."

My jaw drops at the thought of asking someone to make breakfast for me. I've never done that, and the notion feels incredibly selfish and decadent. Still, when in Rome… I shouldn't criticize his lifestyle if I don't want him to criticize mine. No judgement, Scarlett.

Somewhat disappointed that our snuggling time is over, I get up and tug my dress on, Orson opens a door and goes into another room, and I follow him over and stick my head in. Holy shit, it's a walk-in wardrobe. It's as big as my bedroom at home. Wardrobes line three walls, with the fourth once again full of windows that look out over the city.

He slides open one of the wardrobe doors, revealing shelves of T-shirts all neatly folded in every color, jeans of various shades, track pants, cargo trousers on hangers, shorts, and a rail of casual shirts, also in lots of colors. While he pulls on a pair of black track pants, I open the next wardrobe. This contains his suits. I brush a hand along them. "So many," I say. "You're a real clothes horse, aren't you?"

"A bit," he admits, coming over to join me.

"These are a slightly different cut," I comment, realizing the rail is divided into two. On the left, the jackets that hang over the folded trousers are longer, the shoulders are lightly padded, and there's a small pocket above the normal one. The ones on the right are slim and tailored, with no flaps over the pockets.

"British, from Savile Row," he says, gesturing to the left. "Smarter and more formal for work." He indicates the ones on the right. "Italian, from Milan. Evening suits, more flamboyant. I've got more of them at the Club."

"Do you have them tailor made?"

"I do. My English tailor is called Alastair. My Italian one is Elio."

"Have you met them?"

He tugs on a T-shirt. "Of course. You have to, to be measured."

My eyebrows shoot up again. "You mean you actually go to London and Milan to get your suits."

"Yeah. Doesn't everyone?" He gives me an amused look.

Taken aback, I walk along the rail of shirts. Some are plain, others feature stripes, and the last dozen are fancier paisley-patterned ones. There are also two hangers, each holding about thirty ties.

I stop by the last wardrobe. "Can I look?"

"Sure."

I open it. This contains every other piece of clothing a man could ever need—sweaters, non-suit jackets, coats, and racks of shoes—from smart leather Oxford lace ups to Converses to running shoes.

He slides his arms around me from behind, hugs me, and presses a kiss on my shoulder. "Would you like your own one of these?"

"One of what?"

"Rooms."

I laugh. "My clothes would take up about a third of *one* of those wardrobes, if that."

"I'd buy you clothes to fill them up." He kisses my neck, then my ear. "Dresses and jeans and tees and blouses and sexy underwear, although you probably wouldn't wear any of it." Chuckling, he moves away. "Come on." Taking my hand, he leads me out of the room, across the bedroom, and along the corridor.

My mind is spinning a little. It was a throwaway comment, but for the first time I wonder what it would be like to be married to a guy like this. To have your own wardrobe, full of pretty things. To live in a penthouse apartment, or maybe to buy a house somewhere out of the city, on the beach, with a garden that your kids could play in. To wake up every morning next to a man you wanted to make love to, and who wanted to make love to you.

"Gina!" Orson leads me across the living room toward the kitchen. A woman is putting groceries away in the cupboards, but she turns as we approach. She's probably in her early forties, pretty, with blonde hair dyed pink at the ends, lots of black eyeliner, and a stud on the side of her nose.

"Oh," she says, eyebrows rising as she sees us. "Good morning!"

"This is Scarlett," Orson says. "Scarlett, this is Gina."

"Hi," I say shyly.

"Lovely to meet you, Scarlett." She comes forward and shakes my hand. "I'm so sorry," she says to Orson, "you should have texted me to say you had company. You're always alone, so I didn't think."

Her words warm me through. He wasn't lying, then, when he said he hasn't dated anyone recently.

"It's okay." He gestures for me to sit on one of the stools at the breakfast bar. "I was wondering whether you could make us some pancakes."

"Oh." My face flushes. "That's okay, I don't expect—"

"Of course." She smiles. "Banana?"

Orson looks at me expectantly. "Er… um… that would be great," I mumble.

"I'll make the coffee," Orson says, switching on the machine, a huge thing with all kinds of buttons and dials. "How's Jackie?"

"She's good, thanks. It was our anniversary yesterday. Five years."

"Oh, honey, congratulations." He hugs her briefly and kisses her cheek. "Wow, that's gone quick."

"I know. Talk about an old married couple. She's talking about us going to Fiji for a couple of weeks in June. Would that be okay with you?"

"What? Absolutely not."

She ignores him. "Thanks, sweetie."

He chuckles and starts the espresso pouring while she begins making the pancake batter.

I watch them, liking their casual attitude and the fact that they've obviously known each other for a while. What did he call her? His housekeeper. So she buys his groceries, occasionally cooks for him… what else? Cleans, I guess. Well, I suppose if I was a billionaire I wouldn't want to dust and vacuum my own house, either.

Before long, the pancakes and coffee are ready, and Orson sits next to me while we eat, while Gina washes the pans, then continues putting away the groceries.

"These are really good," I say, enjoying the sweet, fluffy pancakes.

"Next time we'll get Gina to add a few of the chocolate truffles," Orson says.

"Naughty boy," she says, putting some packets of pasta in the cupboard. "You can't add chocolate to everything."

"Says who?" He has a sip of coffee, then realizes I've stopped with my fork halfway to my mouth. "What?"

I shake my head.

"What?" he presses.

"You said… next time…"

He has another mouthful of coffee, giving me an amused look. "Yeah…"

"I thought this was… you know…"

"A one-night stand?"

Embarrassed, I glance at Gina. She doesn't look around, but I think she's trying to hide a smile.

Orson just laughs and has another mouthful of pancake as he picks up his phone and brings up a calendar. "I've got a meeting this evening with some investors. And the day after that it's Kingi's birthday and we're having a party at the club in the evening… Oh! Would you like to come?" His eyes light up.

I stare at him. "Go with you, you mean?"

"Yes, Scarlett. Come with me to a party. Be my date."

My jaw sags. My brain has gone blank. "What… what would your father say?"

He gives me an impatient look. "I don't give a fuck. The sooner he gets used to us dating, the better."

"Dating?"

Gina gives him an amused look. He meets her gaze and rolls his eyes. "Help me, for the love of God."

She grins and winks at me. "He's very stubborn," she informs me. "I wouldn't bother trying to fight him."

"I want you to be my girlfriend," he says.

"What if I don't want that?" I say sassily, while my heart bangs on my ribs.

He shrugs. "I'll just kidnap you and handcuff you to the bed." He eats a forkful of pancake, then chuckles as Gina snorts.

My face flames. "Orson!"

He laughs, hooks a foot under my stool, and pulls it toward him. Then he slides a hand to the back of my neck and holds me there while he kisses me. Our lips are all sticky from the maple syrup, but he refuses to let me go, and in the end I have no choice but to give in and let him kiss me.

When he finally lets me go, I sit there, stunned, while he sips his coffee. "Finish your pancakes," he instructs.

"I can't date you," I tell him.

Gina pulls an eek face at him, then says, "I'm going to put some washing on," and leaves the room.

Orson watches her go, then looks at me. "Why not?"

"Seriously? We're from completely different worlds. Our lifestyles, our views, our principles… everything is diametrically opposed."

"We both like sex," he points out.

"There's more to a successful relationship than sex. And no, don't give me that look, you know I'm right. You believe that money is king, and I believe that being part of a community is more important than anything."

"So do I," he protests. "Sort of. The club is a kind of community."

"You said you despise humanity."

"Yeah, okay, I did say that… But I was joking."

"Really?"

"Well, no, but I don't mean my friends and family. I was referring to the man on the street."

"People who aren't part of your elite inner circle, you mean?"

"Yes! Oh, you were being sarcastic."

I glare at him. "Don't tease me."

"But it's such fun." He pulls me into his arms and nuzzles my neck. "You smell so good."

But I push him away. "I'm serious." Tears prick my eyes. "There's no point in us dating. It would never work out."

"You don't know that." He looks puzzled. I bet it's the first time he's ever had a girl refuse to date him. I guess most would say yes because of the money, if nothing else.

"Look, I'm sure the last thing guys want to talk about is Where This is Going on the first date. But honestly, what do you envisage happening if things go well? Would you come and live on the commune with me?" He lifts an eyebrow, and I say, "I didn't think so. So you'd expect me to leave Kahukura and live in the city? Wear a suit, work in an office, eat at fancy restaurants, have my hair styled, my nails done?"

His smile fades slowly, and he looks down at his coffee cup.

I sigh. "What's the point in setting sail on a life raft with no hope of reaching the mainland? I like you. And I know you have the potential to break my heart."

He looks up then and meets my eyes. There's surprise in them, and something else. A kind of steely determination.

"You shouldn't have said that," he says.

"What do you mean?"

He shakes his head and checks the time on his phone. "We should get going. I'll fly us back to Waiheke and then drive you to the commune. You want to have a shower with me?" His eyes gleam.

"Um, no thank you," I say, panicking. For a start, Gina is here. What will she think? "I'll have one when I get home."

"Okay. I won't be long."

I watch him get up and walk away, puzzled by his comment, *You shouldn't have said that*. What did he mean? Which bit was he referring to?

Well, I can't force him to talk to me, so I put it to the back of my mind.

I sit there and chew my bottom lip for about five minutes.

Then eventually I get up and walk through to the bedroom.

The door to the en suite bathroom is open. I wander over to it and lean against the door jamb.

He has already had a shower—wow, that was quick—and he's standing in front of the mirror with a towel around his waist, running a basin of hot water. He glances in the mirror, sees me, and smiles.

"Sorry," I say awkwardly.

167

He gestures with his head for me to come into the room, so I walk in. He wets his face. "Just gonna have a quick shave." He squirts some foam onto his hand, then spreads it across his cheeks and chin.

My dad had a beard, so I've never seen a guy do this in real life. Fascinated, I lean a hip on the unit and watch him.

He wets the razor, then starts drawing it up his throat. I can feel my face growing warm. This is such a masculine act, and there's something incredibly sexy about it. Everything in this bathroom is masculine, in fact. Ana and I have homemade rose petal bath salts, avocado face masks, kawakawa soap, makeup made from coconut oil and natural ingredients, tampons, and other girly items, and all the jars and tins are bright orange and pink and yellow.

Everything on Orson's shelf is black: his tin of male antiperspirant, his razors, his electric toothbrush. The only thing that isn't is the bottle of cologne—Penhaligon's The Tragedy Of Lord George is a dark yellow with a stag's head on the top. I take it down, remove the top, and sniff it. I love the sweet brandy smell.

"I Googled this," I tell him, putting it back. "It says it's 'for the gentleman of distinction,' and 'the perfume notes inspire aristocratic manners.'"

He gives a short laugh as he draws the razor up his cheek. "Sounds like me."

It does, a bit. I don't say it out loud, but I let my gaze drift over him while he rinses his razor in the water, then draws it up his cheek again, accompanied by the scrape of stubble being removed. His biceps are mouthwatering. His chest has just the right amount of hair. Even his back is attractive, not too hairy, and well-muscled. I study the short hair at the nape of his neck and trail my gaze down his spine to the dip just above the towel.

When I look back at him in the mirror, he's watching me.

"Just turning myself on, sorry," I say.

His lips curve up, but he doesn't say anything. He rinses his razor, then washes around the sink.

"What did you mean?" I ask. "When you said 'You shouldn't have said that'?"

He dries his face on a towel. Oh man, the smoothness of that jaw…

"You said I had the potential to break your heart," he says.

"Yeah… I would have thought that was obvious."

"No, it wasn't." He hangs the towel over the rail. Then he walks back to me. He turns me so my butt is against the cabinet, moves even closer, and cups my face. "And now I know that's how you feel, I'm not going to let you go."

My eyes widen. "That's very arrogant."

"Yep." He kisses me. "I want you, Scarlett Stone. And I always get what I want." He kisses me again.

My face warms beneath his hands. I'm half flattered and half furious at his assumption that I'll just fall into his lap. "Stop it," I say when he lifts his head.

He ignores me and kisses me again. I rest both hands on his naked chest, wanting to push him away, but I can't. His skin is warm, and he smells so good, and I keep thinking about how it felt when he made me come with his tongue this morning, and how it felt last night to have him inside me. I want him again. I'm cross with myself for it, but I can't help it.

He lifts his head and looks at me, his eyelids at half-mast. "I'm tempted to drag you into the shower."

I force myself to push him away and turn to put my hair up into a bun. "You need to stop acting as if I don't have a say in this."

He moves up behind me, and I wait for him to grab my breasts where my arms are raised. But he doesn't. He leans on the cabinet on either side of my hips, then presses his lips to my neck, my throat, my jaw, then behind my ear. I shiver, and he moves his arms around me and gives me a hug.

I lower my arms on top of his, and our eyes meet in the mirror.

"You're stunning," he murmurs.

There seems to be no end to the ways this man can surprise me. "Thank you."

He kisses my cheek. "I'm not going to break your heart. I'm going to worship the ground you walk on, until you realize you can't bear to be without me."

I have no idea how a relationship with him could possibly work without one of us completely changing our view of the world and the way we live. And I don't think either of us is prepared to do that.

But it's obvious that he's not used to taking no for an answer. The thought sends a shiver all the way through me.

Chapter Eighteen

Orson

I fly us to the Midnight Club and then drive Scarlett back to Kahukura.

"You can drop me here," she says as we arrive at the gates to the commune.

I ignore her, though. I'm not going to let her slip in as if we've done something secretive and wrong. Instead, I go through the open gates, up the drive, circle the green, and stop right outside the town hall.

"Thanks," she says sarcastically. Then, as a group of people spill out of the building, she mutters, "Oh no."

It's Richard, George, and a few other older people. They fan out as Scarlett opens the car door. Concerned, slightly regretting my decision, I turn off the engine and get out, too.

They watch me walk around the car to join Scarlett. They don't seem hostile, which was what I was worried about. In fact one of the older women is giving her a mischievous smile as she sees Bearcub in Scarlett's hand.

"Morning," Scarlett says. "Is this a welcome committee?"

"We've just finished a meeting," Richard points out. He looks at me. "So… have you come to a decision about the Waiora?"

I nod. "I agree to seventeen and a half million."

All their faces light up. I have no doubt that most of them are well meaning and genuinely want to improve the facilities here, and the retreat for the women and children who need it so desperately.

"Well, I'm guessing we have you to thank for that," George says to Scarlett.

Fury balloons inside me at the implication that she slept with me to seal the deal. I cross the distance between us, and in a second I have him pinned up against the wall with an arm across his throat.

"How dare you," I snarl.

"Whoa!" Richard struggles to pull us apart. "Steady on. Orson!"

"I made up my mind before our date," I snap. I'm not going to let George off the hook that easily after he was so rude to my girl. "I had my business partner check some figures yesterday afternoon, and we both decided to go ahead. You've got a fucking cheek to insinuate anything else."

George struggles to push me away, and as Richard and another guy pull me back, he finally frees himself. Red-faced, his clothing rucked up, he says, "I just meant that I guess she talked you around. I wasn't referring to anything else." He sends her a pleading glance. "You have to believe me, Scarlett. I wouldn't say that."

She frowns. I can't tell if she's pleased or annoyed that I leapt to her defense.

"It was just a misunderstanding," Richard says smoothly. "Let's forget about it. Orson, we have something else to discuss—you kindly offered to send your partner to audit our files for us, and we've decided to agree."

I look at George, who straightens his clothing then glances at Scarlett. He didn't want an audit, so I guess he was outvoted. I thought he'd be mad, but instead there's a touch of fear in his eyes. What will an audit uncover that he wants to keep hidden? I'm pretty sure I can guess.

I glance at Scarlett, wishing I could save her from this. If anything is going to remove her rose-tinted glasses, it's going to be discovering that someone was stealing from the commune. Equally, you can't go through life blindly believing that everyone you meet is honest and truthful. Innocent until proven guilty is great for the law courts, but in everyday life it's best to be cautious.

"I'll talk to Kingi," I say. "Get him to give you a call. He should be able to do it next week."

Richard nods. "Thank you."

"I'll also get him to draw up the papers for the sale of the Waiora, and to lay out the instructions for the stewardship. We can then meet and go through them. I'd prefer to keep things friendly, but obviously if there are any contested points, we might have to get lawyers involved."

"I'd rather that wasn't the case for financial reasons," Richard says. "They'll bleed us dry. I'm sure we can work it out ourselves."

After the way they fleeced me for another two and a half million I'm not so sure, but I nod anyway. "I'll be in touch."

Taking Scarlett's hand, I lead her a little away from the group. I move closer to her, but, conscious of everyone watching, I don't kiss her, even though I want to.

"You okay?" I murmur.

"You shouldn't talk to George like that," she says. "He's been very good to me." Her eyes shine—she's genuinely upset.

I want to tear off her rose-tinted glasses and stomp on them. But instead, I just say, "I thought he was being rude to you."

She glares at me for a moment. Then, to my surprise, her lips twitch. "I thought you were going to challenge him to a duel for a moment."

"I considered it," I reply, relieved she's not mad. "Kingi would happily have brought my pistols over."

Her eyes gleam. "Thank you for defending my honor, even if it was misguided."

"I don't want what happened between us to become ensnared with the commune and the Waiora," I tell her firmly. "Understand?"

"Yes, sir."

"Stop it," I scold.

"Yes, sir."

I give up. "So you'll come to Kingi's party on Saturday?"

She hesitates. "I don't know."

"Please? With a cherry on top?"

"Orson, it's pointless when this can't go anywhere."

I understand her point, and I'm not certain yet how to counter her argument, so I just say, "Well why don't we take it one date at a time? I'll probably drive you mad anyway after a few weeks."

"A few hours, you mean."

"I acknowledge it's a possibility."

"Look, even if I did agree to go, I don't have anything to wear. The women at the club won't be wearing things like this." She gestures at her summer dress.

"You're probably right about the guests," I admit. "But this is a party for family and friends, and it'll be casual, shorts and tees."

"You'll be wearing shorts?"

"Swim shorts, yeah, there's a heated pool and the weather's supposed to be good. So bring a bikini." I cup her face with a hand. "Please?"

She sucks her bottom lip. Then she says, "I'll think about it."

I sigh. "Good girl."

That earns me a wry look. She glances at the others, who are still hovering, no doubt waiting to grill her when I've gone. Then she says, "Thank you for a lovely evening. I had a great time."

"Me too. I'll pick you up at six forty-five on Saturday, okay? The party starts at seven."

"I haven't agreed—"

"And bring your toothbrush. I'd like you to stay the night in my suite."

"That's presumptuous on so many levels."

"Hopeful, more like." I bend my head and let my breath fan over her cheek. "I want to taste you again," I murmur.

"Orson!" Her cheek warms beneath my lips. "You're a wicked man."

"I try." I touch my lips lightly to hers. Then, conscious of the others still watching us, I move back reluctantly. "I'd better go. Firstly though, I've got something for you."

"Oh?"

I go over to the car, open it and reach into the glove box, and bring it back to her. It's a brand-new iPhone. I've taken it out of the packaging, started it up, put in a SIM card for her, and programmed the number into my phone.

She stares at it. "I don't need one."

"You don't have to go on social media or anything. But I'd like to be able to talk to you and message you if I want to. And you can message me at any time." I'm determined to remain in this girl's thoughts as often as I can.

"No thank you," she says.

"Scarlett…"

"You shouldn't try to change me," she says fiercely. "Just because the way I live is different from you."

"I'm not trying to change you."

"Aren't you?"

"I just want to be able to talk to you while we're not together. Come on, it's just a phone, not a loyalty card for the capitalist machine." I pick up her hand, turn it over, and lay the phone in it.

She glares at it.

SERENITY WOODS

I push away a flicker of unease at the thought of the different worlds we inhabit. "I've programmed my number into the contacts, so we're all ready to go. All right, I'd better shoot off. Speak to you later." I wave to the others, get in and start the Aston, and fill the air with its throaty purr as I pull away.

*

The rest of my day is super busy. I take the ferry back to the city, where I have back-to-back meetings until late. I do manage to catch up with Kingi at one point, though, and I ask him if he'll draft up the documentation for the sale of the Waiora, and sketch out an idea for the stewardship. I also tell him that the commune has agreed to an audit of their financial documents. He checks his calendar and says he can start next Wednesday.

A month ago, we attended the wedding of one of our good friends, Lincoln Green, in Wellington. Kingi and I were both groomsmen, and Kingi's affection for Linc was evident in the fact that he shaved off his beard for the occasion. He looked weird without it, so I was somewhat relieved he's growing it back again. Bearing in mind he's six-four and has long wavy hair, he could easily double for Jason Momoa.

"By the way," I tell him, "I'm bringing someone to your party on Saturday."

"You've got a new dog?" he asks.

I give him a wry look. "No."

His bushy eyebrows shoot up. "Scarlett?"

"Yeah."

"You're really trying to piss your father off, aren't you?"

"I don't need to try to do that."

He laughs. Then he smiles. "You really like this girl, don't you?"

"I do. I'd like everyone to meet her. She's nervous about coming though."

"Well, yeah. You said she doesn't leave the commune often, so I get that. We'll all make sure she's welcome though. I'll get Marama to look after her."

"Oh, she's back?" His sister has been traveling and working in Europe for the last few years.

"Yeah, she landed yesterday."

I'm pleased. I like Marama; she's warm and friendly, and I'm pleased to think she'll be here to meet Scarlett.

Kingi heads off to a meeting, but I have ten minutes before my next one starts, so I take out my phone. I messaged Scarlett earlier. To my disappointment, she hasn't messaged back.

Wanting to hear her voice, I call her. It rings half a dozen times, then goes to voicemail.

I leave a brief message saying I miss her and I hope she's having a good day. Then I go off to my meeting.

When it finishes, I check my phone, but there are no missed calls and no messages.

I text her again, telling her I miss her and I hope to hear from her soon. I wait for a moment in case the three little dots appear to announce she's typing. They don't.

Eventually I slide the phone into my pocket, frustrated. She could be busy with her yoga classes, but I have a horrible feeling she won't even have the device on her.

I attempt to put it to the back of my mind and head off to a meeting with Kingi and some business associates from Australia, which continues over dinner and drinks. By the time I leave my office it's after ten, and there's still no message from Scarlett.

I'm not sure what time she goes to bed, but I text her a third time, telling her I'm heading home, and drive to my apartment.

No reply.

I head straight for the gym, run for thirty minutes, and do some weights. Then I go back to my apartment and take a quick shower.

Still no message.

Disappointed, frustrated, and a little bit cross, I pour myself a whisky and take it into my study, where I sit on the sofa, looking out at the city lights. I glance down at Doyle's empty bed and feel a sharp pang of grief. I've spent the last six years with him glued to my ankle, even at work, because I made sure to train him so he wasn't a problem in the office. I do miss him during the day, but I'm so busy that it's only at nighttime that the loss really sets in.

I sip my whisky sulkily. At least a dog is dependable and loyal. A dog would send you a message every minute of the day if it could.

I take a deep breath, then let it out in a long sigh. I miss Scarlett, despite not wanting to. A lot of the women I meet socially, attracted no doubt to my money and position, fawn over me, saying what they think I want to hear. Scarlett doesn't, though. I like the way she teases me and stands up to me. I like that she's different, I love her boho look, her strange views on things, her warm heart. She's like a daisy growing in a nuclear wasteland, a glimpse of nature in a city of concrete and metal and glass. But she'd be easily crushed in that city. She's right; I can't imagine her in my world, any more than I can imagine existing in hers. Meditating and lighting candles and eating kale. My lips curve up at the thought of what she'd say to that. Then my smile fades as I glance at the blank phone screen.

Eventually, I go to bed, but I leave the curtains open and lie awake for a while. I look out at the moon, remembering the feel of her warm body and wishing she was here with me.

It's late before I finally fall into a dreamless sleep.

*

The next day is Saturday. I work at home for a couple of hours, then meet Kingi and a few old friends for brunch at a favorite cafe. It's Kingi's twenty-eighth birthday, and we celebrate over Eggs Benedict, full English Breakfasts, and coffee, reminiscing about our university days and talking about our businesses.

Afterward, I head over to Waiheke to the Midnight Club and spend the afternoon working in my office.

By late afternoon, I'm panicking. I haven't heard from Scarlett, so I don't even know if she's coming to the party tonight. I've texted several times and I've rung her twice, but I'm convinced she's flung the phone away and it's slipped down the back of the sofa.

I call the landline in her house, but she doesn't answer. Finally, I call the commune's main office and ask to speak to her. They send someone off to track her down, but return to say they can't find her, and they think she might have gone off for a walk somewhere.

So is she coming or not?

Gritting my teeth, I head off to my suite in the main hotel building. It's on the top floor, smaller than my penthouse in the city, and consists of a living room with a kitchenette, a bedroom, and a bathroom, but it has a great view over the ocean, and I usually love spending time here.

Today, though, my stomach is full of butterflies. I've never had a girl turn me down before. My father brought me up to believe in the magic formula: see, want, take. If our gaze falls on something I want, it's just a matter of time before I close the deal, because everything and everyone has a price.

Except Scarlett, it seems. A mixture of puzzled and frustrated, I shower and shave, then dress in a pair of dark-blue swim shorts and a light-blue T-shirt. Frowning, I change into a short-sleeved shirt and chinos. Then a long-sleeved shirt with the sleeves rolled up. Finally, exasperated with myself, I put the tee and shorts back on, growl at myself in the mirror, and head out to the Aston.

I drive along the winding road through the rolling hills and vineyards with the Pacific Ocean on my right, arriving at Kahukura just before 6:45 p.m.

I pull up outside Scarlett's house, turn off the engine, and get out. I'm not even sure if she'll be here. I walk up the path, heart racing. I haven't felt this anxious before a date for... well, maybe ever. I feel as if I'm sixteen, about to go to the school ball. I refuse to go the Midnight Club alone tonight. I've told Kingi I'll be bringing her, so I'm going to take her with me even if I have to carry her in a firefighter's lift.

I lift a hand to knock on the door... and it opens.

I lower my hand. She's wearing a short scarlet sundress with a halter top that reveals she has a bikini on underneath. She's pinned up her hair and adorned it with a red rosebud. Her red lips match her dress.

She has a bag over her shoulder, and she comes out now and closes the door behind her.

"Hello," she says, turning to face me.

I stare into her big brown eyes. "I didn't think you were going to come."

"I wasn't sure I would... until I saw you."

We study each other for about ten seconds.

"I missed you," I say, my voice husky. "I called you, and messaged you."

"I know. I did see them."

"Why didn't you message me back?" I ask, puzzled.

Her lips part, but she hesitates and drops her gaze to her red sandals. I think she has honestly been torn in two. She wants to see me. But she's convinced we have no future.

That may be true, but all I can feel is euphoric that she's here and wants to be with me.

"I told you," I say softly, moving forward to cup her face, "I'm not going to break your heart."

"Orson…"

I lower my head and touch my lips to hers. She sighs, her breath whispering across my lips.

When I lift my head, I say, "One step at a time, remember?"

She presses her lips together. Then she nods.

I take her hand. "Come on. We've got a party to go to, and I want everyone to meet you."

Chapter Nineteen

Scarlett

Right up until the moment Orson almost-knocked on the door, I was telling myself I couldn't go with him. I spent yesterday and most of today arguing with myself, getting ready for the party while at the same time convinced I wasn't going to go. I carried his phone in my back pocket and felt it buzz each time he messaged or called. I couldn't bring myself to answer the call, but I did listen to his voice message, and I read the texts he sent. I wanted to reply… but every time I rested my fingers on the keys, I thought of my father and imagined how angry he'd be that I was getting involved with Spencer Cavendish's son.

And yet here I am, in his car, heading over to the Midnight Club. I feel a pang of shame as I think about the rare times that Dad mentioned the Cavendishes, and the way his eyes would light with fury. I don't think he'd understand that neither Orson nor I are interested in their feud. He would say I don't understand the perils of capitalism, and that all Orson wants is to destroy the beauty of the world he created at Kahukura, and I'm betraying everything he worked to build. And I have no doubt that Spencer would say I'm after his son's money.

"Are you okay?" Orson reaches across to hold my hand.

I look out of the window, listening to the Aston purr its way through the countryside. "I'm nervous that your father is going to be at the party." His eyes held hostility the last time we met in Orson's office. It makes me uncomfortable and anxious just to think about it.

"He won't give you any trouble," Orson says firmly. "I'll make sure of it."

I don't say anything. I'm not sure that the pup has the strength to confront the leader of the pack. Spencer's manner commands respect, and I'm convinced his haughty disdain would subdue any confrontation in the workplace. I'm sure he would have discouraged any challenges from his children while they were growing up, and that would naturally have led into adulthood. Orson has his own business with Kingi, and he's obviously successful in his own right, but that doesn't mean he's ready to take on his father.

There's no point in worrying about it, though. Both Mum and Dad are gone, and all I can do is follow my heart and do my best, even if I make a complete hash of things in the process.

Orson swoops around the drive in front of the resort and pulls into a parking space right out the front of the main building that has his name on it. Oh, that's flash.

"Come on," he says, unbuckling his seat belt. "Try not to worry. You look amazing."

Somewhat mollified by his comment, I get out of the car and go to retrieve my bag, but he shoulders it and takes my hand. I decide not to argue and let him lead me up the steps to the lobby.

"Hey, Ash," Orson says to a young porter who comes out to greet us. "Could you take this up to my suite, please?" He hands him my bag and says to me, "Do you need anything from it?"

I have a clutch, so I shake my head. Ash agrees to take the bag up without batting an eyelid, although I'm sure he'll be telling the rest of the staff shortly. I wonder how often Orson brings girls to the club? He insisted he hasn't dated for nearly a year, but I can't quite believe that. He's too handsome, too loaded, and too irresistible not to be fighting girls off with a stick. Surely he must parade a succession of beautiful young things through these doors?

The lobby is busy with guests, some checking in, others sitting having a coffee or an aperitif by the windows overlooking the gardens. A couple of businessmen are heading for the doors to the club. As the doors open, the enticing beat of dance music makes my heart race, and colored lights spill onto the gray carpet as if someone's knocked over cans of paints. My heartbeat rises; I've never been to a nightclub and have no desire to go to one, and if Orson leads me over to it, I'll have to run off in the opposite direction.

But he doesn't—he takes me to the other side of the lobby to a set of doors marked 'Gardens and Pools' with a sign that announces the area is 'Closed for private function'. I guess most of the guests will be at dinner or heading to the club.

The automatic doors slide open, and we go outside. It's a beautiful evening, close to sunset, the air still holding late-summer warmth.

There's a lane pool at the far end, but the one closest to us is huge and kidney shaped, with steps leading into a shallow area at one end and a deeper area at the other. The place is paved with attractive light-pink and white paving slabs, and there are numerous palm trees to give the place a tropical feel. The bar I saw beside the pool is open, with bartenders carrying cocktails and other drinks to the guests who are sitting on loungers or at the round tables. A couple of staff are working at a barbecue that stands in front of the main kitchen, filling the air with the smell of cooked food. The sliding doors that lead to the Midnight Club are open although roped off, so the music is audible, but not too loud to make conversation difficult.

"Kingi," Orson says, and I turn to see the birthday boy approaching with a smile. Orson has previously made the comparison to Bigfoot, and now I can see why—the guy is huge, taller than Orson by a couple of inches, and with big shoulders and a wide chest. He's wearing a sleeveless tee, and he has a full Māori tattoo on his left arm from shoulder to wrist. He has amazing shoulder-length wavy dark-brown hair, and a thick beard. His eyes are an attractive amber color, almost orange.

"You must be Scarlett," Kingi says, his voice deeper than Orson's, like a lion's growl. He holds out a big paw and shakes my hand. "Good to meet you at last."

"Happy birthday!" I take a small parcel out of my purse and hand it to him. Orson's eyebrows rise.

"You didn't have to do that," Kingi protests.

"It's nothing elaborate," I admit. "I made it myself."

He tears off the paper and reveals a miniature canvas attached to a tiny wooden easel. On it I've painted the words 'Te Aranui Developments' and a stylistic landscape of a road disappearing into the distance—the long road.

"It was just for fun," I say bashfully. "You don't have to keep it."

"I love it," he replies, astonished. "I'm going to put it on my desk. Thank you so much." He gives me a big bearhug, grinning as he releases me. "I'm glad you could make it. I don't know what I'd have done with him if you'd decided not to come. He's been *grouchy as* all day."

"No I haven't," Orson insists.

"Moping," Kingi adds. "Pining like a lovesick teenager."

I giggle, glowing with pleasure at the thought that he's missed me.

Orson rolls his eyes. "Where's Marama?"

"She was here a moment ago." Kingi looks around, spots her by the bar, and gestures for her to come over.

"It's Kingi's older sister," Orson murmurs to me as she approaches.

She can only be older by a year or so, because she looks a similar age to me. She has flawless light-brown skin. Her dark-brown hair is long and sleek, and like me she's small and slight, with high cheekbones, a pretty smile, and a Moko Kauae—a traditional Māori tattoo on her chin. A Moko Kauae isn't just a decoration—it's a sacred expression of a woman's connection to her whānau or family, and also illustrates that she has leadership and status within her community.

She also has a tattoo curling around her lower left arm. At first glance it looks like another traditional Māori tattoo, but as I look closer I can see it includes the phases of the moon, maybe because her name, Marama, means 'moon.'

She looks nothing like Kingi, and briefly I wonder if they're adopted until I see she has the same startling amber eyes. I guess she must take after their mother.

"Orson!" She goes up to him, and they exchange a serious hongi, pressing noses in the Māori fashion, exchanging the ha or breath of life. Then she laughs and flings her arms around his neck, and they have a big hug.

"And who's this?" she asks, smiling at me as they move back.

"This is Mahuika Stone," Orson says.

"Most people call me Scarlett," I tell her.

"For the fire goddess?" She gestures at my red dress and smiles, then comes forward. We hongi as we shake hands. "Wait." She moves back and her eyebrows rise. "Stone? As in, Blake Stone's daughter?"

I nod.

Her jaw drops, and she glances at Orson. "Are you two an item?"

"Yes," he says, at the same time that I say, "No."

"Glad we cleared that up," Kingi says.

"We're just… it's a casual thing," I say, flustered.

"Don't listen to her," Orson says, "we're getting married next month."

"Orson!"

"What?" He smirks. He's only joking, I know, but my face still burns.

MIDNIGHT ENEMY

Marama glares at him. "Don't tease the poor girl. Make yourself useful and go and get us a drink."

"Champagne?" Orson asks me.

"Goodness."

He just grins and walks off with Kingi to the bar.

"Men," Marama says. "They're all pains in the ass."

"Absolutely," I agree with feeling, and she laughs.

"You live over at Kahukura?" she asks curiously, leading me to an empty table by the side of the pool.

I nod, taking a seat opposite her. "I hold yoga and art classes there."

"Oh!" Her face lights up. "I'm an artist, too!"

"Seriously?"

"Yeah. Have you exhibited anywhere?"

"No," I say hastily, "I'm only an amateur. I use art as part of a holistic healing program for abused women and children."

Her expression softens. "That sounds amazing. Art can be so therapeutic and cathartic, can't it?"

"That's what I think. I encourage the women to paint what they feel, and to journal and write poetry to help them express their anger and frustration. What about you? Are you professional?"

She nods. "I lived in Wellington for a few years and exhibited down there and did quite a few commissions."

"You paint?"

"I work in lots of media, like clay and collage. My favorite was making stained glass Māori patterns. But I've been traveling across Europe, and it's not been practical to carry too many supplies, so I've mainly been painting acrylics."

The guys come back with our drinks and sit beside us, listening while we continue talking.

"I've never traveled," I admit. "How amazing, to go across Europe."

She drops her gaze to her champagne flute. "Mm, well, I was in a bad place and needed to do something different."

I see Orson and Kingi exchange glances. "It's okay if you don't want to talk about it," I tell Marama softly.

She rubs her nose. "No, it's okay. I'm much better now. I was living with my fiancé—we'd been engaged for six months and were due to get married. This was over a year ago. Then a friend of mine told me she'd seen him at a conference, and said he went to his room with another woman."

I press my fingers to my lips as both men frown. "Oh no."

She continues, "He denied it and got really angry with me for suggesting he'd been unfaithful. We had an uneasy Christmas while I tried to tell myself my friend had gotten it wrong. But on New Year's Eve I was wearing his jacket, and I found an earring in his pocket. He denied it again, but long story short, it eventually turned out he'd been having an affair with a work colleague for several months."

"I'm so sorry," I say with feeling.

"Cheating on her was bad enough," Kingi says, "but gaslighting her like that was just awful." His eyes flash. "I wanted to break both his legs."

"Too obvious," Orson says. "I told you poison would have been easier to hide."

We all chuckle, but it's clear that the two men are mad about what happened, and I understand why.

Marama sighs. "It's terrible when you know in your heart that something is wrong, but the other person won't admit it. I thought I was going mad. Anyway, I was angry and upset when I realized what he'd done. I took it really hard. The apartment was his, so I had to move out. My father suggested I go somewhere completely different to recover and concentrate on my art. So I visited some of the big European art galleries, trying to heal and regain my inspiration."

"Did it work?" I ask.

She nods. "I painted lots of beautiful landscapes. I'm much better now, thanks." She smiles. "Anyway, enough about me. Come on, why don't we get something to eat?"

"Now you're talking." Kingi gets to his feet, and the rest of us follow.

We cross to the tables next to the barbecue where the food is laid out, and a waiter hands us all a plate. I was concerned that there wouldn't be much for me to eat as I'm a vegetarian, but I'm relieved to see they've included some veggie kebabs with zucchinis, bell peppers, mushrooms, and baby tomatoes, and a whole heap of various salads, including a pasta one, a rice one, two different potato salads, and a gorgeous Greek salad with green leaves, olives, and feta cheese. There's also freshly baked garlic bread and herb bread.

We heap up our plates and then return to our table. On the way, Orson introduces me to a few people, including a woman who turns out to be his sister, Helen. I would think she's a year or two younger than him, elegant and graceful, despite the fact that she's heavily pregnant. Is this what his mother looked like?

"Oh, hello," she says, shaking my hand. Her eyes, the same blue as his, are alight with curiosity. "So you're the girl who has him all a flutter?"

"Don't you start," he mumbles, putting his plate down with a thump.

She grins. "Callum wants to know if you're definitely coming to his birthday party?"

"Of course! Wouldn't miss it for the world."

"I'll let him know. Good to meet you," she says to me, then heads off back to her table.

"Callum?" I ask as we sit.

"My nephew. He's three next week. I promised him I'd go to his party and get my face painted with him."

I smile, warmed through at the thought of Orson having his face painted as Spider-Man or something. "Is he here today?"

"No." He's distracted by a man who approaches to wish Kingi happy birthday, and he and Kingi shake hands with him and start talking business.

Marama leans closer to me and murmurs, "This is a child-free resort."

I look around the pool, realizing she's right, and there are no children here today. The youngest person present is maybe twenty, so there aren't even any teens.

"How weird," I say, then suddenly realize how rude that must sound. "Oh, um…"

"It's all right," she says softly. "It takes some getting used to." She nibbles at a seafood kebab. "It's just how we've been brought up—children are seen and not heard. When I was traveling through Spain and Italy, it shocked me initially to see children with the adults at the dinner tables, and they don't tend to have kids' menus—they eat what the adults are having. The children are often up very late. But then I'm guessing that's your experience too, at the commune?"

I nod. "My mother was Māori, and she was keen to include children at all meals and social events."

"The Midnight Club is marketed to the rich as exclusive, a place you can come to escape the noise and frustrations of the family," she says. "We hold lots of conferences here, too, so a lot of business is done, and you don't really want little kids running around screaming, or teenagers causing havoc."

"I suppose. But then—" I stop as a shadow falls over the table. I look up, and my heart skips a beat at the sight of Spencer Cavendish standing there like a stone monolith—tall and imposing. He's wearing chinos, so he looks more casual than the last time I saw him in a suit, but he still has a shirt and tie. Does he wear one in bed?

Orson is still talking to Kingi and the other guy, and he's standing with his back to us, so he hasn't seen his father. Spencer's blue eyes are cold, and my mouth goes dry.

"Ms. Stone," he says.

"Mr. Cavendish," I say in a similar cool tone.

"I understand you managed to persuade Orson to pay an extra two and a half million for the Waiora," he states. He tips his head to the side. "Now how did you manage that, I wonder?"

I meet his eyes. It's the second time someone's implied that I slept with Orson purely to get him to raise his bid, and I get to my feet, feeling a rare surge of anger. Out of the corner of my eye, I see Marama reach across and tug Orson's T-shirt. He looks over his shoulder and sees us, and immediately turns and walks across to us.

"What's going on?" he asks.

"Nothing," Spencer states. "Ms. Stone here was just about to reveal the truth about what she did to get her extra two and a half million dollars."

Orson's eyes flare, and he inhales, clearly with the intention of exploding. Before he can do that, though, I say, "I overheard you, you know."

Spencer frowns. "What do you mean?"

"When you came to the commune," I tell him. "I was in the house. I overheard everything."

Orson opens his mouth, but nothing comes out.

The music is still playing, and around us the sound of laughter and conversation continues. But at the table there's an icy silence.

Orson looks from his father to me and back again. "What does she mean? When did you go to the commune?"

Spencer's brows draw together, but he doesn't reply.

"It was just after Christmas," I say.

"Before your mother died?" Orson asks.

I nod. "You want to talk about the truth," I say hotly to Spencer, unable to keep my anger suppressed any more. "Tell him why you came to Kahukura. Tell him what you said."

But Spencer doesn't say anything. Instead, he turns on his heel, walks away, and disappears inside the building.

Chapter Twenty

Orson

I stare at my father's back, then turn to Scarlett. Her eyes are blazing, but she swallows hard as she focuses on me.

"What the hell was that about?" I demand.

Kingi and Marama hover. They obviously overheard Scarlett's conversation with my dad and are probably unsure as to whether to give us privacy or not. Scarlett glances at them. Her anger fades and she looks suddenly worried.

I've never seen Dad walk away from someone like that. He always has to have the last word, and he wins every argument I've ever seen him have. His reaction is therefore completely unprecedented.

She chews her bottom lip. "I'm sorry, I shouldn't have said anything. I lost my temper, that's all. I don't want to spoil the party."

"It's all right," Kingi says, "we'll leave you to it. Come on, Marama, we'll get a drink." Marama shoots Scarlett a sympathetic glance, then follows him over to the bar.

I sit and gesture for Scarlett to do the same.

"What's going on?" I ask, giving her a direct look.

She studies the table for a moment. Then she lifts her gaze to mine again. "Have you seen The Matrix?"

My eyebrows rise in surprise. "Um... yes." I love the sci-fi movie. Neo, the main character, suspects that mankind is trapped inside a computer simulation. He's offered the choice of a blue pill, which means he'll stay blissfully ignorant of the truth, or a red pill, in which case he'll confront the harshness of reality with the hope of seeking knowledge and understanding.

"Do you want the red pill?" she asks.

I hesitate, just for a couple of seconds. Then I nod. "Always."

"You might not like what you hear," she says softly.

I steel myself. "Do you know why they were enemies?"

She gives a reluctant nod.

"Then tell me," I urge, my heart banging. "I have a right to know."

She picks up her champagne glass and has a large swallow. "The day Spencer came to the commune, Ana was out, but I was upstairs with Mum. She was asleep, but I heard everything through the open bedroom window. When he knocked on our door, Dad answered, but he refused to let him in. They stood in the garden, arguing."

"What about?" I ask, baffled. As far as I was aware, they hadn't spoken in years.

"About my mother. Spencer wanted to see her."

My eyebrows rise. "To see your mum? Not your dad?"

"Yes."

I stare at her. "Why?"

"He said he'd heard that Mum had cancer and was very ill. I don't know how, because I thought hospital information was confidential, but he'd found out that Mum hadn't had Enhertu, and he asked why. Dad was furious and said it was none of his business, but Spencer kept asking. Eventually Dad admitted he couldn't afford it. So Spencer said he wanted to pay for it."

My jaw drops. I'm not totally shocked at the news, because at heart he is a good man, and he's given a fortune to charities and helped many people. But Blake was the one person he hated more than any other. Why would he offer to help his wife?

"Dad refused," Scarlett says.

"Jesus, why?"

"He said he didn't want Spencer to have anything to do with Mum's treatment." She has another big mouthful of champagne.

"How do you feel about that?" I ask softly.

"I was angry then, and I'm angry now. Spencer said it wasn't his choice to make, and he was being selfish, and afterward I told Dad that I agreed with Spencer. But he refused to listen."

I can't believe that Dad was willing to offer to pay for the treatment, but that Blake refused out of spite. Christ, no wonder Scarlett is angry. "So what happened after that?"

"Spencer said he wanted to talk to Mum. But Dad said no, that she'd chosen him a long time ago, and he didn't want Spencer to have anything to do with her."

I stare at her as the words slowly sink in. "She'd chosen Blake?" No… it can't be true. "You're telling me that their thirty-year feud was over your mother?"

"I don't know for sure, but I'm guessing the answer is yes." She tips her head to the side. "You're shocked that love could evoke such passionate feelings?"

"No. I'm just stunned to think my father is capable of such an emotion."

She frowns. "But he was married to your mother. They had two children."

"Yeah, but I don't remember them ever being affectionate in front of me. They didn't even hold hands. It was like a business partnership." The thought of him being in love and out of control makes my head spin.

"Well," Scarlett says, "I think they both fell in love with Mum. She chose my dad, and your father never forgave him for it."

"Holy fuck." I'm completely blown away. "What happened?"

"Spencer tried to force his way past Dad. They had an ugly fight; it was horrible to watch. Dad made Spencer's nose bleed, and Spencer gave him a black eye. I didn't want to leave Mum, so I rang the office to tell them what was going on, and George and Richard came running over to separate them. Spencer told Dad he was a selfish bastard and drove off. That's simplifying it—the argument went on for longer than that, but that's the gist of it."

I look away, not really seeing the pool or the guests. Is it true? Did Dad's feud with Blake really start over a woman? At eighteen? But I know that Dad and Blake were competitive all through high school. Wanting the same girl could have turned into an extension of that competition.

I think about what Scarlett said, about Dad going over to the commune and wanting to pay for Amiria's treatment. Could it be that all these years he's continued to harbor feelings for her?

Dad was eighteen when I was born, so he must have met Mum very soon after his original argument over Amiria. Now, I wonder whether he dated her on the rebound. Did Mum know he'd been in love with someone else?

Young people are often mocked when they say they're in love, and told it's just a crush, and it can't possibly be serious. But clearly his feelings for Amiria must have been powerful for them to have carried on through the years. Her illness and death must have hit him hard.

I study her face, wondering how much she's like her mother. She told me that Amiria 'belonged to everyone, in a way, not just to me.' I didn't give it much thought at the time. What did she mean by it? I thought I had a difficult relationship with my mother because she was so reserved, but now I wonder whether it would have been harder to have a mother who was warm and friendly to everyone, and with whom every man fell in love.

Although Blake and my father were friends at first, and I know they were both smart guys with a similar talent for mathematics and finances, their core beliefs were obviously very different. Blake set up Kahukura in his early twenties with Amiria, so she must have been attracted to his socialist tendencies. No wonder she chose him over my father.

"I'm sorry," Scarlett whispers. "I shouldn't have told you."

"No, you were right to, and I'm glad you did." I get to my feet and kiss her forehead. "But I need to speak to him." I gesture to Marama, who's hovering just out of hearing. "Chat to Marama for a bit," I say to Scarlett. "I won't be long."

"Oh no…" she says, clearly worried I'm going to cause a problem, but I just kiss her forehead again and walk away.

After all this time… I need to talk to my father.

I walk through the lobby and turn into the corridor to the offices. I walk past mine and Kingi's to the next one. Sure enough, my father is in there, looking out at the gardens, his hands behind his back. His dark hair is threaded with silver, which makes the flashes at his temples less noticeable now, but they're still there.

He sees my reflection in the window, but he doesn't turn. I close the door behind me and walk over to his desk. He always uses old-fashioned fountain pens, and one is lying next to an empty notepad. I pick it up and turn it over in my fingers.

"Seventeen and a half million for the Waiora?" He turns to look at me. "Is it really worth that?"

"We'll make the extra money back easily," I reply. "The pool is going to be a huge attraction for the guests, and it'll also smooth things over with the locals. It's a good investment."

"So their ploy worked. She got them what they wanted."

Anger bubbles in my stomach. "It wasn't like that."

"So she didn't open her legs for you?"

I toss the pen onto the desk and put my hands on my hips, but don't trust myself to say anything. He holds my gaze for about ten seconds.

Then he winces, runs his hand through his hair, and says, "That was rude of me."

"She doesn't deserve that."

"I know. I'm sorry."

"She's a nice girl, Dad. And I thought you'd be nicer about her, if only out of respect to her mother."

He looks at me then, startled.

"Yeah," I say. "Scarlett told me that your feud with Blake was because she chose him and not you."

He sighs, sits down on a nearby armchair as if his legs have given out, and massages his brow with a hand.

I sit opposite him. I'm still angry at what he insinuated about Scarlett. But I also know he thinks attack is the best form of defense. And I know him well enough to see that he's hurting.

"Did you love her?" I ask. "Amiria, I mean?"

He lowers his hand. Leaning forward, his elbows on his knees, he links his fingers and studies them. "Yes," he says eventually. Then he gives me a mutinous look. "I know we were only eighteen. But I was crazy about her."

"Will you tell me what happened? With Blake?"

He sighs and looks out of the window. "I guess it doesn't matter now." His gaze is distant. "We met in Year Seven. We were both in the top classes for all subjects. We had lots in common, and we became friends immediately. But we were also fiercely competitive. As we got older, I tended to get higher marks in tests, I was chosen for sports teams before him, I was a faster sprinter, I nearly always had the upper hand… until I met Amiria. We were all in our first year at uni. We met at a party after the first trimester. Blake wasn't there; he was away in the South Island, visiting family."

He leans back and sighs again. "She was stunning, even at eighteen. I asked her to dance, and then at the end of the evening, I asked if I could see her again. She said yes, and I took her to the cinema. A few days later, we went to our favorite cafe. We walked a lot. Just innocent stuff."

"Did you introduce her to Blake?"

"Not for six weeks. Eventually he came back from the South Island, and I told him I'd met someone. They met at another party, the night before the second trimester started. They got on well, and I was pleased—I wanted them to like each other. I didn't worry at first. She was warm and friendly to everyone. Then toward the end of the evening I went off to get us all a drink. When I came back, Blake and Amiria had disappeared. I asked a friend where they'd gone, and he said they'd left. When they didn't come back, I went home alone, confused and angry. I rang both of them, but both their phones went to voicemail. The next day, at uni, he announced they were dating."

"Jesus," I say.

"I was furious at him and said he'd only asked her out because he knew I liked her. He denied it, but he was so fucking smug... I knew I was right. So I hit him. We got in a fight, and we were both suspended. We hardly said two words to each other after that, until the day at the commune."

I don't say anything for a moment. He dated her for six weeks, so it must have only been one factor in the pre-existing feud between him and Blake. After saying that, I know the effect that Scarlett had on me that day at the law firm, so I can't blame him for being captivated.

"So was Mum just a rebound?" I ask softly. "Did you ever really love her?"

His gaze comes back to me. "You can't have two kids with someone and not love them."

"Are you sure? You never seemed in love."

He gives an impatient frown. "Loving someone and being in love aren't the same thing. You must know that by now."

I hadn't thought about it like that, but with some surprise I realize he's probably right.

"Your mother was beautiful," he says. "And she knew how to use her beauty and her love as currencies to get the things she wanted. Namely, me. Even at that age, she recognized my ambition and drive, and knew I was going places, so she got pregnant on purpose because she knew I'd do the right thing."

I stare at him. "Seriously?" I'd guessed I was an accident, but I hadn't considered that my mother engineered it.

"Yeah. She told me she was on the pill and I didn't need to use a condom if I didn't want to. I, like a fool, believed her."

I give a short laugh. "You grilled me relentlessly about using a condom when I was a teen."

"And why do you think I did that?"

With some surprise, I realize it was because he didn't want me to make the same mistake that he did. I'd just assumed it was Dad being Dad, trying to control me.

"I was angry at your mother at first," he says. "But in many ways we were well suited. She was an astute businesswoman, and a suitable companion socially. So I asked her to marry me, and we stayed together. But she doled her love out sparingly, both to me and to her children."

I've only ever thought about the way she treated me and my siblings; I've never given any thought to how it must have felt to be married to a woman who could withhold affection the way she did.

It's the most open and personal he's ever been with me and, while he's in the mood to confess, I ask curiously, "Did you ever have an affair?"

"No, never."

I think about how it must have been for him to be trapped into marrying a woman he wasn't in love with, someone who only wanted him for his fortune and social connections. It explains why he was so worried about Scarlett being attracted to my money. Once again, he was only looking out for me. The thought shocks me.

"Is there anyone else now?" I ask. I've never seen him with another woman since Mum died.

"No one serious. I don't trust easily."

I guess that's understandable if he was tricked into marriage.

He frowns then. "I'm not sure I should have said that about your mother. She was a good woman, on the whole."

"It's okay," I say. "I'm under no illusions about her. But it doesn't mean Scarlett is the same. She's not like either of our mothers. She's very much her own woman."

He gives me a wary look. "You might not think so, but you can't always trust your instincts. She did get the extra two and a half million out of you."

"I agreed to that so she didn't feel she had to sleep with me to get it."

His eyebrows lift; he hadn't considered that.

"I know what I'm doing," I say softly. "I had a good teacher."

His lips quirk up.

We study each other quietly. The sun has set, dusk has fallen, and it's semi-dark in the office. I've always admired both his business and personal instincts, and I'm like him in many ways. I would trust him with my life. But I've never really considered us close. We can't mend that with one conversation, but for the first time I feel we've healed some past rifts. And I have Scarlett to thank for that.

"We should get back to the party," I say. "I don't want to leave Scarlett for too long."

"You go," he says. "I might head up to my suite."

"Ah, come on. Rangi's there, and I saw Huxley and Mack just now. It's going to be fun. Come and have a drink with us."

He hesitates. Then he says, "All right."

We stand and leave the office. As we enter the lobby, we see that the solar lights around the pool have all come on, and the place glows like a beacon through the far windows.

"We did well here," I say to my father. The resort is beautiful and popular, but more than anything I'm proud of the fact that we're able to funnel so much of the profit here into charitable causes.

"We should talk about Kahukura," he says as we cross the lobby. "You were right. We should offer them funding."

I nod, pleased at the thought of telling Scarlett. "Kingi's carrying out an audit of their finances next week."

"Why?"

"The commune is struggling financially. Scarlett told me that their finance director, George, has sole control now Blake's gone, and I said it made sense to get the books checked. I don't know… I have a gut feeling." He stops walking. I stop too when I realize he's not with me, and I turn to face him. "What?"

"I've got something else to tell you," he says.

Chapter Twenty-One

Scarlett

I finish off my champagne, and Kingi brings me another.

"It'll be okay," Marama says, seeing me trembling. "Don't worry."

It's impossible not to, though. I feel as if I've thrown a hand grenade into the Cavendish family, and it's detonating somewhere, and all I can do is wait to pick the pieces of shrapnel out of me when it's done.

"I feel awful," I whisper. "I shouldn't have said anything."

"Yes, you should," Kingi states firmly. "This stupid family feud has gone on for far too long. Orson doesn't say anything now, but I know it upsets him that his father has refused to talk about it. Spencer is a cold fish, though."

"Aw, don't be mean," Marama says. "He's always been very nice to me."

Kingi chuckles. "Sorry. To be fair, he had a tough childhood, and I guess he's just erected a barrier to protect himself."

"Tough in what way?" I ask.

"He came from a dirt-poor family," Marama replies.

My eyebrows rise. "Oh. I didn't realize. I assumed the family was old money."

"No," Marama says, "not at all. Spencer's father worked in a meat processing factory. He and his wife had six children. Spencer was the oldest boy. His father was an abusive alcoholic who used to knock the wife around. As he grew up, Spencer used to try to protect her, and the dad beat him pretty badly on several occasions, I think."

Kingi nods. "Hospitalized him twice. In the end the authorities intervened and put the kids into foster homes. They had to break up the kids into two homes. Spencer and his younger brothers were put into one home and the girls into another. Spencer says that's when his fortunes were turned around. The couple who had the boys were wealthy and supportive and just really nice human beings—I've met them."

"He stayed in touch with them?" Marama asks.

"Yeah. The guy had had problems when he was young and someone helped him in the same way, so it was a sort of pay-it-back kind of thing, I think. He got the boys into a decent school, encouraged them with their schoolwork, and when he saw that Spencer had a talent for figures, he got him extra tuition and pushed him hard."

"He got Eleanor pregnant when he was really young though, didn't he?" Marama says.

Kingi nods again. "He was only eighteen I think. But Peter and Joyce—his foster parents—paid for everything, and Peter pushed Spencer to go to university even though he was a young dad. Spencer flourished there. He discovered he had a talent for investment, a kind of sixth sense for what would be profitable. He created an online financial advisory service in his second year of university, and he invested all the money he made through it. Then when he graduated, he created Cavendish Investments, Cavendish Property Developments, and several other companies. Started on his own, gradually grew his staff. Made an absolute fortune over the years. He's totally a self-made man."

"So why doesn't Orson work for him?" I ask, puzzled.

He tips his head from side to side. "He was always keen that Orson made his own way in the world. He wanted his children to be independent. I think he'd have found Orson a role if he'd wanted, but right from when we were young at school, Orson and I would talk about setting up our own company. I think he wanted to impress his father and prove that he could do well on his own."

"Fascinating," Marama says. "Do you think Spencer is proud of him?"

"Of course," Kingi replies. "But he's not the type of guy who's open with his affection or praise. Like I said, he's a cold fish."

Marama shrugs. "I don't believe it's because he doesn't have feelings. I think he's just learned over the years to keep them under control. And I admire that in a way. A man in his position."

"Orson and I run companies and we're not like robots."

"Spencer isn't a robot."

"He's totally a cyborg. The dude never smiles."

197

"Of course he does!"

"Well, he'll smile at you," Kingi says with a snort.

She blinks. "What do you mean?"

He just flicks his eyebrows up. Marama instantly turns scarlet.

I smile. "He is very handsome, and—" I stop as I see Orson and Spencer come out of the building, and all words flee my mind.

To my relief, neither of them looks angry. As they approach, someone stops Spencer to talk, so Orson joins us and sits beside me.

"Are you okay?" I ask.

"Fine." He squeezes my hand. "It's all good, don't worry." Despite his assurance, though, he's frowning. "I'll get us all another round of drinks," he says, and gets to his feet again. "Kingi, give us a hand?"

"Sure." Kingi rises and goes with him. Before they reach the bar, though, they stop and have a conversation. I wonder what that's about?

"Hey." It's Helen, Orson's sister. She joins us at the table, lowering down heavily with her pregnant belly. "Everything all right? I saw Dad and Orson walk off."

"Yes, fine," Marama says, presumably deciding to leave it to Orson to tell her what's going on. "Having a good time?"

"The food is fantastic," Helen says. "I just adore the chef here."

"Those oysters are to die for."

"I know, with the mignonette sauce."

I'm not sure what that is, so I don't say anything. I like these women, but I am conscious that they come from a very different world from me.

"Hello." Spencer stops by the table. He slides his hands into the pockets of his chinos and hesitates. "Scarlett… I want to apologize. I was very rude earlier, and it was unforgivable, I'm so sorry."

His apology surprises me and takes the wind out of my sails. Conscious of Marama and Helen watching, I say, "Oh… um… it's okay."

"I carry thirty years of resentment and hurt with me," he says, "and it's time I let it go. It's clear that Orson is very fond of you, and you're special to him. I've started off on the wrong foot with you, and I'm sorry about that."

It's true that Spencer was rude to me. And it's also true that my father was hardly the sort to forgive and forget. But the Cavendishes aside, he also taught me and Ana that human beings make mistakes.

We all say and do things we regret. And it's the ability to forgive that makes a person worth knowing.

"It's okay," I say softly. "I understand."

He looks surprised, as if he expected me to tell him to go fuck himself and storm off.

"Oh," he says. "Right."

"Why don't you join us?" Marama suggests. "Orson and Kingi are getting drinks."

He looks at me. "Is that okay with you?"

I nod, trying not to wince as I think about what Dad would say if he knew I was sharing a glass of champagne with Spencer Cavendish.

He pulls out a seat and sits. Then he smiles at Marama. Kingi's right—he doesn't smile often, but he's definitely smiling at her. "So how long are you back for?" he asks.

"About a month," she says. "Then I'm going to do some more traveling. I want to go to India, and Japan, and maybe the States."

"Still concentrating on your art?" he asks.

"Yes. Going to galleries, and seeing some beautiful places and painting them too."

Helen sips her champagne. "Are you going to exhibit your work here again in New Zealand?"

"Maybe. I'm seeing someone in Wellington next week to talk about it and show her my paintings." Marama gives a look that says she's nervous but excited.

I smile. "I hope they like them."

"Of course they will," Spencer says. "She's terrific."

She pushes him playfully. "Oh, you. You have no idea what my art is like."

"Of course I do," he says, amused. "I have one of your stained-glass works at home."

Her eyebrows shoot up. "What?"

"I bought one from the exhibition you held last year."

Her jaw drops. "I didn't know you went to that."

He just smiles.

Clearly flustered, she says, "Which one did you buy?"

"Parson-Bird," he says. It's a nickname for the tui bird, which has white feathers at its throat. "It's beautiful," he says to me and Helen. "All blues, greens, and purples. I've hung it in one of the windows and it throws colored light across the whole room."

"Clearly you're a woman of many talents," Spencer tells Marama. There's a slight hint of mischief in his tone.

"Wouldn't you like to know?" she replies, her tone flirtatious as she gathers her wits together.

His lips curve up. Luckily, at that point, Orson and Kingi show up with a tray of drinks.

"Everything all right?" he asks, handing them out.

"Fine," I say, and smile. "We were talking about how Spencer bought one of Marama's stained-glass pieces."

"I'm not surprised," Kingi says. "They're fantastic." He knocks his glass as he puts it down and half of it spills across the table. "Dammit."

"I'll get a cloth," Marama says, and goes off to fetch one.

"She likes you," Helen says to her father with a mischievous smile.

Spencer just gives his daughter a wry look.

"You should ask her out," Helen says.

"She's in her twenties," Spencer says, in a voice that suggests she should change the subject.

"She's twenty-nine," she scoffs. "Nearly thirty."

"Still too young for me," he says. "And she's also the daughter of my business associate."

"And Kingi's sister," Orson points out.

"Kingi wouldn't mind if Dad dated his sister," Helen says, "would you?"

Kingi looks startled. "Er…"

"Enough." Spencer throws her a glare, then picks up his glass. "Have a great evening." He gets up and walks off.

Helen giggles. "Oops. I probably shouldn't have teased him."

Marama comes back with a cloth and starts mopping up Kingi's spilled drink. She glances around and says, "What?"

"Nothing," Helen says innocently. She meets my eyes and winks.

Orson snorts and changes the subject, and the conversation moves on. But I spot Marama's glance drifting across the pool several times to where Spencer is sitting talking to a couple of men his own age. He doesn't look back, though. He's obviously very aware of their age difference and her family, and I can't imagine he'd be interested in a romantic relationship with her.

*

It turns out to be a great evening. Orson introduces me to lots of people whose names I soon forget, most of whom are business associates. But it's clear that some are good friends too, especially the two couples who join us at our table early in the evening. I soon realize the two guys are part of the Midnight Circle.

The first of his friends is called Mack Hart, a dark-haired, intense kinda guy with very unusual eyes that are blue speckled with green, like planet Earth. It turns out he's the inventor of the fastest supercomputer in the country. I find it more than a little intimidating to be surrounded by all these smart guys, and I wouldn't have said a word all evening if it wasn't for his wife—a beautiful, curly-haired beauty called Sidnie, who seems very normal and is determined to include me in the conversation as often as possible.

Orson introduces the other guy as Oliver Huxley, although everyone seems to call him by his surname. He tells me that Huxley runs a business club in Auckland, and I remember then that this was the guy who approached Orson with the idea of setting up the first Midnight Club. He's about Orson's height and build, a bit stockier maybe, and incredibly affable, clearly used to putting people at ease.

His wife, Elizabeth, is around my height with dark hair in a sharp bob. It turns out that she runs some kind of company that does drug research, and they've won awards for the work they've done with IVF.

"What do you do?" Elizabeth asks me politely when Orson introduces us.

It's impossible not to feel daunted by all these powerful people. But I'm proud of my work, so I lift my chin and say, "I help run the retreat at Kahukura."

Her eyebrows rise. "For abused women, right? Part of Women's Refuge?"

I nod, pleased she's heard of it. "Yes. My father created it. I hold yoga and art classes there. We believe in the healing power of creativity."

I wait for them to exchange mocking glances, but they don't, and Huxley says, "Incredibly worthwhile work," while Elizabeth adds, "I can only imagine how that helps them to rediscover their equilibrium."

"That's it exactly," I say, pleased. "I like that description."

"Important for them to regain power over their own lives, I would think," Huxley says.

"Yes, very much so." I relax after that, and Orson squeezes my hand, obviously recognizing that I feel better.

We eat, and drink, and after a while we have a swim, during which Orson lifts me in his arms and threatens to dunk me, but he ends up kissing me, prompting Kingi to yell from the table, "No petting in the pool," to which Orson yells back, "You're just jealous."

After that, there's more champagne, and Orson feeds me a variety of sumptuous desserts. I sit and listen to him and his friends and family chatting around the table, thinking about what a different life we lead. I really like everyone present—Kingi, Mack, Sidnie, Huxley, Elizabeth, Helen, Marama, and even Spencer, when he comes over for a while, as he's very like Orson—quick-witted, smart, and warm when he chooses to be.

But I'm not sure I can ever see myself existing in their world. It's impossible to change your core philosophy, and mine is so at odds with Orson's. I look around at all this wealth—the women's jewelry, their designer clothes even though they're wearing shorts and tees, the sumptuous food and the expensive champagne, the numerous staff waiting on their every whim… And it's so different from my life, where you're encouraged to do everything yourself, where everyone is considered equal, and where extravagance is frowned on, because every extra cent spent on something opulent is money that could be used to help someone less fortunate than yourself.

I'm not saying it's not attractive… There's something wonderful about being waited on hand on foot, and not having to do your own cooking and cleaning and washing. Imagine being able to buy any piece of clothing or jewelry or household item that you liked the look of. And not having to worry whether your car was going to break down because yours was brand new and you'd just take it back to the garage and get them to mend it. Of being able to buy a huge house or an exquisite apartment. Of having the freedom to travel without having to backpack or scrimp and scrape and not worrying about health insurance or running out of money in a foreign country.

I feel a bit differently about the Cavendishes too now I know that Spencer is a self-made man. I don't know why it makes a difference, but it does. He's obviously decided his family isn't going to suffer the way he did—and I can't blame him for that—while at the same time attempting to instill values in his children so they appreciate their wealth and don't take it for granted. Orson told me he works fourteen hours a day sometimes, and so even if he doesn't quite appreciate the difficulties we go through at the commune trying to make ends meet, he isn't a playboy.

"How are you doing?" he asks now, jolting me out of my reverie.

"I'm fine," I reply. "A little tired." It's late and I've had several glasses of champagne.

"Shall we head off?" he asks.

"I'm happy to walk home if you'd like to stay with your friends."

He gives me a look. "This late? In the dark? I don't think so. If you want to go home, I'll get someone to drive you." He gets to his feet. "Come and see my suite and have a coffee or something. I just want to spend some time alone with you."

"I bet you do."

His lips curve up. "Just to chat. If after that you want to leave, I'll call my chauffeur. Come on." He gets to his feet and extends a hand. I slide mine into it and get to my feet.

"We're off," Orson says to the group. "Happy birthday, bro."

Kingi stands, and the two of them exchange a bearhug.

"I'll see you Wednesday," Kingi says to me. "For the audit." His gaze slides briefly to Orson's dad. I follow his gaze and look at Spencer. He just lifts an eyebrow.

I want to ask what's going on, but Orson takes my hand again, and everyone calls, "Goodnight," and we wave and head for the main building.

"Thank you for inviting me," I say as we walk through the lobby. "I had a great time."

"Really?"

"Yes. I liked all your friends and family. It was good to put faces to names."

He leads us across to another corridor that goes outside under a covered walkway, heading for the main hotel building.

"Is there something I need to know about the audit?" I ask.

"Why do you say that?"

I shrug. "Just got a feeling."

"Don't worry about it. No point in worrying before the audit's done." His tone is not dismissive, exactly, but I know he's telling me he doesn't want to discuss it further.

I open my mouth to protest, but the double doors open automatically, and we go inside. "I love this building," he says. "We took a long time to plan it. Kingi wanted something biophilic—it means connected to nature. He'd visited an office in Christchurch that had a biophilic design and loved it, and we decided to incorporate the architecture here."

The lobby is full of indoor plants and even has a tree in one corner. The construction materials all look to be natural—wood, bamboo, and cork. There's a water feature in the middle, and I can see from the large windows that during the day the place would be filled with natural lighting. The wooden panels are all carved with Māori designs. It's beautiful.

Somewhat stunned, I let him lead me to the elevator, which is all glass, and it takes us up to the top floor. Here there's a corridor with half a dozen doors, and he goes to one of them, touches a key card to it, and opens it.

I go inside. It's smaller than his apartment in the city, but it's beautiful, with a similar design to the lobby—lots of carved wood and green plants. The windows face the ocean, and the rising moon casts a silver path, as if tempting me to cross the sea. The furnishings are all natural too, simple but elegant and made from wood and bamboo. The walls are what fascinate me, though, as they've been painted with natural scenes—trees, grass, flowers, and animals. I feel as if I'm in a cabin way out in the bush.

"It's fantastic," I say, turning around to see the kitchenette and, through a door, the bedroom.

"Not huge," he says, "but I usually only stay here once or twice a week." He goes into the kitchen and opens the fridge. "Champagne? Or would you prefer a coffee now?"

I walk over to join him. "You were serious about the coffee?"

He closes the fridge and turns to face me. "Of course. I thought we could sit and have a chat. And then… you know… you can decide whether you want to stay…"

His voice trails off as I move up close to him, put my hands on his chest, and push him up against the fridge. "You really think I've come up here to talk?" I murmur, pressing up against him. He smells amazing; even though he's been swimming, the scent of his cologne lingers on his clothes.

"Well, I didn't want to assume…"

He stops speaking as I reach up onto my tiptoes and kiss him.

Mmm… he tastes sweet, a mix of chocolate and whiskey, along with the enticing smell of his cologne, a blend that goes straight to my head and fires up all my nerve endings. I lift my arms around his neck and touch my tongue to his bottom lip, and when he obediently opens his mouth, I plunge my tongue into his mouth.

"Mmm," he murmurs with an approving growl deep in his throat. Taking me by the hips, he turns me and pushes me up against the fridge with enough force to make all the bottles inside it rattle. Unapologetically, he kisses me, until I'm breathless, and my knees are trembling, and I can't think about anything else except the touch of his lips on mine.

Chapter Twenty-Two

Orson

Fuck.

I'd promised myself I'd go slow. That I wouldn't try to pressure her to stay. That I'd let her go at her own pace.

Well, it looks as if she's doing that; it's just that her pace is a lot faster than I imagined.

Heat sears through me, and I'm hard in seconds. Briefly, I debate whether I should slow this down, move back, insist on a drink, tell her she doesn't have to do this. But somehow, I don't think she's faking it to impress me. She's sliding her fingers through my hair, and when I move my hand up her ribs, she arches her back to push her breast into it. I brush a thumb over the nipple, then tug it gently, and she gives such a sexy moan that I nearly come on the spot.

"Bed," I tell her firmly, moving back. "Now."

She resists though, pulling me back toward her. "Here," she says, linking her arms around my neck.

My eyebrows shoot up. "In the kitchen?"

"Yeah." Her eyes sparkle. "Please."

She wants to try it somewhere else other than the bed. Well, I'm not going to argue with her. "I'll fuck you anywhere you want," I murmur back with feeling before thinking maybe that was a bit ungentlemanly, but she just laughs and crushes her lips to mine again.

Oh man… I hadn't expected this. She was so reluctant to come to the party, and she's so resistant to the idea of a relationship, that I assumed she was just curious about the club, and afterward she'd want to go straight home. I know we had a good night together at my apartment, but I didn't think she was interested in anything more.

It looks as if I was wrong.

Of course it doesn't mean anything. Girls like sex as much as guys, and she's new to it, and probably curious. Once she's gotten what she wants, it's likely she'll be distant again.

Right now, though, I'm not going to worry about it. She's in my arms, and all I can do is try to show her how I feel about her, and make sure she enjoys herself.

With that in mind, I turn her and push her up against the kitchen counter, still kissing her, while I slide my hands beneath her dress. She's wearing her bikini beneath it, and I find the elastic of the bottoms and tug them down her legs. She steps out of them, and I toss them away, then drop to my knees in front of her.

"Orson... oh!" She gasps as I lift her leg over my shoulder, and then I lean forward and slide my tongue into the heart of her. "Oh my God..." She moans and grips hold of the counter, tipping back her head.

She's bare, soft, and silky smooth, and I groan as the pure, natural scent and taste of a woman fills my mouth, slightly salty, slightly sweet, and creamy, which makes my erection strain against my shorts. I bring up a hand and stroke my thumb lightly down the center of her, then when I reach her entrance, ease it into her, just a little way, to collect her moisture. I use my thumb to brush it across her skin and spread it over her clit, before finally lowering my mouth to it.

She slides a hand into my hair as I circle my tongue over the tiny button, and her fingers tighten as I keep up the rhythm. I lick and suck, and tease the rest of her with my fingers, enjoying every second of being so intimate with her. I love the way she moves her hips to match the movement of my tongue and fingers, and eventually how she slips her hand to the back of my head and pulls my head closer. Oh yeah, baby, fuck my face, that turns me on so much... I groan and suck harder, and she gives such a sexy moan that I can't bear it any longer.

I pull away and push up to my feet, and she trembles and says, "Oh God... I was so close..."

"I know. I need to be inside you when you come." I go to slide my hand into my trousers, then realize I'm in my swim shorts. "Damn, I don't have my wallet. Hold on, I'll just get a condom."

She catches my arm. "My doctor put me on the pill a few years ago because I had heavy periods. If you want to... um... you can leave it."

I hesitate. I've never had sex without a condom. My father drilled that into me when I was young, and now I understand why.

Her face flushes. "I'm sorry, that was probably inappropriate. I know it's best to think about STDs…"

"It's not that," I say hastily. "I'm clean, and you obviously are. It's just… my dad told me tonight that my mother got pregnant on purpose. She told him she was on the pill, and she lied."

Her eyes widen and her jaw drops. "Oh shit! Really?"

"Yeah. He said she suspected he'd do the right thing and marry her."

We study each other for a moment. My brain is working furiously, trying to tell me I'd be stupid to fall for the same trick, and my father warned me for a reason. But all I can think is how much I'd love to be inside her without barriers, and how incredibly sexy it would be to fill her up.

Her expression softens, and she says, "I understand. It's not a problem at all. We can wait thirty seconds for you to find a condom."

Her openness and understanding seals the deal. I trust her, and I don't think she'd do to me what my mother did to my father.

It crosses my mind that he would point out that the several glasses of champagne and whiskey might have something to do with my decision, but I shove him out of my mind.

"Fuck it." I bend, lift her, and deposit her on the kitchen counter.

She squeals, then laughs as I push open her legs and move between them. "Naughty boy," she scolds. "Honestly, I don't mind waiting."

"I can't wait another second." I peel her dress up her body and over her head, then reach behind her and undo the ties of her bikini top behind her neck. I pull each tie down, and the triangles gradually peel away to reveal her generous breasts. The material clings hold of the tips tantalizingly, and then I pull it down to expose her light-brown nipples.

"Fuck." I'm so hard. "You have amazing breasts."

"Why, thank you."

"I mean it." I lower my head, cover a nipple with my mouth, and brush my tongue over the tip. She moans and lets her head drop back, threading her fingers in my hair. Ahhh… I love doing this, teasing her velvety soft nipples and feeling them harden on my tongue, and I suck harder, feeling smug pleasure as she tightens her fingers.

"Orson…" she whispers. "Oh God…"

I swap to the other nipple, teasing her to the edge again, wanting her aching for me, and only when she's breathing in deep gasps do I move back. I tear off my tee, push my swim shorts down my legs and kick them away, then move back and guide my erection between her legs. Her eyes light up, and she watches as I slide the tip down through her slick skin and press it against her entrance.

I cup the back of her neck and kiss her as I slide inside her.

Ahhh... man, she's so tight, and it feels soooo sensitive without the condom. I groan as I give a few thrusts, coating myself with her moisture and slowly easing into her. She closes her eyes and tips back her head again, and I kiss her neck while I slowly ease back and push forward.

She exhales, then breathes in again and holds it while I sink in the final inch. Now our bodies are flush, and I'm buried deep inside her.

I wait for a moment, just reveling in the sensation of being encased by all that warm, soft flesh. I press my forehead and nose to hers in a hongi, exchanging the ha, our lips just touching, our breaths mingling, and she gives a quiet, "Ohhh..."

Gradually, I start to move, almost withdrawing, then sinking back into her with long, slow thrusts.

"You feel fucking amazing," I tell her, my voice husky with desire.

"Mmm... you too." She frowns as I pull all the way out. "Aw, don't stop."

"I'm not. I just like to watch you take me."

Obviously realizing it turns me on, she leans back on her hands and widens her thighs, totally opening up for me, watching me with wide eyes. I can't tear my gaze from where I'm penetrating her, though, and I groan as I press the head back into her and observe how her body resists the invasion for a moment before welcoming me in. Fuck, that's so hot.

"Jeez, Orson..." She tips her head back again, her lips parting in a long moan.

This girl is so fucking hot, I'm going to self-combust. I slide inside her as slowly as I can bear it for as long as I can, but eventually my body refuses to wait any longer, and I start picking up the pace.

"You feel so good," I murmur, "I love how you open up for me, you're amazing."

"Mmm..." She falls back onto her elbows. "Oh God, I can feel you all the way up, right to the top..."

"Yeah, baby, you're taking me so well, look, every single inch of me, all the way inside you... And you're so wet, it's exquisite."

"Ah, don't embarrass me."

"It's not embarrassing, it's fucking hot. Look at you." I withdraw, lower a hand between her legs, and slide two fingers inside her. I remove them, coated with her moisture, insert them in my mouth and suck the wetness off, then kiss her, plunging my tongue into her mouth so she can taste herself.

She laughs and gives a muffled protest, then gives in and lets me kiss her deeply while I enter her again. Ohhh… I'm not far now, pleasure building as if she's fanning the flames of the desire inside me. Luckily, her breaths are becoming more ragged, her chest heaving, and when I cup her breast and tug on her nipple, she groans.

I lower a hand between us and tease her clit with my thumb, and it only takes twenty seconds of that before she whispers, "I'm going to come."

"Yeah, baby…" I kiss her and thrust harder, unable to hold back any longer, and she screws up her nose and comes with a squeal, giving deep, heartfelt gasps as I pound into her and let my body go at the pace it wants.

She clamps around me, so incredibly tight, and I'm so sensitive without the condom that there's no way I'm going to be able to hang onto my self-control. She's just finished her climax when mine hits, and she slides a hand to the back of my neck and holds me there for a kiss as I come, spilling inside her without barriers, filling her with my seed.

"Fuck…" I gasp, my hips jerking, my cock twitching, as delicious spasms ripple through me.

When I'm finally done, I wrap my arms around her, and we exchange a long, luscious, sensual kiss.

"I'm so sorry," I murmur when I eventually lift my head.

"Why?"

I kiss her nose, her cheeks, her eyelids. "For being so quick. I wanted to take you to bed and spend hours just kissing and touching. You get me so riled up."

"My work here is done." She giggles, then groans. "I'm all sticky now."

"The one downside of not using condoms." I grab a piece of kitchen towel for her.

"It wasn't a complaint." She lets me help her down. Then I pull her into my arms again. She slides her arms around my waist and snuggles right up against me, and we stand there like that for a while, feeling our heartbeats gradually slow.

I kiss the top of her head, then lift my hands to cup her face. I kiss her mouth, long and slow.

"Mmm," she murmurs.

"What would you like to do?" I say softly. "Have a drink of something? Do you want to go home? Or would you like to stay the night?"

Our eyes meet, and she swallows. "Stay the night."

Joy fills me. "Good. Come on, then, let's get ready for bed."

We brush our teeth standing next to each other, then climb into bed and pull the cool cotton duvet over us. Scarlett turns onto her side facing away from me, and I pull her close and wrap my arms around her so she's cuddled right against me.

"Beautiful night," she says, and I'm not sure if she's referring to the party, what we've just done, or the moon rising slowly over the Pacific Ocean. Maybe all three.

"I'd like to do this every night," I tell her. The confession surprises me—I must have drunk more than I thought. Or maybe it doesn't. It's only what was in my heart.

She doesn't agree, though. I kiss her hair and ask, "Wouldn't you?"

"Nothing's changed," she whispers. "We're still worlds apart."

I feel a deep ache inside. I know she's right, but it hurts to hear her say it.

I refuse to think that's it, though. "Nothing is unsolvable," I point out. "There's a solution to every problem."

"Not this one, Orson. It goes too deep."

"I don't believe that."

"That's because you think you can change me, and it's not fair."

"It's not about changing you. It's about finding a compromise."

"Meaning what? We build a house halfway between the club and the commune?"

"I don't know yet. I know we have very different values and ways of living. But that doesn't mean we can't both make changes if we want to be together. Just saying 'this is the way I am' isn't compromising."

"That's fair. But that's not the only problem."

I frown. "What do you mean?"

"I know my father would be deeply hurt and angry at the fact that I'm spending time with the man he considered his worst enemy. And

I know he's gone now, but I loved and respected him so much, and it makes me feel uneasy to think how I'm going against his wishes. I'm not sure I can move past that."

For once, I don't have an answer. I can't change the past. I truly think my father—while not being cured of his lifelong hatred—might be ready to move on, but Blake is no longer here to be convinced that the feud should be put to one side.

"Maybe we should just take it day by day," I suggest.

"And what? Wake up three months down the line, in exactly the same position? It'll hurt ten times as much to break up then. A hundred times, even."

I don't say anything, because there's nothing to say.

Half of me expects her to get up and leave. After all, what's the point in staying if she's decided this isn't going to work? But she doesn't, and after about ten minutes, her breathing deepens, and I realize she's fallen asleep.

I relax into the pillow now I know she's not leaving, and tighten my arms around her. I have a suspicion for how this might work out, but the very act of it coming to light is going to cause a tsunami of emotion to come crashing down over her, and I'm not sure she'll still be standing once the worst is over.

I'm not big on hope, or faith. I prefer to be in control of my fate. But for once, all I can do is wait for it to play out, and promise myself I'll do my best to help her survive.

*

Despite her words, I manage to talk Scarlett into seeing me again on Monday. I take her into town to watch a movie, and then out for dinner. I make sure to keep our conversation away from anything deep and meaningful, and we talk about books, movies, and music, and just concentrate on getting to know one another better.

Afterward, she agrees to come back to my apartment with me, and this time I take her into the bedroom, and we spend a long, long time making out, just kissing, cuddling, and touching, for as long as we can bear before I finally slide inside her.

I make love to her again in the night, ducking under the covers to give her an orgasm with my mouth first, and then taking her in as many positions as I can think of, prolonging her pleasure until she begs me to take her and let her come.

I want to brand myself into her skin, mark her as mine, and make it impossible for her to leave me. But I can't. All I can do is imprint myself on her memories, and hope that when the moment comes—as I know it will—she won't be able to forget me as easily as she thinks she can.

*

I don't see her on Tuesday as I have an evening meeting. On Wednesday, Kingi heads off to the commune to start his audit. It's a relatively small business, so neither of us is expecting it to take more than a week.

I talk Scarlett into seeing me that evening and take her to see a band we both like at the Spark Arena. Afterward, I tell her I'll happily fly her home, but if she wants to come back to my apartment, I promise her that I've bought a tub of mint choc chip ice cream especially for her, and I'll smear it over her and lick it all off, or she can do the same to me if she wishes.

She chooses to spend the night.

I don't see her Thursday, but I've managed to organize tickets to a performance of Midsummer Night's Dream on Auckland domain on Friday evening, and even though she protests that we shouldn't prolong this, she's unable to resist the thought of seeing a Shakespeare play in the open air. I tell her I'll pick her up at six to give us time to fly over and get to the venue by seven thirty.

I'm busy all morning, although I manage to have a quick call with Kingi. I ask him how the audit's going, and hear him walking, and then a door closing. The sound of birdsong tells me he's gone outside, probably out of earshot of anyone at the commune.

"Between you and me it's not well run at all," he says. "The accounts are all over the place. It's going to take a few weeks to fully analyze everything." He hesitates.

"What?" I ask, sensing he has something more to say.

But he says, "My spidey senses are tingling, but I need to finish the batch of documents I'm working on at the moment. I'll speak to you later."

I frown, but I have a business lunch, so I say goodbye, then return to the office and work for the rest of the afternoon. I'm just getting ready to pack up and head over to Waiheke when Kingi calls.

"It's me," he says. "You need to get over here. Now."

Chapter Twenty-Three

Scarlett

I've just finished my last yoga class of the day, and I'm on my way out of the retreat to go home to change when to my astonishment I see a silver Aston Martin pulling up out the front of the main office.

Orson wasn't supposed to arrive until six. Have I gotten the time wrong? I check my watch—no, it's only three thirty. I cross over to him, my heart racing as he gets out. He's not dressed for the theater; he's in a navy pin-striped business suit—one of his British-cut military-style ones that's beautifully tailored, so I know he bought it in Savile Row. He must have come straight from the office. I'm suddenly conscious that I'm wearing leggings, and my light-gray tee has a dark V of sweat between my breasts.

To my surprise, though, he doesn't comment on it. Instead, he looks serious as he says, "Hey."

My stomach flutters. "What are you doing here?" It sounds accusatory, so I soften it with a smile.

He doesn't smile back, though. Instead, he hesitates. Then he says, "Kingi called me."

I check on Kingi from time to time, asking him if there's anything I can get him, but he always says no, and has seemed happy enough being up to his ears in documents and folders.

"He asked you to come in?" I ask. "What's going on?"

"Not sure yet. Will you take me to see him?" Something about his manner seems official and reserved. He doesn't offer me his hand or come and give me a kiss.

Puzzled, I lead the way into the office building. The woman on reception checks him in and gives him a visitor sticker. Then I take him through to the finance offices at the back.

My father used to work in the biggest office, and George worked in the one next door. He's yet to move into the main one, maybe out of respect for me and Ana, but I'm sure he will eventually, as it has a pleasant view of the vineyards. Today, Kingi is sitting behind the desk, looking at the computer screen and tapping on the keyboard while he talks to George, who's sitting in another chair in front of the desk.

George looks across as we enter. His face is pale, and he looks terrified.

"Hey," Orson says, nodding at Kingi. He then goes over to George and offers his hand. George looks at it as if he doesn't want to, then shakes it out of politeness.

"What's going on?" I ask while Orson brings two more chairs over in front of the desk.

Kingi doesn't answer. Orson gestures at one of the chairs, and I lower onto it and perch on the edge, my spine stiff. Finally, Kingi looks over at me. He's also in a suit, but he's ditched the jacket and rolled up the sleeves of his white shirt, revealing the tattoo on his left arm. His long hair looks as if he's spent time running a hand through it. He also seems serious.

"Guys," I say, "you're scaring me. What's going on?"

Kingi glances at Orson, who nods. Kingi squares the folders on his desk, thinking, before he finally looks at me. "I've carried out a pretty thorough investigation of the commune's books. I haven't finished the audit; that will take about another week. But I think I have a good take now on the finance situation here, and on why the commune is struggling."

"Okay." Part of me wonders why they aren't presenting his findings to the Elders. Why are they telling me?

"As you know," Kingi continues, "Kahukura is a commune rather than an intentional community. This means that its members' income and resources are shared."

"Yes, I understand."

"It's a relatively complicated system. There are several different entities here: there's the vineyard, the retreat, and the commune as a whole, and the money is set up to flow between all of these."

"Okay."

"George and your father looked after the finances between them while your father was alive."

"Yes, I know."

"I'm just trying to explain but it's quite confusing, and—"

"Kingi," I say, "spit it out."

He hesitates. Glances at Orson. Then says, "I found something."

"Something?"

"A discrepancy."

"What kind of discrepancy?"

Orson leans forward, his elbows on his knees and his hands linked. "There are funds missing," he says gently.

I open my mouth, but no words come out. I close it and wait for one of them to explain. When they don't say anything, I finally find my voice. "How much?"

Orson looks at Kingi, who says, "One hundred and twenty-three thousand, four hundred and sixty-two dollars."

My jaw drops. "*What?*"

"The money has been transferred from the vineyard and general commune funds," Kingi states. "Not from the retreat. That's important for you to know."

I'm shocked and baffled. What's he trying to say? I look at Orson, who's watching me, frowning. "I don't understand," I say, switching my glare to Kingi. "Are you saying that someone has taken money from the commune? I don't believe it." I'm starting to grow angry. "We've all worked hard to make Kahukura a success. Nobody here would steal from the others. You're wrong. You have to be. You've missed something, a deposit, or a transfer somewhere."

"It's not one transfer," Kingi says. "It's over fifty smaller ones conducted over a period of a few months so they're harder to spot."

I'm shaking a little now. "You've… you've mixed up the figures, or misunderstood, or—"

I stop as George lets out a long groan and puts his face in his hands. I stare at him, shock making me speechless.

"It was me," he says. "I'm sorry, Scarlett. I'm so sorry."

I stare at the top of his head. He has a kind of tonsure, a bald spot in the middle of a ring of gray hair. I hadn't realized that.

"It was you?" I say eventually. "You've been taking money from the commune?" I look at Kingi, who's sitting with his elbows on the desk, hands clasped, his mouth resting on them, then at Orson, whose expression is undecipherable.

I look back at George. He's now lifted his head, and he's staring at the floor with glassy eyes.

"Why?" I whisper.

I'm not stupid, and whatever Orson thinks, I'm not completely naive. People steal for many reasons. Some do it for mental health reasons, some for the thrill, others are attention seeking, but mostly they don't have the resources to get what they need or desire because of financial hardship.

As far as I know, George doesn't have a psychological disorder. He's not a thrill seeker—he's told me he would never bungee jump or skydive and hates going on rides at theme parks. I can't see he's doing it for attention. It can only be because there's something he wants or needs, and due to the fact that we don't have our own finances, he's felt the urge to take from the commune.

I could sort of understand it if he'd taken fifty bucks or a few hundred or even a few thousand for some luxury item he'd missed, like Scotch or jewelry for his wife or… I don't know… a piece of technology. But a hundred and twenty-three thousand?

"I was going to leave the commune," George says. "And I needed money to do that, for a deposit on a house."

My heart bangs on my ribs. "You were going to leave?" My voice is small enough to fit in a snail shell. Since my father's death, George has been like a rock for me. The thought that he has been considering leaving me is a huge shock.

His eyes meet mine, shining with tears. His shoulders are hunched and he looks in pain, as if he's drunk a beaker of acid and it's eating away at his insides.

"What about Jeannie?" I ask. His wife is amazing, and I always thought she adored the commune. They couldn't have kids, and she loves helping out at the school.

He winces as if he's bitten on a sore tooth. Then he says, "Her too."

It makes sense, I guess. "But don't you get to withdraw your initial investment anyway if you leave?" I ask, confused. I'm sure there's some clause in the agreement everyone signs when they come to Kahukura. George and Jeannie were among the founders of the commune with my parents, and I know they had a house in Auckland that they sold to come here, and they would have put that money into the commune.

"A percentage of it," he says, "and it wouldn't be enough in today's market. I'm so sorry."

"Stop saying you're sorry," I snap. "I don't believe this. You wouldn't do that, not to the commune."

"People do strange things when they're in trouble," he says, and Orson and Kingi exchange glances.

The back of my neck prickles. There's something they're not telling me. I can feel it. My brain works furiously. If he was going to leave, what's stopped him? Why hasn't he taken the money and run? Could it have been the fact that knowing Ana and I would be alone made him think twice?

That raises a question in my mind. "Did Dad know?"

I can tell immediately by George's face that I've guessed correctly. My lips part as realization settles in. "You talked to him about it on the day he died." It's a statement, not a question. I know immediately that I'm right.

"Yes," George says. He brushes his hand over his face. "He'd discovered the discrepancies, and he broached the topic with me. I denied it at first, and tried to think of other reasons the funds could have gone missing, but he knew I was lying."

"Oh God," I whisper. "The shock gave him the heart attack."

He puts his face in his hands again.

Tears well in my eyes in seconds and spill over my lashes, as fast as a tsunami hitting the shore. "You as good as killed him," I say, the words falling from my lips as if I'm hurling stones at him.

"I know." He's shaking. "I'm sorry."

"Stop it! Stop saying that!"

Orson gets suddenly to his feet. "Nope," he says. He puts his hands on his hips, shakes his head, and states again, "Nope."

"Orson…" Kingi also stands. "Don't."

The two of them stare at each other. Orson's chest heaves, but he doesn't say anything.

George lowers his hands and looks at them. "You should leave," he says to Orson.

Orson just shakes his head.

"Go," Kingi says. "I'll deal with it."

"Nope," Orson says a third time. He doesn't look at me, but he squares his shoulders as if bracing himself for a fight.

I get slowly to my feet. "What is it?"

Finally, he looks at me. He thinks for a moment, his blue eyes blazing. Then he says, "Blue pill or red pill?"

Oh shit. He's asking whether I want to stay ignorant, or whether I want to know the truth. He's leaving the decision up to me.

I tremble. Do I want to know? I love my life. I'm happy living in my own small world. Being naive and innocent.

But that's the very definition of cowardly, surely? To refuse to listen to the truth, and wanting to stay oblivious? I'm a better person than that, surely? Orson, like Neo in the Matrix, chose to embrace reality, and I have to do the same.

Besides, how bad can it be?

I swallow hard. "I want to know."

"You're sure?"

"Yes." I'm shaking now.

He looks at George. "Tell her."

George gets up. We're all standing now. George's expression slowly morphs into pure fury. "Get out," he says to Orson. "This is none of your business."

Kingi walks around the table. "He's right. You need to go."

"I'm not going," Orson states. "She's an adult, and she needs to know. Tell her."

"Tell me what?" I stamp my foot like a toddler. "If one of you doesn't tell me what's going on, I'm going to scream, I swear!"

They ignore me, though. George and Orson continue to glare at each other, while Kingi hovers, clearly unsure what to do.

"Tell her," Orson says again.

"This is none of your business," George snaps.

"Tell her!" Orson yells.

"I don't want this," George replies, his voice also rising. "This is my choice."

"If you don't fucking tell her, I will!"

Without warning, George swings at him. Orson—twenty-five years younger and forty pounds lighter—steps back, and George's fist misses his chin by half an inch. George yells and lunges at him, Orson crashes into the desk, sending papers flying, and the two men grapple at one another.

I burst into tears.

"For fuck's sake." Kingi lifts George off Orson as if he's a rag doll and sets him aside. Orson springs to his feet and moves forward, but Kingi positions himself between them and says, "Stop it! You've made Scarlett cry."

Immediately, both men look at me, and I press a hand over my mouth, trying unsuccessfully to stop sobbing.

"Baby," Orson says. He glares at George then. "Look what you've done."

"I haven't done anything—this is your fault."

"Guys!" Kingi yells. He blows out a long breath and gives George a pitying look. "Come on. I understand why you didn't want her to know, but it's pointless. Just tell her, for fuck's sake."

George looks at me, and his expression is filled with such pain that it physically hurts me.

"Scarlett," he says. "Sweetheart…" He shakes his head, unable to speak, too overcome with emotion.

I give Orson a pleading glance.

"It was your father," he says. "Who took the money. I'm so sorry."

I blink. "What?"

George sinks back into his chair. Silence falls in the room.

Orson flicks back the sides of his jacket and slides his hands into his trouser pockets. "Your father was the one who siphoned off the funds. I'm guessing he was trying to find the money to pay for your mother's treatment, but he wasn't able to get enough in time."

"After she died," Kingi says, "he started to transfer it back into the accounts, disguising it as donations, but once I knew what to look for it was easy to find."

"You're wrong," I say, trembling. "Dad wouldn't do something like that. He wouldn't steal from the commune."

Orson and Kingi don't react, though. Kingi's face creases with pity, and Orson just frowns. They truly believe it.

It can't be true, though. Dad would never have done anything like that. The whole ethos of the commune is that everything is shared so nobody has to go without. He would never have stolen money.

And yet I would never have thought that George would have either…

I force myself to confront the truth. Mum was dying. The treatment that was most likely to cure her cost a little more than the missing amount. Dad had turned down Spencer's generous offer. What if he took the money out of desperation? Oh God…

I stare at George. "Aren't you angry that they're saying this? Tell them that Dad wouldn't do it!"

George sends me a look that's heavy with sorrow.

"George was going to take the blame," Orson says. "Even though it would almost certainly have meant going to prison."

My jaw drops for the umpteenth time. "That's why you were upset when the Elders agreed to the audit."

"I didn't want you to know," George says miserably. He glares at Orson. "It was my choice. You had no right to tell her. Kingi said you loved her. He said you'd want to protect her."

"I do," Orson says, shocking me. "But not at the expense of an innocent man going to prison." He looks at me then. "I thought you should know the truth."

I'm still sobbing, and I'm finding it hard to catch my breath. My heart is racing, I feel dizzy, and I have an odd sensation in my hands, which spasm, the fingers curling toward the palm. I sway, and the room spins.

"Catch her," someone says.

"Did she faint?"

"Jesus, is she okay?"

"Put this behind her."

"She's hyperventilating. That's all."

"Sit here, honey. You're okay." Orson's voice wraps around me like a blanket. "Lower your head. That's it. Now remember how you taught me to breathe properly? From the belly, not the chest. Here, breathe with me." He takes my hand and puts it on his body, where his diaphragm would be.

I feel his belly rise and fall and attempt to breathe with him.

"You'll be okay," he murmurs. One of his hands is resting over mine. With the other, he reaches out and strokes my head. "It's just the shock. You'll be fine."

I breathe with him, I don't know for how long, but eventually my sobs slow, and I start breathing regularly again. The world stops spinning, my fingers unfurl, and I become aware of my surroundings again. Orson has dropped to his haunches before me, and as I raise my head, I look into his eyes.

He smiles, cups my face, and brushes my tears away with his thumbs. "You're so fucking beautiful."

"I'm sorry," I whisper.

"Jesus, I'm not surprised you felt faint after a shock like that." He kisses my forehead. "I'm so sorry. Did I do the right thing by telling you?" His brows draw together.

I remember then—my father stole a vast amount of money from the commune. He stole from his friends—from people we considered family. I feel as if someone has stuck a dagger in my throat and dragged it all the way down through my body to my stomach. I would give anything to un-know that knowledge.

But then I look at George, at the misery on his face, and my heart goes out to him. He was prepared to go to prison for my father, and to protect Ana and me. The thought makes me want to bawl my eyes out.

I rise and walk away from him, and he slowly pushes himself up. I stop a few steps away, fold my arms, and turn and face the three men. Orson is frowning; George looks devastated; Kingi's expression shows concern and pity.

"So what's the situation?" I ask, lifting my chin. "How much did Dad pay back, and what is left owing?"

"Don't worry about that now," Orson says.

"I'm not a child."

"I know." He gives me a steady look. "Kingi will complete the audit and then deliver a report."

"To the Elders?"

All three of them exchange glances. "We haven't decided that yet," Orson says.

"Are you going to call the police?"

Again, he says, "We haven't decided."

I nod. "Well, I'll leave you to it. I need to get some fresh air." I turn and walk out of the room.

I've just reached the main office when Orson catches up with me. He slides a hand beneath my arm to stop me, but I move it away, and the woman on reception glances at us. She's obviously heard the yelling and commotion, and she saw him take my arm. We deal with women who've suffered trauma every day, and all of us here are very sensitive to men being physical in that way.

"Everything all right?" she asks me cautiously.

I nod stiffly. "I'm fine."

"You want me to call Lee?" Our maintenance guy and a couple of his friends double in the commune as security on the rare occasions that the women at the retreat have male relatives turn up looking for them.

Orson looks startled, and I say hastily, "No, thank you." I gesture with my head for him to follow me outdoors.

We go out into the late summer sun, and it's only then that I realize how cold I am. The warmth of the sun's rays penetrates my tee, and I rub my arms with my hands, feeling goosebumps.

"I'm so sorry," he says, "I shouldn't have caught your arm like that."

"It's all right."

"Honey, let's go somewhere quiet and talk."

"I just need some time on my own," I whisper.

"Please…"

"I can't." I'm shaking with the effort of holding in my emotion. "I need to go home." I turn and walk away.

I stride out, heading for my house, and I assume he's stayed at the office until he suddenly appears at my side, matching my pace.

"Go away," I tell him.

"We need to talk."

"I just want to be alone."

"We're a couple, sweetheart, and that means we talk to each other about what's bothering or upsetting us."

"We're not a couple," I snap. "We've fucked a few times, that's all."

If I hope to have shocked him into leaving me alone, I'm about to be disappointed. "Bullshit," he says. "I love you."

I stop as we reach my house, and I unlock the door. Then I turn to glare at him as he moves forward as if to follow me in. "Go away. You don't love me. You don't even know me."

"I know enough to love what I see."

"Stop it. You don't love me."

"Don't tell me what I feel."

"See, want, take? That's what this is. You want me, so you've decided you're going to have me. But don't my feelings factor into this equation?"

His lips twist. "Of course."

"I like you, Orson, but I don't want any part of your lifestyle. Or your world, which values money and belongings above people."

"Jesus, come on…"

I'm so upset that my words flow like water out of a broken pipe. "You think money can buy anything, including affection and love. You think throwing money at me—taking me to nice places, eating good food, buying me expensive jewelry—will make me fall in love with you, but you're wrong."

"That's not what I think at all…"

"Look what money did to my father." Tears well in my eyes again. "It's like acid. It eats away at all the decency in a person. He was a good man, and he opened this commune and the retreat because he wanted to help people, and to live with others without the burden of money and capitalism weighing us down. He wanted us to be a real community, and rely on and help each other. To be like a family. But then Mum got sick, and he was terrified of losing her. The real world doesn't care about who gets the treatment, though does it? As long as the drug company gets its money. Your mum got her treatment because you could afford it, but my family couldn't."

He looks away, across the green. I feel a twinge of guilt deep inside—it's not his fault that he has money. If we were rich, Dad would have gotten the treatment without a second thought. But I've gone too far to stop now.

"He would never have done it if it wasn't for Mum," I say.

Orson looks back at me. He hesitates. Then he says, "Blue pill or red pill?"

I start shaking. "What do you mean?" Surely there's nothing more?

But he says, "Do you want to know everything?"

I swallow hard. "Yes."

He nods. "It wasn't the first time."

I blink. "What?"

"It wasn't the first time he'd stolen money."

Chapter Twenty-Four

Orson

Scarlett's jaw sags. "What are you talking about?"

I pause, having second thoughts about telling her. She's very upset, and this is only going to make things worse. But it's too late now. She wanted to know everything.

"Dad told me on the night of Kingi's party, after I confronted him with what you'd told me. I said Kingi was auditing the commune's finances because it was struggling, and I said I had my suspicions about George. And Dad said there was something I needed to know. That his feud with Blake wasn't just about Amiria. He said when they were in their first year at uni, one of their courses involved developing a business proposal for a university incubator program."

"A what?"

"It's a business development initiative run by a university that helps students turn ideas into real businesses. Because of what happened with his birth parents, Dad had this idea for setting up a retreat for women, and Blake thought it was a great idea and was really excited about the notion of helping others with their business knowledge. The initiative offered seed funding—that means a small amount of money to get started, as well as mentorship and networking opportunities. It was organized as a competition, and winning it would have meant money for their new company, as well as kudos in the business community. Dad said he brought the drive and numbers, while Blake brought the big-picture vision."

"Kahukura was Spencer's idea?"

"Yes, but they also both had a friend at uni who'd been abused by her partner, and Blake fully supported the idea."

She looks dumbfounded. "So what went wrong?"

I take a deep breath. "Blake stole from the project fund to buy materials, and he fudged the results to make the project succeed. He said they were going to win anyway, and he just gave them a little push. Dad was furious when he found out what Blake had done because he wanted to win on merit, not manipulation. He believes in hard work, integrity, and earning everything. Blake said he believed in helping people and fixing broken systems, even if it meant bending the rules. That the end justifies the means. This happened in the same month as your mum choosing your dad over mine."

She presses a hand over her heart. Hopefully she won't faint again.

"Blake went on to set up Kahukura when he left university," I continue. "Dad was angry because he felt Blake took all the credit for it when it was actually his idea. He hated the way Blake made the retreat part of the commune because he felt it turned it into some kind of bohemian safe haven, as if trauma could be cured with incense and group hugs. He was convinced it became a utopian mess that was more about ideals than a place for real recovery. At the time he wanted nothing to do with it. He thought they worked together well and that they could have created something amazing, but Blake ruined it. So he walked away—both from their friendship and from the retreat. He turned his talents to making money from property, but it's why he embraced the idea of the Midnight Circle so wholeheartedly. He believes in helping those less fortunate than himself, and he's brought me up to be the same. But he acknowledged that despite not agreeing with many of your father's actions, he has helped a lot of women."

It's a long speech, and I'm a little breathless when I finish. I so want Scarlett to believe me and to understand that Dad doesn't think Blake is all bad.

She's trembling now, though. Oh shit…

"I don't…" She can't get the words out. "Why…" She gives up and starts crying—great heart-rending sobs that punch me right in the stomach. Her knees give way, and I catch her just before she falls to the floor.

I lift her into my arms, open the door, carry her inside, and push the door shut behind me. I take her into the small living room and over to the sofa, and I turn and sit on it, cradling her on my lap.

She curls up into a ball, and I hold her while she cries, and cries, and cries. I don't move. I rest my lips on her hair, while outside the sun sinks toward the horizon, and the shadows creep across the grass.

At one point, I hear footsteps outside. I'd texted Kingi quickly before I caught up with Scarlett, suggesting he and George give us some space, so I don't think it's him. It turns out to be Ana, already looking concerned, so I assume she's heard of the kerfuffle at the office. She slips into the house, sees us immediately, and comes over.

"Scarlett," she whispers, dropping to her knees in front of us. "Honey." She puts a hand on her back, but Scarlett turns away from her and buries her face in my shirt.

Ana withdraws her hand. "She's been so strong," she says. "She's held us all together with both hands since Mum died. She hasn't allowed herself to grieve."

So it's all pouring out of her in one go.

"What happened?" Ana whispers.

I look at Scarlett, who's still sobbing. "You'll have to talk to Scarlett about that."

"All right." Ana says. "I'll make a cup of tea." It's the cure-all for everything, and she goes into the kitchen.

The sound of the kettle and the clink of a spoon in the mugs somehow grounds me, and it must do the same to Scarlett, because she gradually relaxes in my arms. She turns her face and rests her cheek on my shoulder, her lips close to my throat, but she doesn't attempt to move away. I keep my arms tight around her, happy to hold her.

Ana comes back out with two mugs of tea and leaves them on the low table in front of us.

"Thank you," I say softly.

She smiles, her expression softening as she looks at us both. "I'm going to take a shower." She bends and kisses Scarlett's head, then walks out, and soon I hear a door closing.

"How are you doing?" I murmur.

"I'm okay." Her whisper is so soft I almost miss it.

"You want a sip of tea?"

She clears her throat, then pushes herself up. She wipes her face, gets up, and retrieves some tissues from a box on the table. For a moment I think she's going to sit in one of the armchairs and put some distance between us. But after she's blown her nose and wiped her face, she picks up her tea, then comes to sit next to me, turning toward me. She sips the tea, then rests her temple on the back of the sofa and lets out a long sigh. She looks incredibly sad and defeated.

I unbutton my jacket, move forward to slip it off, pick up my tea, then sit back again.

It occurs to me that I don't experience high-emotion situations very often. At work I defuse tension with humor and I'm careful to deal with any hot tempers by deflecting and distracting the upset person. Socially, my friends and family are mostly high achievers who are also keen to remove drama from their lives. Most of my relationships have come to a mutual end. So this whole experience has unsettled me. Maybe I'm more like my father than I care to admit.

I can't imagine what she must be feeling. She hasn't asked me to leave, but other than give her a hug, I'm not sure how to comfort her. How can I make things better, when she must feel as if her whole world is falling apart?

"Did I do the right thing in telling you?" I ask. She didn't answer me in the office, and I feel a heaviness inside at the thought that I'm the one who's crushed her.

She looks down at her mug and traces a finger around the rim. "I wish I didn't know. But that's not the same thing. It would be hypocritical to tell you that truth is the most important thing to me, then to say you shouldn't have told me."

"It doesn't make it any easier to handle."

"No, it doesn't."

We sit there quietly, sipping our tea. I hear the bathroom door open, and Ana's footsteps heading down to what I presume is her room, and the door opens and closes.

There's maybe an hour until sunset. The sunlight pouring into the room is the color of treacle. Scarlett gives a little shiver, as if she's cold, although it's warm in the room. Or maybe it's a shudder as she thinks of what she's learned today. I feel as if a cyclone has blown through the village, and now the wind is dying down, and it's time to deal with the fallout—fixing all the fences that have blown over, and replacing the tiles that have been ripped from the roofs.

"Talk to me," I say.

She scratches at a mark on her mug. "You said my dad thought that helping people was the most important thing, even if it meant bending the rules. Do you agree?"

I inhale, then exhale slowly. I need to answer this carefully. "I understand why your dad took the money. He loved your mum, and he didn't want to lose her. But I think he should have gone to the

Elders and asked if he could borrow from the funds. I thought that was what the idea of the commune was about—dealing with problems together."

She gives a small nod. "He could also have accepted your dad's offer of the money."

"Yes, true."

"Pride stopped him. That stupid feud. If he'd accepted Spencer's offer, both of my parents might still be here." She wipes fresh tears from her face.

I don't reply to that because she's not wrong. Instead, I say, "How are you feeling now?"

"Hurt. Sad. Ashamed. Angry."

"At George?"

"No. He's a sweetheart. He just wanted to protect me and Ana."

"Are you angry at me?"

She gives a small smile. "No, of course not."

"At my dad?"

"No. At myself."

Now I'm baffled. "None of it is your fault."

"Maybe not, but I'm embarrassed and ashamed about what a fool I've been. Ever since we've met, I've talked to you as if we at the commune are somehow superior to you. I said you are married to money, and we are all about family, and community, and love, and roses, and blah blah blah…" Her voice holds a ton of sarcasm, and her cheeks flush.

Pain flares inside my chest. I wanted to remove her rose-tinted spectacles, but I regret it now. I loved her positivity, and the way she always found the silver lining in every cloud. I thought that her naivety would eventually cause problems, and I was right, but that doesn't make it any easier to watch. I feel as if I'm observing a scientist carrying out vivisection on a baby rabbit. The aim might be to make sure a drug is safe for consumption, so the outcome is a positive one, but that doesn't mean the process isn't cruel and heartbreaking to watch.

"I feel so incredibly foolish," she whispers. "I thought my dad was perfect."

I smile. "Every girl does."

She carries on as if I haven't spoken. "Everyone must have been laughing at me. Stupid, innocent Scarlett, thinking we'd built something worthwhile here."

"You have," I say firmly. "What's happened today hasn't changed that."

"I thought my father had values, and integrity, and principles, but it was all just a house of cards." Tears tip over her lashes. I don't think she's even aware of them.

"Do you believe there are times when the end justifies the means?" I ask. "I mean, I know you think the same healthcare should be available to everyone, regardless of whether they have money or not. So do I, as it happens. So bearing in mind that the system sucks, do you understand why he did it?"

"I understand. But he shouldn't have stolen from his friends and family. Mum wouldn't have wanted that."

"No, I suppose not."

She looks away, out of the window, across the green. "Your analogy of The Matrix was very apt."

"Maybe. But don't forget that the moral of the movie is that knowledge and self-awareness lead to positive growth and change, even if the truth is painful and uncomfortable."

She looks back at me and wipes her face again. "I understand. But I wish it didn't hurt quite so much." She starts crying again.

I take her mug and put it with mine on the table, then pull her into my arms again. I turn and lie back on the cushions, stretching out and bringing her with me, turning a little so she's tucked against the back of the sofa and can't fall off.

Both her parents have died. She has a younger sister she's obviously felt the need to look after and protect, and she also found out that she owns the land that Kahukura is built on, which is a huge responsibility. And now she's discovered something about her father that has shaken all her core values and principles like an earthquake. She'll have to deal with the aftershocks for a long while. But hopefully when she rebuilds, the foundations will be stronger for it.

Half an hour later, Ana comes out, leans over the sofa, and sees that Scarlett is asleep. She goes off, returns with a blanket, and covers us both.

"Thank you," I whisper.

She gives a small smile and returns to her room.

I fall into a light doze, only stirring when Scarlett finally wakes. It's dark now, the only light from the moon outside, which casts us in a silvery light.

"How are you doing?" I ask as we both sit up.

"I'm a bit stiff." She gives a watery smile. "I need to go to bed. Do you... want to come with me?"

I'm tempted, but I say, "No, I'll head back to my apartment. I think you need some time alone, and to explain everything to Ana. So I'll talk to you tomorrow. Is that okay?"

She nods. "I'm sorry we missed the play."

"It's fine. Try to get some sleep."

"All right."

I pick up my jacket and car keys, and we cross to the door. She opens it, and I go out, then stop on the doorstep.

I turn and cup her face. "Everything's going to be okay," I tell her.

"It doesn't feel like it at the moment," she whispers.

"I know. But you'll be fine. You're strong Scarlett." I lower my head and press my lips to hers, just once, soft as a feather. "Trust me."

"I do."

Surprised, I kiss her nose, then lower my hand and move back. We study each other for a moment. Then I give a small smile, turn, and walk away, hearing the door close behind me.

Chapter Twenty-Five

Scarlett

I open Ana's door, but she's already asleep. I'm dog tired too, exhausted and emotionally wrung out, but when I go to bed I find myself lying awake in the darkness, my brain and my heart locked in battle.

As the night wears on, I work through a plethora of emotions, from hurt to shame to anger to confusion. How can someone spend a lifetime teaching the goodness of people and the importance of friends and family, only to steal from that community when he felt like it? Did he spend weeks agonizing over whether he should do it? Or did he move quickly once he discovered we couldn't afford Mum's treatment? Orson's announcement that Dad had stolen before suggests it wouldn't have taken him long to decide.

I think about when I asked Orson's thoughts on whether the end justifies the means. He was very diplomatic and said he understood why Dad had taken the money, but that he should have gone to the Elders and asked for their help. I agree with him—I thought that was the idea of living in a commune, too. We're supposed to solve problems together.

I feel as if the world has tipped on its axis, and the south pole is now the north. I thought Spencer was heartless and cruel and thought only of money, and my father was the one with outstanding values and principles. But it turns out that Spencer is honest and sincere and has integrity, and my father was… what? A thief who bent the rules if it meant he could get what he wanted.

I cry for a while, feeling lonely and full of self-pity. Then, as I lie there and let my tears dry on my cheeks, I remember the phone Orson gave me. It's on my bedside table, and I pick it up and touch the screen. Sure enough, he texted me, over an hour ago, so he's probably gone to bed now. It's just a short message, but it touches me to think he was thoughtful enough to send it.

Thinking of you. You were right to take the red pill. Be like Neo, and embrace the truth and use it to shape your own destiny. I love you. O x

I put the phone back on the bedside table, then pick up Mr. Bearcub and bring him under the covers. I haven't hugged a teddy bear since I was a kid, but I wrap my arms around the soft toy, enjoying the comfort he brings.

Orson is right. Regardless of how painful and uncomfortable it is, it's still better that I know the truth.

All children are innocent, but they all lose that purity at some point. Everyone has to take that step into adulthood. I thought I'd grown up, but I realize now that although I'd passed through puberty, I hadn't matured. Being brought up in the commune was always going to affect my ideologies and views. Orson said I was wearing rose-tinted glasses, and he was right. I've been naive and idealistic, and I haven't seen the world the way it really is.

It's hard not to feel foolish. But I feel as if I have two choices. I can let the truth eat away at me like acid, become cynical, decide that everything I've learned and the person I've been up to this point has all been a sham, and turn my back on my beliefs and my way of life.

Or, in Orson's words, I can embrace the truth and use it to shape my own destiny.

I take a deep breath and let it out slowly. I mustn't wallow in self-pity. The fact that Dad stole money doesn't mean the work he did at Kahukura was pointless, or that our way of life here isn't commendable and worth pursuing. We help a lot of women at the retreat, and I don't believe my healing program is worthless.

My father has fallen off his pedestal, and as he's crashed to the ground, he's brought my life down in the process. But the world isn't really falling apart. Like a pile of children's bricks, it was never built on a solid foundation. *I* put him on the pedestal. And even though he has to take some of the blame for forming my ideologies, it's been my choice to stay at the commune and isolate myself from the world. Ana is less idealistic and naive than I am because she travels to the city frequently and has a phone and is on social media. I'm the only one I can blame for my innocence.

I think of the things I've said to Orson and wince. No wonder he's mocked me from time to time, saying things like *I don't want my chakras located*, and *I don't need to know if the moon's in Uranus*. That was at the beginning though, before we got to know one another.

He got angry with George because he thought he insulted me. He wanted me to meet his friends and family. He defended me in front of his father. And he said *I love you*. Yes, he's an elitist capitalist who believes some people are superior to others. Yes, he thinks everything and everyone has a price, and that money can buy anything. But he and his father give so much to charity. I feel in my heart that he's a good man. Or am I being naive again?

I'm frightened of trusting my gut, because it's led me astray so wildly. And I feel panicky at the thought of dating Orson, because how will I ever be able to convince him, his father, or myself that it has nothing to do with his money? I've glimpsed into his world and seen what money can buy—safety, security, and comfort. I'd be lying if I said I didn't find that attractive.

And yet… that's not why I want to be with him. I'm shallow enough to be drawn to his biceps and his gorgeous hair, but that's not the only reason I like him—I find his confidence attractive, even though it borders on arrogance, and I adore his hard-working attitude, his philanthropic heart, and his deep-rooted desire for justice and fairness, which was evident in the way he defended me.

Am I going to let what's happened spoil something that could be real and beautiful?

My eyelids are drooping. It's very late, probably near to two a.m. Mr. Bearcub is soft in my arms, and I bury my nose in his fur, remembering how wonderful it felt to cuddle up to his namesake in bed. I miss Orson so much. I wish he'd stayed. But I know he was right. I need to talk to Ana, and we have to decide what we're going to do about the funds that Dad stole. We need to talk to George, and the Elders too, probably, because I can't imagine keeping it from them. Only when I've sorted out that part of my life will I be able to think about my love life, and where I go from here.

I don't know what the future holds. I can't picture it. I'm in love with Orson, I think. I miss him. I want to be with him. But I can't envisage how it would work. Despite what's happened, I don't know that I can transfer myself to his world, and he certainly wouldn't want to live in mine.

I fall asleep, and I dream of flying, of escaping into the bright blue sky, and leaving all my fears and worries behind me. And then I spend the rest of the dream searching for a bearcub in the forest, sad because I'm unable to track him down.

*

The next day, I rise when my alarm goes off at seven, even though I've only had five hours' sleep, make Ana and me some coffee, and sit with her and go through everything. She's shocked and upset, but probably less than me, which just reinforces to me how innocent I've been.

We talk for a long time about what we're going to do, and eventually decide the best thing is to talk to George and Kingi, get them to prepare a brief report on their findings, and then take it to the Elders at their meeting this evening.

I have yoga and Jiu Jitsu classes today, and I'm taking several groups to the Waiora, but after I shower and dress, I make time first to deliver the message to George and Kingi where they're working in the main office, despite it being Saturday. They both promise they'll have the report ready by six p.m., which is when the Elders are meeting. After that, I head off to the retreat for my first class.

Orson texted me this morning asking if I managed to get any sleep. We exchanged a few messages, and then he said he had to go to a meeting, and I haven't heard from him since.

I'm therefore surprised when I come out of my class and see his Aston Martin parked out the front of the office. I go in and look down the corridor to see that the door to the finance office is closed.

"Is Orson here?" I ask the woman on reception.

She nods. "They've asked not to be disturbed."

Maybe Kingi needed some help with the figures. I hesitate, wondering whether to knock on the door or text him and let him know I'm out here, but I figure that he'll come and get me if he needs me. So I leave them to it and return to the retreat, collect my first healing group, and take them to the Waiora.

It's a blustery day, the wind whipping the clouds across the sky, but it's still warm. I feel the need for healing as much as the women I'm with, and so I spend a long time at the pool, leading them through a guided meditation, and hoping that the spirit of the rainbow falls will help me heal and guide me forward.

When we return, Orson's car has gone. I text him, but although he replies, it's only to say that he's in a meeting and he'll catch up with me later.

I don't hear from him for the rest of the day, but I keep myself busy with classes, with helping at lunch, and with trips to the Waiora.

At 5:45 p.m., Ana wishes me luck, then heads off to the refectory to help with the evening meal. I still haven't heard from Orson, and I feel oddly unsettled because of it.

I go into the town hall, walk through the lobby, and cross the main hall to the Elders' meeting room. I hear someone speaking as I approach, then a murmur of voices, so it sounds as if the meeting has started already. It surprises me, as it's not quite six and someone is always late.

I pause in the doorway—and stare at the table in surprise. The eight elders are there, including George. And so is Kingi and, to my surprise, Orson. My jaw drops—I hadn't seen the Aston and had no idea he was there.

The center of the table is filled with the remains of a meal—plates with leftover sandwiches and flakes of pastry, as if they've all been there for several hours.

"Scarlett," Richard says, spotting me. "Come in, dear. Take a seat."

My heart races, but I force my feet to move and walk forward to take the empty chair at the other end of the table to him. Orson sits halfway along the table on my right, next to Kingi. George sits opposite them. Orson meets my gaze, gives a small smile, and winks at me. I don't respond, though, feeling too panicky and unsure of myself.

I look around the other faces, at the people I know so well, and I'm relieved that there doesn't appear to be any anger evident. I can see that a couple of the women's faces are red, as if they've been crying. But most of them also smile at me as our eyes meet, including George, who looks better than he did this morning.

"Am I late?" I ask, convinced they told me six p.m.

Richard shakes his head. "No, no. George asked us to come in earlier." He leans his elbows on the table and his mouth on his hands for a moment, and gradually the others fall quiet. "Scarlett," he begins, "George has told us about the initial findings of Kingi's audit. He says he made you aware of this yesterday. Do you understand what has happened?"

I give a stiff nod. "Over a period of time, my father withdrew funds from the commune, the vineyard, and the retreat, probably in the hope of paying for my mother's cancer treatment."

To my surprise, he shakes his head. "That's not quite correct. Yes, he took money from the commune and the vineyard, but he did not take anything from the retreat's account."

I frown. "Isn't that just semantics?"

"No, we don't believe it is. We actually think it's very important." He blows out a long breath. "Obviously, the news has shocked us all. Despite setting up the commune and encouraging us to help one another, Blake was a very private man, and none of us had any idea that the best treatment for your mother's cancer would have been available privately. My guess is that he didn't want to admit a desire to pay for private treatment, because that goes against our ethics here. But of course he didn't want to lose your mother, either, which is why he attempted to find the money himself."

"He told me he would have paid it back over time and nobody would even have noticed," George states.

"It's all very unfortunate," Richard says. "We're a family here. We miss them both, and we all understand why he felt driven to help your mum, even if we don't agree with it."

I glance at Orson. He's leaning on the arm of his chair, his fingers resting on his lips, so I can't tell what he's thinking.

"Kingi has kindly written up his initial findings in a report for us," Richard continues, putting a hand on a manila folder that lies open on the table in front of him with a few sheets of paper inside.

I clear my throat. "How much money is outstanding?"

Richard tidies the sheets of paper, closes the folder, then looks at me. Finally, he smiles. "Nothing."

My eyebrows rise. "What do you mean?"

"Orson spent a few hours with Kingi and George this morning," Richard says, "in order to gain a full understanding of the commune's financial situation. Then he called an emergency meeting of the Midnight Circle. He put forward a proposal, and all the members of the Circle signed the agreement form on the spot. The proposal includes seventeen and half million dollars for the sale of the Waiora, and a further charity donation to the retreat of seven and a half million dollars. So the proposal is for twenty-five million dollars."

MIDNIGHT ENEMY

My jaw drops. His initial offer was for fifteen, which is much more than it was valued at. George pushed him to seventeen and a half. But now he's offering twenty-five? Fifteen million more than what the Waiora is worth?

I look at Orson. He meets my gaze steadily, not moving.

"The proposal includes a clause that Blake's remaining debt be wiped," Richard continues.

My throat tightens. Oh God. Orson…

"Scarlett," Richard says gently, "we know this has been a huge shock to you. The land that Kahukura is built on belongs to you, and you have every right to close the commune and keep the money from the sale of the Waiora for yourself. The charity donation would go to the retreat, or in the event of its closure, to the Women's Refuge. But we're hoping that you will stay, and keep the retreat up and running."

"We've talked a lot about the commune and our way of life," George says. "Obviously there have been hurt feelings, and some loss of trust because of the events. So we're putting forward the idea of changing the commune into an intentional community. This would mean that the members have control of their own finances, but that we would continue to work together to run the retreat, to collaborate on tasks and the maintenance of Kahukura, and to share resources. Does that make sense?"

I nod, because I don't trust myself to speak.

"I would promote David to joint financial director," George says, naming one of the men in the commune who is an accountant, "and from now on we'll always have two people looking after the finances."

"We would like to spend the majority of the money from the sale on improving the site," Richard says, "repairing buildings, building new ones, and maybe on encouraging some new blood into the community. The donation would be spent entirely on the retreat—on improving the facilities and enlarging the accommodation so we can accept more women and families."

"But it all depends on you," George says. He takes the manila folder from Richard, rises, and brings it over to me. He puts it on the table before me, opens the folder, and shows me the contents. "This is the proposal." He points out the clause about wiping my father's debt, and the way the money is to be broken down into the sale and the donation. He turns the page to reveal a space for my signature. "You don't have to sign now," he says. "You're welcome to take it to the lawyer you saw, or someone else to get independent advice. We don't want you to feel pressured in any way."

I swallow hard and look around the table. Despite his words, I can see the fear on their faces. They're worried I'm going to say that I want to take the money and run. That I want to close the commune and the retreat, which would essentially leave them all homeless.

I'm not surprised they're afraid. Many of them have been here over thirty years. They've built what they thought was a solid foundation for a place to live and bring up their children, formed around a common purpose and ideology, which is basically that if we pull together, we can achieve more than if we work alone.

What my father did hasn't destroyed that. All he did was prove that he was human.

I look at Kingi, who's frowning, but who smiles briefly as he sees my gaze fall on him. Then I look at Orson. He's not wearing a suit, and instead has donned dark chinos and a navy shirt. He wanted to dress down to put the Elders at ease. He's a smart guy who knows how to read a room.

He's offered to pay off my father's debt and make sure that Kahukura is safe and secure for the foreseeable future. If it's what I want. *If* I decide to stay. Again, he's leaving the choice in my hands. He's not pressuring me to leave. Quite the opposite, really. If I stay, it means the divide will remain between us, because even if the commune does become an intentional community, our ideologies will always be different.

But I have to put aside my personal feelings right now. I have to decide what's best for the people in this room, for the members of the commune, and for the women and children who come to the retreat.

And there's not really a decision to be made, is there?

"Can I borrow your pen?" I ask Kingi.

There's a collective intake of breath around the table. Kingi picks it up and passes it to me. What a shock—it's a Montblanc. Ana has a thing for stationery, and she showed me their website once. I remember this one—it's a limited-edition Muhammed Ali pen. I swear it was worth seven thousand dollars.

I slide off the cap, turn it in my fingers, then sign on the dotted line. Then I glance up at Orson, who smiles.

Chapter Twenty-Six

Orson

After Scarlett signs the contract, the Elders want to talk to Scarlett about the allocation of the new funds. Kingi and I have no more to contribute, so we tell them we'll leave them to it and pack up our briefcases.

Scarlett rises with us, informs them she'll be back shortly, and accompanies us out.

Outside, the sun is heading for the horizon, and the commune is bathed in a marmalade light, thick and a deep yellow-orange. The solar lights around the duck pond and outside the buildings have come on, and the place glows in the peace of the dusky evening.

"I wanted to say thank you," Scarlett says to Kingi. "For everything you've done."

"I'm sorry for any distress it's caused you," he replies.

"It's better to know the truth," she says. "Red pill, right?"

He nods. "Always." He glances at me. "I'll see you back at the club?"

"Yeah, I'll head over shortly."

He smiles at Scarlett, then heads off to his car.

I look back at Scarlett. She has dark shadows under her eyes, so I don't imagine she got much sleep last night. But I'm thrilled that she's signed the papers. It means she's not going to sell up, close the commune, and flee. It means she's probably staying.

"Thank you," she says, looking into my eyes. "For your incredibly generous donation."

"You're welcome. You run a worthwhile cause here. We should have included you ages ago."

"Your father signed the papers?"

"Yes—all members have to agree to every donation."

"I know he said he wanted to let go of his resentment, but I have to admit, I didn't think he'd be able to."

"He said that the way you forgave him for his behavior that night convinced him. And also the fact that I told him I love you." I smile.

She blinks up at me. "You can't say that. We've hardly dated at all."

"My dad said loving someone and being in love aren't the same thing, and maybe he's right. Perhaps love is something that comes with time. But I'm definitely *in* love with you. Are you in love with me?" I tip my head so I can look deep into her eyes.

Her lips part and a light flush, pink as the sunset, appears in her cheeks. "Maybe. But I don't know how it could possibly work between us."

"We'll make it work," I say firmly.

Her brows draw together.

I take her hands. "Tell me what's on your mind."

"I can't."

"Why?"

"It doesn't make sense to talk about Where This is Going so early on…"

"I don't see a problem with having a map to follow on the journey. Doesn't mean you have to stick to it."

She swallows hard. "It's just… I'm afraid you're going to make me leave the commune."

It's my turn to frown. "I'm not going to make you do anything you don't want to do."

"But I don't see how it can work unless I do, because you're not going to want to come and live here."

"Well, I have to point out that you haven't asked me…"

Her mouth opens, but no words come out.

I blow out a long breath. "Look, you're right in that I have no great desire to live in a commune. But good relationships involve compromise, right?"

She nods.

"So for now maybe a few times a week we could go on dates. Go to the city for a meal or a show, or you could come to the club and spend some time with Marama and Elizabeth, who both really liked you, and I'm happy to come and meet your friends here. If you want to, sometimes you can stay with me at my apartment, or at the club, or I can stay with you here—I have no objection to that. And then maybe, down the line, we could… I don't know… get a place of our own a mile or two away, on the coast? Close enough so you could walk or ride to the commune every day? But somewhere of our own so we'd have the privacy I prefer?"

She presses her fingers to her lips. "Do you mean that?" she whispers, her voice husky with emotion.

"I do. I mean obviously it's one step at a time. But I want you to understand that we have a future, if we're prepared to make it work. And I want it to. I want to be with you, Scarlett. I want you in my life."

I cup her face and move closer to her, and she looks up into my eyes. Hers are shining, and her bottom lip trembles, but she doesn't let the tears fall.

"You've been so brave," I murmur. "I know you've had George and the others at the commune to help, but you've had an awful lot to deal with, and what's happened over the past few weeks has been very hard on you."

"I've felt so alone," she whispers.

"I know. But you're not alone now. I'm here. I don't want to interfere at all, but I would like to help you and the others make Kahukura a well-run institution that funds itself, with a strong financial structure."

"You've already been so generous…"

I hesitate. Then I say, "I have something to admit to you."

Her eyebrows rise. "Oh?"

I rub the back of my neck. Then I confess, "My pain has gone."

Her mouth forms an O. "Really?"

"Yeah. I only realized yesterday, when I went to take my morning painkillers and realized I didn't need them. Look, I'm a man of fact and figures. I believe in proof and evidence, and science over mysticism. Despite this, I know you won't believe me, but I like to think I'm open minded. Something that's happened over the past few weeks has helped my pain. Maybe I've just healed naturally. Perhaps it was being at the Waiora, or you laying your hands on me. It could just be being with you." I smile. "Or maybe it's because I've finally made peace with my father, and like you said, it was internal stress and tension causing the pain. But the fact is that I feel better. I've seen you at work, and I truly believe you can help people in trouble. I believe in what you do, and I want to help you make the world a better place." I wince. "Don't tell Kingi I said that. I'll never hear the end of it."

She gives me such a beautiful smile that my heart fills with joy.

"Thank you," I tell her sincerely. I kiss her, briefly, a couple of times. Then, when she lifts her arms around my neck, I give her a longer kiss, wrapping my arms around her.

When we're done, she lowers her arms and laughs as she rubs her nose. "Will I see you tomorrow?"

"Definitely. You can tell me how the rest of the meeting goes."

"All right." She moves backward, holding my hand until she has to let it drop. "See you soon."

I wave goodbye. I walked over from the club, and I head back the same way, lit by the setting sun, feeling a lightness inside I don't think I've ever felt before.

*

The next day is Saturday. I know Scarlett holds a couple of classes in the morning, so when I wake up, I send her a text saying I hope she's slept well and tell her I'm going for a run, then don a tee, shorts, and trainers. We have a gym at the club, but today I feel like being out in the real world, so I head outside.

We've put in a circular path around the club that's approximately a kilometer long for guests who like to walk, and I put my earbuds in, stick the Arctic Monkeys on, and head off. It's early enough that I only meet one or two early risers, and we politely exchange nods before continuing on our way.

It's a beautiful morning. The sun is rising in front of me, and the whole complex is flooded with lemon-colored light. The air is fresh, denoting that we're moving into autumn now, but I know it'll be warm enough by lunchtime to go out without a jacket.

I feel light of heart, lifted by the sensation of being without pain. My knee is still a little stiff, but after about fifteen minutes that wears off, and I revel in the feeling of my muscles warming and my body moving fluidly.

As I run, I reflect on the events of the past few weeks. I've been cynical and judgmental, blindly believing what my father told me about the commune. It led to me believing that everyone there must be foolish and gullible. I assumed that George must be the one who'd been stealing, despite Scarlett insisting he was an honorable man, and it turned out the guy was willing to go to prison to defend his friend and to protect Scarlett and her sister.

I won't make that mistake again. I'm not going to be able to rid myself of my core beliefs overnight, but I'm going to make sure to listen to Scarlett and be as open-minded as I can, and to try to judge others based on my experience rather than what other people tell me.

I hope she was able to think about the possibility of us having a relationship last night. I think I convinced her, but I haven't heard from her since, so I don't know what's going through her mind.

My phone buzzes in the running bag I wear strapped to the top of my left arm, and I take it out and look at the screen. It's a text from Scarlett in reply to mine. It just says, *Super busy this morning. Catch up this afternoon. Will you be at the club all day?*

I text back, *Yes but I can come over any time.*

I wait for her to reply, but after a minute I realize she's probably not going to, and I slot the phone back into the bag and continue running.

*

I spend the morning working. There's always something urgent that needs doing, and it's after one before my stomach rumbles, reminding me I should find some sustenance before I pass out. I call the front desk and ask if they can get the chef to send me something through, and five minutes later someone turns up with a plate of chicken salad sandwiches, a bowl of homemade kumara crisps, a piece of apple pie and custard, and a piping hot latte. Nice.

Kingi comes into my office, says, "Ooh, lunch," stuffs half the crisps into one of the sandwiches, and has eaten half of it before I have the chance to protest.

"Help yourself," I say sarcastically, which earns me a grin. I pick up my phone and check the screen, then put it back on the table.

"Anything from Scarlett?" Kingi asks.

"I texted her about half an hour ago, but I haven't heard from her. She's probably taking a class." I'm sure she said she didn't have any in the afternoon, though.

"Yeah, she's probably just busy." His eyes sparkle.

"What?"

"Nothing."

"Kingi, I know that look. What's going on?"

"I have no idea." He gets up and steals another sandwich. "You staying here?"

"Yeah. If I haven't heard from her by three p.m., I'll head over to the commune and find out what's going on."

"All right. Let me know when you leave, okay?" He goes to have a spoonful of the apple pie, sees my glare, holds up a hand, and heads out.

It gets to two thirty, and I start packing up my stuff. I close my laptop and lock it in my desk, pocket my phone, and toss my coffee cup in the bin. I'm just about to walk out when I hear voices in the corridor. I know Kingi is here, but I'm pretty sure the rest of the offices are empty.

I glance at the door, and my eyebrows shoot up as Scarlett comes in, followed closely by Kingi, who's carrying a medium-sized cardboard box.

"Hello," Scarlett says, smiling.

"Oh, hey! What are you doing here?"

She walks up to me and slides her arms around my waist, and I give her a hug, warmth spreading through me.

She lifts her face for a kiss. Then she moves back and says, "I brought you a present."

"Really?"

Kingi brings the box over and puts it on the coffee table. He grins at me. Then he winks at Scarlett and says, "I'll leave you to it," and goes out.

"If it's a cake, I'd have preferred it if you'd jumped out of it," I point out.

She gives me a wry look, then gestures at it. "Aren't you going to open it?"

"It's not my birthday."

"It's a thank you, Orson, from all of us at Kahukura, for everything you've done for us."

Frowning, I go over to the box. "You didn't need to do that. I don't expect—" I twitch, startled, as the box moves. "What the fuck?"

I stare at her. She just grins. I look back at the box, only noticing then that the top has a series of air holes in it. My heart racing, I lift the side flaps, which aren't stuck down, and open the front and back.

My jaw drops. Inside, sitting up in a small bed, is a tiny puppy.

Its tail, which curves up over its body, is wagging at a million miles an hour. The puppy stands and puts its front paws on the side of the box. Worried it's going to tip it forward, I reach in, pick the puppy up, and lift it into my arms.

It's tiny—only about six inches tall—and white with light-brown patches. It looks like a Jack Russell, but its coat is rough, and its face has an adorable small shaggy beard. It's wearing a blue collar. I look underneath—it's a boy.

"His name is Bearcub," Scarlett says. "He's eight weeks old."

"What breed is he?" My voice is suspiciously husky.

"He's a Parson Russell Terrier. They have a longer head and a larger chest than the Jack Russell. He'll probably double in size by the time he's an adult, but he'll still be small enough to ride on your bike. Apparently they have a lot of energy… like someone else I know…" She smiles. "I thought he could go running with you."

He puts his front feet on my chest and licks my chin. Jesus, he's so small, but his brown eyes are full of spirit.

I think about Doyle, and my eyes fill with tears. "I don't think we'll take you on the bike," I whisper. "We're going to keep you safe, little fella."

"One of the guys at the commune knows a local breeder," Scarlett says softly. "I've got all the paperwork." She fondles the puppy's ear. "He can't go for a walk until he's had his last injections at about sixteen weeks, but the garden is fine."

He climbs up my chest, then sinks down and rests his chin on my shoulder. For a moment, I can't speak. His body is tiny and warm, and where my hand is supporting him under his chest, I can feel his heart beating against his ribs. I love his coloring, his whiskers, and his tail, which doesn't stop moving. He's beautiful, and he's exactly what I needed.

Kingi comes back into the room, and he says, "Aw, now, isn't that the perfect scene?" He lifts his phone and takes a photo, and I laugh, blinking the tears away.

"You knew?" I ask.

He nods. "Scarlett called me this morning and asked me to make sure you stayed in the office until she arrived." He comes closer and reaches out a hand to stroke the pup. "He's gorgeous."

"He'll never replace Doyle," I say, feeling a brief stab of guilt.

"Of course not," Kingi replies with a smile. "This little guy has his own personality, you can see that already. He's going to be a major pain in the ass."

"Like me," Scarlett says, and giggles.

"Both making my life a misery." I chuckle and kiss Bearcub's head.

Kingi heads for the door. "Scarlett brought some stuff for him, and I've asked the porter to take it to your suite, I hope that was okay."

"What kind of stuff?"

"A small crate," she says, "new food and water bowls, a couple of toys, and a leash. I wasn't sure whether you'd want to use Doyle's, so I thought if he had new ones…"

"That's great," I say. "Thank you."

Kingi smiles and goes out.

I get to my feet and take Bearcub over to the sliding doors that lead out into the garden. It has a fence around it, so he's safe. I put him down, and he immediately runs over to the tree and has a pee against it.

Scarlett comes out and stands beside me, and we both watch him investigating his land, sniffing stones and pots and trying to eat a flower.

"He's gorgeous," I tell her. "Thank you so much."

"You didn't mind not choosing him yourself?"

"Not at all. I couldn't quite bring myself to make the decision, you know? I needed someone else to do it for me."

She slides her arms around my waist again, and I hug her. The afternoon sunlight slants across us, banana yellow, and it warms me through.

"How has your day been?" I ask her.

"Good. Richard and George want to talk to you about contacting your designer and asking her to draw up some plans for new building developments for both the village and the retreat."

I kiss her hair. "Are you okay with that?"

"Yes, I think it's a good idea. Dad's vision was great but idealistic. This new vision is much more practical and sustainable, I hope."

"I think you're right."

"The donation was so generous—I think we'll be able to double the number of women we have staying at the retreat."

"That's fantastic."

"And I also want to talk to you about the Waiora. I'd like to help you with the design of that. You're right—it does need to be made safer, and it makes sense to have facilities, as long as they're not too much of an eyesore. I'm excited about taking classes to the gazebos, and decorating them to reflect the peaceful nature of the pond."

"We'll make sure to have plenty of signs that stress the importance of it being a place of quiet reflection."

"That would be great."

We stand there, smiling as we watch Bearcub bark at a fantail in the tree.

Then I look down at her. "Have you given any more thought to what I said last night?"

She nods. "Of course. I haven't been able to stop thinking about it." She looks up into my eyes. "I'm so touched that you want to be a part of Kahukura. And I wanted to say that I'm keen to be a part of the Midnight Club, too. I mean, I'm not sure I'll ever be comfortable in a nightclub, or in your world. But I will try. I thought that maybe, eventually, I might be able to do some work with the Circle. I know quite a lot about the donation side of things, and I have a slightly different perspective, having worked for a charity."

"That would be fantastic." I kiss her nose. "Thank you for trying."

"I want to make it work. I'm trying to do what you said, and use the truth to shape my own destiny."

I kiss her lips once, twice, and then a longer third time. Then Bearcub barks, making us laugh, and we look over at where he's tugging on a piece of wire fence around the base of the tree.

"The sun's really bright," Scarlett says, shielding her eyes.

"Like our future."

"That's really cheesy."

"Yeah, I know." I chuckle and go over to rescue Bearcub, and lift him up and kiss his nose. I bring him back to Scarlett, and she strokes his head, slipping her other arm around my waist, and holding me close.

Newsletter

If you'd like to be informed when my next book is available, you can sign up for my mailing list on my website, http://www.serenitywoodsromance.com

About the Author

USA Today bestselling author Serenity Woods writes sizzling New Zealand billionaire romances. A reader once called her the Queen of Happy Endings because her books have no cheating and no cliffhangers, just super-soppy HEAs!

She likes to describe her heroes as 'nice guys doing naughty things,' so if you like your men hot, rich, funny, and respectful out of the bedroom but wicked beneath the sheets, you've come to the right place!.

Website: http://www.serenitywoodsromance.com
Facebook: http://www.facebook.com/serenitywoodsromance

www.ingramcontent.com/pod-product-compliance
Ingram Content Group UK Ltd.
Pitfield, Milton Keynes, MK11 3LW, UK
UKHW020642210725
6984UKWH00022B/318